Advance praise for James Van Pelt's

## Strangers and Beggars

"James Van Pelt's short story collection may have Beggars in the title, but it's actually full of riches—a treasure trove of stories on everything from baseball to sorrow to the surveillance culture. And above all Van Pelt's insightful and unique perspective on everything from highway congestion to compulsion to school administrators. A varied and absorbing collection by a versatile and talented author."

— Connie Willis, author of *Passages*

"James Van Pelt is one of those writers who should be a lot better known than he is. He's been flying below most people's radar, because his wonderful, inventive, moving short stories have been appearing hither and yon. But that should change now that the best of them are here, in a single volume, that belongs on every SF fan's shelf."

— Robert J. Sawyer, author of *Hominids*

"James Van Pelt has a gift for opening strange new windows on familiar events, revealing the world from a perspective you never knew existed. Read these stories and feel your mind stretch."

— Jerry Oltion, author of *The Getaway Special*

"Equally adept at science fiction, fantasy and horror, Jim Van Pelt is one of those rare writers who swoop effortlessly across the landscape of the fantastic. I read him with admiration and envy. Discover a new master of the short form in the pages of *Strangers and Beggars*."

— James Patrick Kelly, author of *Think Like a Dinosaur*

"James Van Pelt is that rarest of beings, an author who combines a deep understanding and passion for humanity with a sense of wide-eyed wonder. These stories provide a stunning glimpse of a talent at home in any genre, from horror to modern fantasy to science fiction, one who confidently weaves unforgettable characters and situations into a tapestry celebrating what it is to be human. A moving, triumphant collection. Highly recommended.

— Julie E. Czerneda, author of *In the Company of Others*

# Strangers and Beggars

## James Van Pelt

**Fairwood Press**

Auburn • Seattle

*Strangers and Beggars*
A Fairwood Press Book
July 2002
Copyright © 2002 by James Van Pelt

*Fairwood Press*
5203 Quincy Ave SE
Auburn, WA 98092
**www.fairwoodpress.com**

Cover art and design © Getty Images/The Image Bank

ISBN: 0-9668184-5-8
First Fairwood Press Edition: July 2002
Printed in the United States of America

To my first readers (and there are a *lot* of you), to Gary and Mike for keeping me sane or at least not completely crazy, to my family for supporting and encouraging me, but most of all to Tammy who confirms that all things are possible with love.

# Acknowledgements

The stories in this anthology first appeared as follows:

*Altair*:
"Voices"

*Adventures in Sword & Sorcery*:
"Nine Fingers on the Flute"

*After Shocks*:
"Parallel Highways"

*Analog*:
"What Weena Knew"
"The Comeback"
"Nor a Lender Be"
"Ressurection"

*Asimov's*:
"The Infodict"

*First Publication Anywhere*:
"Finding Orson"

*Pulphouse*:
"Eight Words"

*Realms of Fantasy*:
"Happy Ending"
"Home"

*Talebones*:
"Miss Hathaway's Spider"
"The Death Dwarves"
"The Yard God"

*Transversions*:
"The Diorama"

*Weird Tales*:
"Shark Attack: A Love Story"

# Contents

## Foreword:
### Bruce Holland Rogers

## Stories:

### Teaching

### Love

### Death

### Time

# Strangers
## and
# Beggars

# *Introduction:*
# New Maps Out of Hell
## by Bruce Holland Rogers

Welcome to the world of James Van Pelt, a world of invisible shotgun-toting dwarves, psychic baseball consultants, sharks under the carpet, and giant spiders. The world of "imaginative literature." Or, to put it another way, welcome to heaven, hell and assorted realms in between.

Of all the territories you're about to enter, the ones that may linger longest in your memory are the infernal ones. That's not because Van Pelt is a particularly dark writer. In fact, it's his treatment of light-in-darkness that makes him so worth reading.

Thus, it's thoroughly unfair of me to stand at the gates of Van Pelt's fiction with the word hell on my lips. First, the territory that I have in mind is more akin to Ray Bradbury's *October Country* than Dante's *Inferno*. Second, most of these stories aren't the least bit infernal. "The Death Dwarves" may be darkly funny, but funny it is. "The Comeback" is a baseball tall tale. "Nor a Lender Be" is about that rare sort of teacher who makes the classroom a little bit of heaven for the lucky few who find themselves enrolled with him. And I certainly don't mean to suggest that reading these stories is going to be a torment. No, you have hours of pleasure ahead of you. But some of your enjoyment may come from the special pleasures of Things Gone Very Wrong.

One of the first important critical works about science fiction was a collection of lectures-turned-essays by Kingsley Amis called *New Maps of Hell*. Up until this 1960 book, the thinking was that science fiction was a literature about technology. Amis pointed out that science fiction was more a literature about society, especially about society gone wrong. SF is largely dystopian. It is the literature of alienation, changes for the worse.

Most of the stories in this collection are more fantasy than SF (and some are neither). And not every story in this collection is about things gone very wrong. But by my count nearly half of them are—things gone wrong in a great variety of ways. "What Weena Knew" borrows its dystopia from H. G. Wells's *The Time Machine*. The dystopia of poor Miss Hathaway and her spider is a bureaucratic one. The purgatories of "Happy Ending," "Eight Words" and "Voices" are the interior realms created from regret. Owen's unhappy neighborhood in "The Diorama" is unhappy because Owen is unhappy and does his best to drag his neighbors down with him. Of these dystopias, "Parallel Highways" is the one nearest to a true hell of demons and brimstone, but the demons drive big rigs and the brimstone vapors are really diesel exhaust. These stories may have a common dystopian theme, but it's a theme worked with variety and surprise—the sort of variety and surprise that Ray Bradbury dished up. In fact, "The Diorama" reminds me a great deal of Bradbury's classic story, "The Veldt," but with one key difference.

That difference is where Van Pelt shines. Lots of writers explore the territory of dystopia, but don't imagine that all you get with Van Pelt is a tour of hell. While there may be some value in simply mapping the infernal regions, where would that leave the reader? No, Van Pelt cares about his readers too much to just give us a tour of the dark places. Ultimately, this collection is more about *emerging* from the darkness.

One of the great movie moments of all time is in the biopic, *Ghandi*. In the midst of the violence surrounding India's partition, a distressed Hindu man tells Ghandi, "As for me, I am going to hell."

"Why are you going to hell?" the mahatma asks him.

"I killed a Muslim child. A little child!"

"There is a way out of hell," Ghandi says. He instructs the man to find another Muslim child, one who has been orphaned in the violence, and bring him up in his own home as a Muslim. And the man leaves to find that child. He recognizes the road to redemption when it is pointed out to him.

For someone in a living hell, what gift could be greater than a map with the escape routes marked? Whatever the ultimate realities of heaven and hell may be, hell can be present for us here and now. One of the things fiction does is help us understand the path to here-and-now redemption. My favorite stories in this collection do just that. They aren't new maps of hell. They are new maps *out* of hell.

Not half of these stories are about the dark regions of imagination. Of that minority, not every one ends with redemption. (Some characters who have made terrible choices are still living with the darkness of those decisions at the story's end, but there's a least a hint that the exit light is visible —if not to the character, then to the reader.) But these maps out of darkness are the essential James Van Pelt, the trait that makes him an inheritor of Ray Bradbury's "The Veldt." Both the Bradbury story and Van Pelt's "The Diorama" cover similar imaginary ground, but Bradbury's story ends in terror. Van Pelt's tale ends in hope.

There are other pleasures on these pages. Van Pelt can dazzle with technique or tantalize us with a mystery, but there's more to his stories than showmanship. Experimental fiction is too often only about experimentation itself, but "Happy Ending" is a morality play that is effective because of its experimental form. "Voices" is a mystery about more than solving a puzzle.

So welcome to these assorted territories of James Van Pelt's imagination. Here you'll encounter the popcorn and peanuts smell of the stadium, the perfume of a beautiful woman you can't get out of your mind, the chalk dust of classrooms, and an office that smells of the sea. Don't mind the occasional tang of brimstone. You'll be glad you came.

*"All strangers and beggars are from Zeus,
and a gift, though small, is precious."*

—Homer, *The Odyssey*

# Teaching

# Miss Hathaway's Spider

*-knowledge-*

**M**iss Hathaway first noticed the spider on a cool September morning, before the students arrived, as she dusted the chalk trays with her canary-yellow feather duster. No other teacher cleaned the chalk trays, but she knew that was a reflection of their lack of professionalism, for no one was as meticulous, as orderly, as conscientious as she. Not that she considered cleaning the chalk trays a part of her job, but the janitor never did them. She had written a memo to him once, folded it neatly into thirds and placed it in his box in the faculty mail room.

> *Dear Mr. Clean,*
>     *I would like to commend you on the appearance of my classroom, but would it be possible for you to pay closer attention to the chalk trays? They do become awfully dusty. High school students are acutely aware of an untidy environment, don't you think?*
>                     *Sincerely,*
>                     *Miss Hathaway*

But even after her letter, in the morning the trays were dirty, and, annoyed, she cleaned them out.

She saw the spider clinging to the underside of a web a foot above the carpet in the corner of the room farthest from the door when she bent to drop broken pieces of chalk into the trash can. She jumped back, a tidy little jump; her hands flew to her face below her wire-rim glasses and cupped her cheeks. "Oh," she said.

Miss Hathaway, who at five-foot-one and a hundred-and-two pounds and filled with the authority of her fifteen years of teaching experience, who had broken up fights between football players, who faced lunch room duty with the bravery of any soldier on Iwo Jima, who had at the beginning of this school year moved a cabinet full of books from one side of her room to the other, was afraid of spiders.

She knelt cautiously to observe it and realized that someone coming into her classroom at that moment would see her  crouched in a corner at the front of the class and might think she was praying. But the presence of the remarkable spider pushed that thought from her head, and she scooted closer. Its size struck her first; at least three inches from toe-tip to toe-tip. And then its color: black and spit-shine shiny. The spider's body and the black, metallic legs reflected the fluorescent light from the ceiling in tiny star bursts.

But even a remarkable spider, she thought, had no place in a classroom. She pushed herself up from the floor, smoothed the front of her skirt, then pressed her intercom switch and asked for the unhelpful Mr. Clean.

When he arrived, she said, "Class begins in one half hour, and I do not believe the spider should be here."

He crouched down next to the web. The spider vanished into a hole in the wall. "It's a big one... " He poked a greasy, chewed pencil into the hole.  A crumbling of rotten sheetrock drifted to the carpet. " ...and we probably ought to call the exterminators... "

"Well?" Miss Hathaway crossed her arms across her chest, wrapping her fingers around her elbows. She could feel the sharp crease she had ironed into her blouse sleeves.

" ...but we're out of funding." He stood up and pushed his pencil into his shirt pocket. "You'll have to kill it yourself."

She squeezed her elbows. "But this is why I called you."

He sniffed."Our job's floors, boards and desks."

"You can't take care of the spider?"

"The exterminators are union; janitors are union, just like teachers. You wouldn't want me to scab, would you?"

"Of course not. Wouldn't dream of it. I understand our positions exactly." She picked up her feather duster, turned her back to him and began dusting an already clean chalk tray with short, brisk strokes. "Thank you for your attention."

Mr. Clean paused at the door on his way out. "I'll suck her right up, if I catch her on the carpet."

*-comprehension-*

*T*wo weeks later Miss Hathaway sat on the front three inches of a chair before Vice Principal Book's desk. The chair came from the elementary school and forced her to sit with her knees higher than her hips and her eyes level with the top of the desk.

Vice Principal Book, a large man with beefy upper arms that strained the sleeves of his battleship-gray jacket, gazed down on her. Behind him, six certificates, their frames butting up one to the other and lined up so precisely that they looked like one long brass and glass display, hung from the green cinder block wall. "So, let me see if I can put this in a nutshell. You have a spider problem in your room, and therefore you can't teach?"

"I'm sorry to bother you with this, and I wouldn't, but I talked to the janitor, and he said it wasn't his job. I don't see how it is properly mine either." She kept her neatly manicured hands still. Vice Principal Book made her nervous, even though he was once only a Driver's Ed instructor.

He smiled. "Miss Hathaway, Miss Hathaway, you *are* one of our best teachers." He consulted an open manila folder on the desk. "Spotless record. Perfect paperwork. Up to date lesson plans. Never tardy to faculty meetings. And, most important, you don't send students up to me for discipline problems." He chuckled. "How distracting can a spider be?"

It wasn't distracting at all, at first, thought Miss Hathaway; the only reason she didn't kill it was because the janitor should kill it; he didn't clean the trays; at least he could get rid of the spider. Miss Hathaway thought of the web, now a yard wide, that clouded the corner of the room, the eight inches of glistening spider that hung there, and the mysteriously larger hole in the wall. She thought of the three times in the last two days, while lecturing on the funnel paragraph, she had pirouetted in mid-sentence, convinced the black spider was creeping up on her. "Maybe if you came down and looked at it?"

"I don't think we'll need to go that far. There isn't an educational challenge that can't be solved, if we put our heads together, right in this office, Miss Hathaway."

"This does seem to be an extraordinary situation, though." She wanted to squirm forward on the chair because her blouse had come untucked from the back of her skirt, but she was perched on the edge already. The thought of tucking the blouse in with Vice Principal Book watching made her queasy.

He leaned back in his chair, squeaking the springs, and laced his fingers across his stomach. His jacket pulled into a series of wrinkles radiating away from the single button holding it closed. "Remember the Miracle Worker?" He continued without waiting for her to answer. "She taught that little girl who couldn't see, hear or talk. The Miracle Worker didn't have a beautiful classroom, did she?"

He looked at Miss Hathaway expectectantly. "Uh, no, she didn't."

"She didn't have class-sets of brand new expensive Harcourt Brace Jovanovich English texts, did she?"

"No," she answered. He was caught in his rhythm now.

"No, she didn't! She didn't have video tapes or record players or computers to help her. Think of the primitive conditions she worked in, and think of your own situation. Why, if she had the advantages you have, she could have really done something with that little girl. So, I believe that what you need to do is to reconsider your situation. Believe in your own abilities. Do you believe, Miss Hathaway?"

"Yes," Miss Hathaway whispered. He beat the top of the desk with his fist to emphasize his words.

"Believe in the school. Believe that the principal and I are behind you all the way. Believe that the school board knows what it's doing. Believe in the goal of every child in its place. I have that dream." He lunged out of his chair and loomed above her. "Sure, you have a spider, but you have so many positives. You can stand tall in your classroom, like a pillar of fire, like a burning bush, like a tower of Babel. Can you do that?"

"Oh, yes!"

"In the teaching profession we can't dwell on the negatives; we have to accentuate the positives. Be a team player. Keep a tight lid on the boat, and your ship will come in."

He slapped her folder closed. "Be a Helen Keller for us Miss Hathaway. You can be a miracle worker like her, if you'll put your mind to it."

Momentarily engulfed in his enthusiasm, she rose. She said, "I think I can," and marched down to her classroom.

*-application-*

**M**onday, the week after Homecoming. Melba Toast raised her hand, and Miss Hathaway thought, as she often did, of how cruel parents can be.

"There is web on my desk," Melba said. The web stretched from ceiling to floor now, and its intricate structure of thick threads anchored to points as far as ten feet from the corner of the room, including Melba's desk. Its form sprang from the corner without order, random, not a neat lattice work of geometry, but a chaotic mess of lines and darkness.

"Isn't that interesting?" Miss Hathaway said. "But I don't believe we need to consider that now. What we should think about is a topic for our next essay." Miss Hathaway felt distracted, unfocused. She knew what the next essay *should* be—the lesson plans she had used for the last fifteen years were perfectly clear—a comparison/contrast essay on abortion, but she didn't want to assign it. The whole idea of thirty essays like essays from years past exhausted her. But this attitude put her in a weird position, she realized: for the first time in her teaching career, she didn't know exactly what she was going to do next. It disturbed her. She paced the front of the classroom, her hands behind her back, avoiding the mass of web to the left of her podium. The two-foot long spider crawled along the ceiling of the room. Students under it watched warily. "Your essays on gun control were fine. Really, they were. But they lacked something... immediacy perhaps. If we wrote about a topic closer to home your writing might be livelier."

The spider paused above Jim Bag, a mediocre student with a tendency to dangle his modifiers, who turned every writing assignment into an essay on football. He clenched the edges of his desk and looked ready to bolt if the spider should make a move towards him. "Jesus Christ, that gives me the creeps," he announced.

Miss Hathaway stopped pacing. Here was something she could deal with. No one talked in her room without raising a hand. In fact, she thought, no one should ever talk. After all, this was a writing class. "While I am deciding what our next subject will be, why don't all of you take out a pen and in one paragraph write your feelings about the spider. Make sure you include a distinct thesis sentence. I'll collect them in fifteen minutes." They pulled paper out of notebooks and busied themselves at the assignment. While they were writing she studied the spider, and the distraction, the unfocusing, came back.

She thought about it being black. But it was blacker than black. Midnight black. No, blacker than that. It was black with depth. Cave black. Blind black. Not like a black mirror, but like outer space. Black like a neutron star defying color. Denying color. Fall into the pit black. A black from the back of the dream black.

And the shape, a dark, dismembered hand. Black bone fingers beating gravity. Clinging to the ceiling. Nothing that big should be able to walk above you, she thought. Each joint clearly articulated. Multiple leg knuckles, bent, full of promise. Full of threat.

And the long abdomen, packed, round. The skin taut, pulsing faintly, rising and falling, never still. At this size she could see it always moved. She envisioned her hand reaching out, stroking it.

She jerked her eyes away. Breathing hard, face flushed, she walked up and down the straight aisles between the desks, studied the students' papers and forced herself not to look up as she passed beneath the spider.

Later, at the podium, she read a sampling of the essays to the class.

"'In today's modern society, spiders are seldom thought of.'" She gazed at them in their orderly rows before her. "Can anyone make a suggestion for improving this lead-in sentence?" No one spoke. "Generally, we don't approve of ending sentences with prepositions." They looked back at her blankly. "This might be a good test question," she said, and many of them wrote down that sentences should not end with prepositions.

She read the next one. "'In the current, modern world of today, spiders are very important.' Can anyone think of a better verb than 'are' for this sentence?" No one spoke; she suggested a different verb.

Before the bell rang, she said to them, "Think about strategies to develop your paragraph on the spider into an essay. Invent ways to turn this negative into a positive." She was pleased with herself for having heeded Vice Principal Book's advice.

At the bell, they hurried to the door. "Jim!" she called. "I need to talk to you about your language."

After he left, she was alone, and the spider was with her. It moved up the wall and onto the ceiling with a cool, slow grace; and its movement made her think of a glacier creeping into an ancient civilization's valley, sliding with weighty patience inch after inch, covering roads, pushing aside viaducts, smoothing away the lines of irrigation ditches. She shook her head and realized minutes had passed. The spider had crossed the room.

*-analysis-*

*B*efore class, the day after Thanksgiving break, Vice Principal Book slapped a sheet of paper on Miss Hathaway's podium.

"We don't need to involve the principal in this now, do we?" His open jacket and tie that hung to one side exposed his belly pushing through the gaps between the buttons. "A memo like this insults my office."

Miss Hathaway had never seen Vice Principal Book in her room before, and his sudden appearance startled her into dropping her gradebook. She pushed her glasses up from where they had slid to the end of her nose so she could look at him.

"But you can see the problem," she said and waved her hand at the web-choked corner of the class where hundreds of translucent-gray, rope thick strands originated to connect to every solid surface in the room. The ruler straight rows of desks, except for Melba's, and the podium were the only areas relatively free from sticky web. The ceiling lights filtered through and cast abstract, bizarre shadows. On the wall behind Vice Principal Book, the four-foot long spider delicately picked its way from strand to strand; its body covered a poster diagramming a key-hole essay. When she saw the spider, her attention wavered from Vice Principal Book, and it suddenly occurred to her that she hadn't been able to see the hole in the wall behind the web for weeks, and she wondered how large was it now? And where, exactly, did it lead?

"What I see," said Vice Principal Book, "is that you need to distinguish facts from fiction. The facts are that the principal runs this building with a system. The system includes a hierarchy of command. He does not deal with teachers—I deal with teachers. When you subvert the hierarchy, then the system doesn't work."

Miss Hathaway faced him. "I have to deal with this spider every day!"

Vehemently he said, "You have to deal with *me* every day. Spiders come and spiders go, but I'm here forever. You have a bad history of this kind of memo writing." Confused, Miss Hathaway looked at him. "Oh yes, I know about your memo to the janitor. Nothing is too small for me to notice, Miss Hathaway."

Early students walked into the class and put their books under their desks. The Vice Principal lowered his voice, but his tone stayed angry. "A parent complained about your essay assignment on the spider. Parents don't want their children to think—and you know this as well as I do—about things that make them uncomfortable. I don't want you drawing attention to it. As far as you and your students are concerned, it doesn't exist. No more essays. No discussions. There is no spider!" He marched out of the class, stiffly ducking his head under low strings of web that crossed from wall to wall.

Miss Hathaway grabbed a stack of essays from a shelf in the podium, crunching the first page of the top paper. They were the spider essays, each with neatly red-penned comments in the margins and a grade written in the upper right hand corner (a "happy face" drawn next to the pleasingly many "A's" and a "sad face" next to the surprisingly few "F's").

She wanted to return them today. That was what her lesson plan said: "Hand back graded essays and discuss."

She stood rigid at the podium, thinking an unthinkable thought: I will hand them back anyway. And she waited for the tardy bell to ring, but as she waited she grew less sure. He is the vice principal, after all, she thought, and the more she considered this, the sadder she became. He had never yelled at her before; hadn't he said she was "one of the best teachers?" Who would want to lose that?

She sighed, smoothed the wrinkle she had made in the top essay, placed the stack deep in the podium and opened her *Warriner's English Grammar and Composition* text to find an exercise as an alternative lesson plan.

The last few students entered the room and made their way to their desks.

And that might have been the end of it, except that when Melba Toast took her seat she did what no student, what no janitor, what Miss Hathaway herself, had not done—she brushed against a piece of the web.

"Uh oh," said Melba, and all eyes turned to her; in the spotlight of attention, she was alone. No one moved. Then the spider swarmed down from the ceiling, an avalanche of legs and dreamy black motion.

During the brief struggle, while Miss Hathaway did nothing, she suddenly realized she knew the facts, she always had. The problem was the fiction, and how was she to separate them?

*-synthesis-*

The next day, Miss Hathaway marked her roll sheet mechanically, making tidy black checks in the exact middle of each square until she came to Melba Toast's space. Her desk was empty, but Melba herself, wrapped in a long white cocoon, hung from a net of threads coming out of the confusion of web above the class. Only her eyes peeked out, open, awake, but unfocused, as if she were seeing things beyond the walls.

After a long moment, Miss Hathaway marked Melba tardy, reasoning that although she was not in her seat when the bell rang, she was in the room.

The class labored over a four-page worksheet on subject/verb and pronoun/antecedent agreement as Miss Hathaway finished her paperwork and began to stroll up and down the aisles; but wherever she walked, and no matter how hard she tried not to look, her eyes kept finding their way to Melba.

Someone knocked on the door, startling Miss Hathaway. It was Guidance Counselor Mitty. They talked in the hall.

"You sent for me," he said as if he had somewhere else to be that was much more important. A slight man, barely as tall as Miss Hathaway herself, he struggled to keep straight an armful of manila envelopes

"I've lost a student."

"I heard. I heard. Terrible thing. But what can we do?"

"I don't know. I thought you people had special training. It's time we did *something* though." Miss Hathaway looked back into her classroom where the students were working quietly.

"These are awful times Miss Hathaway. They always are. But we have a saying up in counseling, 'Don't lose the school, saving a whale.' Sometimes one of them slips away from us, but we can't knock ourselves out. Buck up. We win more than we lose."

"You're saying to not worry about her?"

He shrugged. "I'm doing a study. If you'll write a report on her case, I'll pull her files, and maybe we can work up a profile of what to look for next time. Keep the rest of your ducks in a row, and the sharks won't get them. But if this episode starts to bother you, come on up." He looked fatherly. "The district sponsors a support group for teachers. It's wonderful, really. I go twice a week myself, not that I need it, but I always feel refreshed after others speak about their problems."

"But what of her parents? Won't her parents want to know what happened to her?"

"Oh, we're right on top of that. Any time a student is in danger of not graduating we send a letter to the home, and, of course, failure notices come out next week, so they'll know. We are committed to communicating with parents."

Miss Hathaway opened her mouth and shut it, opened it and shut it. She raised her hands and dropped them. Guidance Counselor Mitty backed away from her. "Have you tried talking to the vice principal?" he said.

Miss Hathaway closed her eyes and thought about violent acts, of slapping his papers out of his hands, of kicking his manila folders down the hall, of tearing his reports into hundreds of pieces. She opened her eyes; he was gone.

Later, the bell rang, dismissing class. Trembling, she studied the spider high in its corner.

Each leg rested on a firm line of web, balancing the spider perfectly, leaving it poised to go in any direction, the center of stillness. She stepped towards it, and the spider elevated its two front legs as if to embrace her. She stepped back, and the legs dropped down.

She sat on the stool behind her podium and thought about Guidance Counselor Mitty, Vice Principal Book, and Mr. Clean, and she couldn't make any sense of them. And the more she thought, the angrier she became. She wrote their names on a sheet of paper and tried to sort them out. What did they want? Then she crumpled the sheet, wrote the names again, added her own name and drew lines from name to name, and then from letter to letter until the sheet was a maze of lines. Finally she stood, and then stalked around the perimeter of the room, muttering. Web touched or covered the posters, the intercom, the bulletin board, the book shelves and the blackboards.

She stopped in front of the spider and stared at it again, and she realized she was sweating. Her forehead was wet with it; hair stuck to the side of her face; she felt sweat on her back and belly. She untucked her blouse. She wanted to take it off, to throw it on the floor, to kick her shoes away from her, to unbutton the skirt and drop it, to peel off everything. Then the spider moved toward her, not quickly: slowly, barely seeming to lift its legs, placing each exactly on the next strand. Like a vision of a black tidal wave rolling up in slow motion across a gray beach, she saw it. Larger and darker, blotting out the sky, covering the sun, sweeping up the sand. Like a hand sliding under the covers, reaching closer and closer. To what? she thought. To what? And she realized a funny thing: at this size the spider didn't scare her. It was rather...rather...lovely. She stepped forward, reached out with both hands; she stroked the spider's sides between pairs of legs, drew it toward her, and the spider wrapped gently around her.

She was so warm.

*-evaluation-*

Miss Hathaway felt as if she were a blind eye opening for the first time, like she had never been in the world before.

She floated in the spider dream, down each line of web, from wall to wall, from ceiling to floor. She connected everywhere, could move everywhere, felt air drifting, individual molecules bouncing, sounds vibrating. On the outskirts of her perception she heard Melba Toast singing a tune Miss Hathaway didn't recognize, a happy song.

Through the hole in the wall, a hole that she now knew opened beyond her classroom, a hole that was more a door than any she had ever gone through, she saw light. And beyond the door she believed waited a world she had never considered, and she could feel in herself the power to go there. Who knew how far she could go in the spider dream? But for now the spider itself delighted her. She felt its presence as a huge pillow of soft sounds, and its blackness transformed into gauzy yellow, green and blue lights with no center. No one point more interesting than any other. None of it bad or good. None of it comparable to any other thing. No degrees of complication. No head. No base. The spider was an entirety. Words were too weak. Words themselves, as soon as she thought of them, limited whatever it was. Whatever it is. She laughed. There was so much she wanted to understand, but there was no rush. She had time, she knew, she had time. A spider is nothing if it is not patient.

Then a shape moved below her and Miss Hathaway focused her eyes and realized that her body dangled from the ceiling of her own classroom. A person she had never seen before, a small angry woman in a neatly pressed blouse, hair tied tightly back in a bun, was digging into the podium, examining each piece of paper closely, then piling it on the floor in increasing exasperation. Finally, she glared up at Miss Hathaway. "Lesson plans?" she shouted. She searched through the last stack of papers. The first students came in and sat in their desks. "Where are your lesson plans?"

She was the substitute.

# Finding Orson

O she doth teach the torches to burn bright.
                    —*Romeo and Juliet*

P atty tried to ignore Elaine's contentment, but it broadcast like orange campfire light from her desk across the otherwise empty office. Patty looked away and filled the umpteenth bubble on the student evaluation sheet. Her grade book lay open beside her, the quarter's penciled percentages covering the sheet in gray smudges. Each student's final test, the quarter grade and a comment had to be marked in the appropriate bubble for the computer to scan. The grades came from her book; the comment she took from a possible comments list taped to the book's inside cover. Assigning grades weighed on the first year teacher.

She considered one student, Fran, whose talent levitated tissue papers and twisted them into odd shapes in the air. Since Fran paid attention and turned in her work, Patty marked forty-five, "Works to capacity." Patty filled the two circles (the forty and the five). Fran had declared earlier in the week she wanted to read Juliet's parts and her boyfriend William should play Romeo, but she changed her mind when Patty said they couldn't act out the lines, "O then dear saint, let lips do what hands do—" in act I. Patty moved to the next name to repeat the process.

Patty noticed the thirty year veteran, Elaine, worked at twice her speed.

"How do you manage to do these so fast? I put the darn grades in the wrong circles, and I have to erase."

"Don't do that," Elaine said without looking up. "The computer will mis-read and you'll have to redo the whole sheet. Leave the mistake and correct it when they print the confirmation copy. The secretary will hand-enter the new grade."

Patty bent over her work and finished three more students. "Well, it's not the mistakes that slow me up, anyway; it's the comments." She tried to decide if Matt should get a fourteen, "Fails to complete assignments," or a sixty-two, "Absences affecting performance."

"Give everyone an eight. It's just one bubble."

Patty ran her finger down the list. "'A pleasure to have in class'? That doesn't describe everyone."

"Sure it does, honey." Elaine looked at her kindly. "Some are more pleasurable than others is all. Besides, they don't have the comments I *really* want like 'Your parents must be cousins,' or 'Not allowed to operate heavy equipment.' What are you going to put for Bobby Beddows? Is he controlling that talent any better?"

Patty wrinkled her nose. "I handed back their essays Monday, and when he saw my corrections, he made a smell like a paving operation. I thought I'd have to evacuate the room."

"Freshmen can produce some pretty repellent odors without it being their gift. Better you than me. Think of it as paying your dues. Oh, you might ask Rachael Yashita to help. She can raise a breeze to clear the air. Last year at the middle-school the counselors scheduled the two together."

"I'm more worried about Orson. He hasn't displayed any talent at all yet."

The bell rang, ending their planning period, and they gathered their books and materials. Elaine said, "Be patient. I've had a couple like him, and it's rough to develop late. Kids can get cruel about it. Besides, isn't your formal evaluation today? There's something to worry about." She paused at the door. Behind her students streamed to their next classes. "Well, I'm off to beat back the boundaries of ignorance. Oh, and don't forget we have a Career Days assembly at 1:00." She stepped into the traffic flow and disappeared.

A video camera, cables and boxes filled the door to Patty's room. She watched her step to avoid tripping.

"Don't mind me," said Vice-principal Drabbe. "You won't even know we're here."

A student assistant waved to her from behind the camera. Drabbe had pulled a desk from the circle and put it next to the camera. Evaluation tools spread across the desk top: a large stopwatch, a log to record observations, a memo pad, and a hand-held tape recorder. Most students sat in their desks, and she could see Drabbe had already written in the log. He scribbled a memo, folded it and handed it to his aid to deliver. Drabbe's memos were famous for their inscrutability. Elaine still joked about one she'd received the school's first week that read, "Remember the hats rule." She'd said, "And all along I thought it was the principal."

Students chattered about the Career Days assembly, and Patty walked around the circle, greeting each one before the bell rang beginning class.

Inga, whose talent caused intestinal cramps, said, "I want to learn about taxes. I hear I.R.S. agents make money galore."

Her friend Natalie said, "Someone told me a horticulturist will be speaking. That sounds interesting to me." Natalie's talent made plants hum. The first day of school, she'd waved her hand over Patty's African Violets on her desk, and they'd sung low, musical tones for ten minutes.

"Hi, Ms. Epson," said Thomas. He stood a sheet of paper on edge, stacked a second one on top and was tried to get a third to stay in place. An odd talent, but it made him proud. "I'll get them to the ceiling before the end of the semester," he said.

"I'm sure you will, but class is about to start. Can you put those back in their folder where they belong?"

Drabbe mumbled into his tape recorder and scribbled into his log. The red light on the camera glowed, and class hadn't begun yet.

When the bell rang, Drabbe started the stopwatch. Patty collected the *Romeo and Juliet* project proposals she'd assigned for today, took a deep breath and launched into act II. She'd cast student parts earlier, and after they'd read for a while, she stopped them to write in their journals on the topic, "Imagine a conversation between Juliet and her dad if he had seen her kissing Romeo at the masquerade." Patty turned to her desk to make sure everyone had submitted project proposals.

Drabbe said into his recorder, "Journal writing at twelve minutes and twenty-one seconds." He smiled genially in Patty's direction when she glanced at him.

Everyone had turned in a proposal except Orson. The students bent over their journals while Patty walked behind them, peeking over shoulders to see what they wrote. Her own talent worked well today. When she passed close enough to each student she picked up a wash of emotion, which she sensed as a colored cloud surrounding them. Most were neutral, cruising along in what Patty considered "the gray mode," not ecstatic or depressed, but functioning normally. A nice-feeling light blue shade wrapped itself around Inga. Patty had heard the swim-team captain had asked her to Homecoming before first hour. Pink tendrils flowed through the blue, reflecting her good mood.

But a frightening black fog surrounded Orson, an ebony-haired, serious boy, a half-head shorter than the next shortest student in the room. The color circled him, obscuring him as she drew closer. Patty held her breath, not wanting to breathe it in. He wrote methodically, pencil thumping the paper at the end of sentences. Patty bent to whisper to him, "I didn't see your proposal." He'd been writing the same sentence over and over, filling the sheet: "Consider the Romeo solution." Goose bumps prickled the back of her neck. She stood behind him for a bit, half-bent at the waist until he looked at her, his eyes a dark brown with darker circles beneath them.

"I don't like tragedy," he said, and then without pausing, as if on the same subject, "Everyone else has something." This close to him, so deep in his cloud, the lights from the room dimmed. She'd poked her head into a sad, twilight world, and they were alone.

"Maybe you could work with that as your project." She put her hand on his shoulder.

The muscles under his shirt knotted, as if the boy strained against some internal explosion, but as soon as she rested her hand on him, his color lightened.

Drabbe spoke into his recorder again. He mumbled, and it sounded like, "Touched a pupil, " but Patty kept her hand there.

"How could I do that?" Orson whispered. She strained to hear, but he always spoke softly, and she'd grown used to it.

Patty glanced up, thinking. The other students continued to write. Behind them, the Globe theater and Stratford on Avon posters decorated the walls. Earlier the class had written sonnets, and examples filled the bare spaces. Underneath the clock, a sign from a teacher who'd had the room the year before said, "TIME WILL PASS; WILL YOU?"

"Well, maybe explore what it means to want something and not have it. That's what Romeo and Juliet went through. It's their tragedy in the play. Remember at the beginning when Benvolio asks Romeo what sadness lengthens his hours? Romeo said, 'Not having that which, having, makes them short.' Sometimes I think Shakespeare wrote this play about yearning. Do you know what yearning is?"

Orson nodded.

"So maybe you could write about something you yearn for. If that's what the play is saying to you, you could write about it."

Orson turned his head and squinted one eye as if considering the idea. His color faded to gray. Then he said in the same, quiet voice, "Fly."

Patty straightened. "Excuse me?"

"Fly." Orson pointed to a fly buzzing against a ceiling light panel.

Before Patty could stop it, Harmony, a plump girl whose face always looked flushed, aimed her finger at the insect and said, "Bang."

With a loud snap, the fly disintegrated into a tiny cloud. Its disembodied wings fluttered to the floor.

Giggles erupted from all sides for an instant, then stopped. Students covered their mouths and glanced at Mr. Drabbe and his video camera.

The camera's single eye stared at Patty. Drabbe's pencil in one hand poised over the log, and his other hand held the recorder, ready for comment. For a moment all waited, then Vivian said, "Ew, gross, Harmony. You got fly guts in my hair."

Dead cat smell filled the room. Patty's eyes watered from the strong odor. "Bobby, this is inappropriate."

For five minutes chaos reigned.

Bobby claimed innocence. "Sometimes my emotions get away from me," he announced straight faced, then spoiled the effect by snickering.

Harmony blamed Yonda. "She's always summoning flies. She knows it drives me crazy."

Yonda flipped Harmony the finger.

"You know where to find me, girlfriend," said Harmony, and they both laughed.

In the midst of Patty's attempts to restore order, a student from the nurse's office delivered notes for four students to report for hearing tests. Patty delivered the notes, tried to dismiss the four with as little disruption as possible and failed while asking the class to resume their journal work. Drabbe wrote on the pad, dictated notes and directed the camera with frantic intensity. When Patty passed his desk, she saw his emotions: bright, sunshiny yellow. He was a happy man.

Then, when all had calmed down and the class turned to the play's next act, the intercom clicked loudly and dismissed the students for Career Days assembly in the gym.


*E*laine asked Patty about the evaluation. In the teacher lounge's bright light, surrounded by the coffee pot's and pop machine's comforting normality, Patty's unease about Orson faded a bit.

"You might try a clapping trick I learned from a kindergarten teacher," said Elaine. Her lunch, a rice and vegetable mixture, smelled of cayenne pepper, which she stirred before dipping her fork in. "You clap your hands once and say, 'Anyone who can hear my voice, raise your hand.' Then you clap your hands twice and say the same thing. It sounds childish, but when it works all the kids will have their hands up, and class will be quiet."

Patty had bought a cafeteria chicken-fried hamburger topped by a mashed potato scoop, drowned in gravy. The roll beside it glistened with butter and weighed at least a quarter of a pound.

Elaine said, "I don't know how you can eat that. If I have a school lunch, I spend the afternoon running to the rest room."

"What am I supposed to do about Drabbe? He's got the whole disaster on videotape. The lesson self destructed."

Elaine leaned back in her chair. "Oh, Drabbe is okay. You should see him handle problem kids. Once he stopped a fight between three football players, and by the time he finished talking to them, right there in the hall, before a huge crowd, the three cried and hugged each other."

"Wow, that's quite a talent."

"It's a skill. His talent alphabetizes objects. He showed me once. If you put any three items on his desk—say a paperclip, a stapler and a note-book—they'll slide around into alphabetical order. He minored in German in college, and he told me when he thinks in German the items line up in Germanic, alphabetical order."

Patty laughed. "It fits him."

"He can be a little anal. If he were a student, I'd mark a forty-seven on his bubble sheet."

"What's that?"

"Does not work or play well with his peers. He'll give you all kinds of advice about your class you can ignore, and what he writes down on your evaluation will be so full of educationalese Andrew Carnegie wouldn't be able to make heads nor tails of it. You're going to be a fine teacher. Pay attention to the kids. They'll let you know if you're good."

Elaine checked her watch. "I've got bus duty." She shoveled in the last few spoonfuls of lunch, then dumped the dish and silverware on her desk.

"It's lunch. What buses?"

"The kids from the vocational center. Hard to believe a Master's de-gree and thirty-two years of experience qualifies you for a fifteen minute lunch and a chance to watch the bus unload." She grabbed a handful of student notebooks as she went through the door.

Patty looked at her meal. None of it appeared appetizing, so she walked to the Counseling office.

Ms. Reed, the freshmen counselor greeted her with forms and bro-chures. "I'm the building's union rep, and I see from my membership list you haven't joined yet. Let me tell you about the benefits."

For ten minutes, Reed talked about step raises, maternity leave, the sick day bank, insurance breaks and other items "...your hard-working teacher's union has earned for you."

"As a first-year teacher," Reed said, "you can't afford not to join."

Finally, Patty told her about Orson.

"Students write self destructive journal entries all the time. I wouldn't worry about the boy quite yet. If you see other signs of depression, though, let me know." Reed handed her a pamphlet entitled, *Permanent Solutions to Temporary Problems: Teens and Suicide*, and it reminded Patty of Orson's journal entry, "Consider the Romeo Solution."

"I don't know why you English teachers have to give them *Romeo and Juliet*. Seems every other year someone's in here thinking he's Romeo or she's Juliet. I wish you could give them a positive classic like...*Mary Poppins* with Julie Andrews."

Patty puzzled on how to answer. It seemed like such a non sequitur. Finally she offered, "That's a movie."

"Oh, really? Well, what do you know. Anyway, Orson's a youngster. His talent hasn't come in, and that's sure to bother him. But youngsters' lives are filled with ups and downs. You watch: tomorrow he'll be high as a kite about some good event."

Patty thought about the cloud around Orson. Funeral black, a palpable sadness. She'd seen depressed students before, but nothing to compare to the moment in class when the cloud swallowed him.

Reed said, "I'll schedule an appointment with him if you're that worried."

When the bell rang, sending Patty to her next class, Reed piled more union information onto the stack she carried. Reed said, "Remember, students come and go, but if you stay with the district, you could be in this building your whole career. The union has your best interests at heart."

A directive Patty found in her mail-box before school started dictated the day's lesson. The administrators and the Counseling Department had decided a good follow-up to the Career Days assembly would be for all the English teachers to administer a career interest survey to their students and then to discuss career possibilities with them. The memo was signed, "Educationally Yours, Mr. Drabbe."

Patty sighed. She'd worked well past midnight preparing material for today's classes, and a half-page memo wiped out half the lesson.

As class began, she passed out the survey, and the students laughed at some of the questions like, "Do you take drugs?" and "Do you know more than two foreign languages."

Alice asked, "Does Pig-Latin count?"

Stephanie added, "I know Shakespearean English, forsooth. That dost sound foreign to me."

Thomas said, "The question is, do you know two foreign languages while you're taking drugs? That would make you employable."

Patty looked forlornly at the *Romeo and Juliet* Project Progress Reports she'd prepared for the day, so after the class completed the surveys, instead of leading a talk on career choices, she asked them to write about them in their journals, figuring they'd finish writing quicker than they'd finish discussing. She walked behind the circle of desks, reading over their shoulders while they worked. Most wrote about jobs that related to their talents in some way or another. Zach, who could calm angry animals, wrote about veterinary medicine as did Charles, who could make dogs howl. Jen wrote about becoming a writer. Her pens and pencils talked, and if Patty listened, she could hear their squeaky, little voices (always with a slight British accent) giving corrections like, "'Ere, wot makes you think a comma goes there, deary?" Stephanie wanted to become an electrical engineer, which went along with her ability to amplify static discharges. Her hair always flared away from her neck, and the other kids had learned to not brush against her, or they'd be zapped.

Orson scribbled, and Patty sidled beside him to read his journal. His cloud disturbed her again. Although not jet-black as it had been before, black tendrils snaked through it. Other colors roiled in the cloud too, oranges and reds. He wasn't writing about careers, and he covered the page with his hand.

"I'm working on the project you suggested," he whispered. He didn't meet her eyes. "You know, the one about yearning? I don't have a clue what I want to be anyway." His cloud darkened.

Patty put a hand on his shoulder again, but this time his colors remained. "That's okay, Orson. I didn't know what I wanted to do until college. What's the project?"

"I'm rewriting *Romeo and Juliet*. I don't think it has to be a tragedy."

"Really?" Patty squatted beside him to be on the same level. "That's ambitious. How are you going to do it? It's a long play, and it would take a lot of changing."

He paused for a moment, as if struggling with how to answer. "Maybe not so much. You said yesterday the difference between comedy and tragedy is the ending, but I don't think that's all. It starts earlier in the play."

Patty leaned toward him. She could feel her eyebrows raising. This differed from the way most kids approached their projects. Elston and Katy were working together on *Romeo and Juliet* flashcards. The card's front contained a quote, and the back identified the speaker. Uma wanted to draw a balcony scene poster. Quenton had brought a shoe-box and a macaroni noodles package to make a diorama of Verona. The other projects seemed elementary compared to this one, and Orson's reasons for doing it worried her. She thought about her adolescent development classes, but couldn't remember a matching case.

She said, "Tomorrow everyone reports on their progress. Are you going to finish in time?"

Orson whispered, "Ask for me tomorrow and you shall find me a grave man.'"

Patty started to say, "That's Mercutio, isn't it, act III? You're reading ahead," but a fire alarm went off. Smoke and burning smells swept through the room, and for a second Patty almost panicked. She imagined flames outside her door and reached for a chair to throw through a window, but the kids laughed, and Bobby looked at the ceiling as if something interesting had appeared there.

"Bobby," she sighed, "this is not appropriate."

Then everyone scrambled for the door. As she joined the crowd in the hall, she tossed away the day's lesson. Even if this were a drill, they'd lose ten minutes standing outside, and it would take ten more to get class on track again. Later, as she shooed kids farther from the building, it occurred to her Mercutio was dying as he said those words, and she looked for Orson in the faces around her, but he had vanished.

At the day's end, a student senate announcement reminded everyone to support the Career Days assembly tomorrow by wearing clothes that reflected a career choice.


After school in the English office, long after the halls had cleared and the janitor's vacuum whined in a distant classroom, Elaine said, "So do you think he's suicidal?" She plucked a spiral notebook from the pile beside her, put it to her ear for a second, then dropped it onto the stack by her desk. Books spoke to her. They told her how many words the students had written, and whether they'd completed the assignments.

"He's scaring me. Ms. Reed gave me a pamphlet on suicide, but the warning signs are so vague they fit half the kids most the time. Mood swings, for crying out loud. Behavior changes. That's *normal* freshmen."

Elaine chuckled. "You don't sound like a rookie to me. Is there any popcorn left?"

Patty checked the bowl. "Nope, just some kernels."

"Those are the best." She pinched one from the salty buttery mess at the bottom and crunched it between her teeth. "If you're genuinely worried, you might call the boy's parents. You could find out if there's something going on there."

Patty tried a kernel, but it was like sucking on a greasy pebble, and she couldn't bring herself to chew it. "Maybe I should." She spit the kernel into a napkin. "Have you seen this yet?" She held a form in triplicate from the administrator's office. "We're supposed to put every course we've ever taken on it with a brief explanation of its impact on our instruction. Why does it seem I never get to teach English? I thought all my time would be spent wallowing in the classics, but instead I deal with distractions."

Elaine said, "You teach the kid, honey, not the subject." Elaine reached for the form, and Patty handed it to her. "This is a recertification questionnaire. You're not supposed to have one until your teaching certificate expires. It must be in your box by mistake. Give it back to the secretaries. Did you fill out your new emergency contact card? That was due today."

Patty put her head in her hands. "No. Nobody told me this would be a part of my day when I chose education as a career. What happens if I'm late with it?"

Crunching another kernel, Elaine said, "Nothing except Drabbe will record it on your evaluation. It's the part that deals with professional responsibilities." She leaned back in her chair and laced her fingers across her stomach. "You know, education is like the old joke about the pigeon that plays checkers. What amazes is not that it wins a game every once in a while, but it can play at all. Are you calling Orson's folks?"

Patty put the form on the pile of other forms on her desk. "I don't know. What would I say? Your son admires Romeo? My talent reads emotions and your son looked black yesterday? Keep him away from the apothecary? People are pretty uncomfortable with that anyway. It's too close to telepathy."

"How was he today?"

"He doesn't know what he wants to be. The Career Days assembly didn't help. But a little better, I think. He stayed busy in his journal until the fire alarm. Said he's rewriting *Romeo and Juliet* so it won't be so sad."

"Working in class is a good sign, I believe. As long as it's not a good-bye letter. While he's at it, ask him to rewrite my contract. I shouldn't have to monitor the lunch room the same year I'm the Junior class sponsor."

Patty grinned. "Okay I'll talk to him. But if he does that, I'll want him to rewrite Drabbe's evaluation. I'm afraid it will read like *Hamlet*. I'll get to the end, all these bodies will be strewn across the stage, and they'll all be me."

"Goodnight, sweet prince," said Elaine.

"Parting is such sweet sorrow."

"Don't forget to dress like your career choice tomorrow. I think I'll wear cowboy boots, a ballet skirt, a medical smock and a fireman's hat. I always tell the kids I can't decide what I want to be when I grow up."

After Elaine left, Patty sat alone in the office for another hour, deciding how to grade the *Romeo and Juliet* projects when they came in. She'd made the assignment and tried to give the students several ways to complete it, but she hadn't thought all the way through to how they would be evaluated. If Orson rewrote the play, as he said he would, that would require tons more time and effort than the Shakespearean word search Paul had proposed or Harmony's crossword puzzle project.

She looked at tomorrow's lesson plans: "Students to present proposals to the class. Discuss." It was one of those dangerous plans that might take ten minutes to finish, and then they'd be left with the rest of the hour to fill, or she might not get through half the class. It depended on how talkative they were. Hopefully, though, the students would find things to respond to in each other's proposals, and she would serve as a discussion facilitator. She thought about Orson. Would he stand in front of the class and talk? The students knew he'd exhibited no talent so far, and even if they didn't tease him, he knew they knew. That could be enough to keep him from speaking. A professor she'd had in a teaching methods class the year before had said, "A sense of isolation can be a contributing factor to failure in the classroom. It can even provoke desperate actions."

She put her plans away and looked up Orson's phone number, connected to an answering machine, then left her name and number.

In the hallway before class the next morning, Patty turned the corner to see Mr. Drabbe striding toward her. No place to hide, so she kept walking. A couple student senate members hung a Homecoming poster. One wore a clown suit, and the other dressed as a policeman. The halls were empty otherwise, and their voices echoed.

"Ms. Epson, how are you?" He grinned like a shark circling the lifeboats, she thought. "Could you come by my office after school today? I'd like to discuss your evaluation."

Patty tried to remain calm and professional, but she could feel herself freezing up. "Certainly." She noticed she'd crossed her arms across her chest. If she could sense her emotions as she could others, she believed she'd be a bilious green.

"There's some very interesting conclusions I've made from watching your video," he said.

Patty closed her eyes briefly. "I'll look forward to hearing your thoughts."

He nodded and continued on his way.

In the mail room, she checked the day's announcements. As far as she could tell, no assemblies scheduled, no dismissals for any sports teams, no field trips that would suck students from her classes, no standardized testing, no medical screenings, and nothing else that would interfere with her lessons. In short, it looked to be an unusual day. She thought about Orson. If all went well, he would explain his project in the middle of the hour. Assuming no fire drills, bomb scares, power outages or student senate interruptions, he'd get a chance to present a unique project for the class.

This provoked a new worries, however. Freshmen were mercurial. They might find Orson's unique proposal interesting. *She* thought it interesting, but she taught English, and she'd already discovered the lessons she loved weren't always what students loved. Also, "unusual" meant one of two things to freshmen: "cool" or "stupid." She prayed they'd go for "cool," and forget for the moment Orson had no talent. It would do his self image so much good. But she couldn't shake the feeling of the cloud around him, that dark moment when his despair almost blocked the light. She had an image of it tightening around him, absorbing him so he'd be lost within and never come out.

A new lesson plan excited Elaine, and Patty envied her as she busied around her desk, gathering books and papers. When the warning bell rang for first hour, Elaine said, "There are days I can't believe they pay me. Well, I'm off to be the wizard."

Patty wished she felt a third as industrious, but mostly she thought about Orson. She sketched out strategies to preempt any possible disasters with the class. If she prepped them right, maybe they'd stay positive and give Orson a break. So much depended on Orson, though. If he screwed up, the kids would go after him. It wasn't they were cruel; it was just freshmen's nature. They were beautiful, young timber wolves. You could sense their nobility and strength, but if you seemed the least bit weak or sick (or different), they'd pull you down.

Of course, Orson might decide not to present at all. Like Melville's Bartleby, he might say, "I prefer not to," and that would be the end. The kids would brand him a loser again (not because others might not do their homework, but because it was Orson). He'd sink deeper in the cloud, fulfilling the conclusion they'd reached about him by believing it himself. She wrote in her plan book, "Be ready, Orson!" like a little prayer.

Class started with an interruption. Patty announced the order of presentations, and when Rachael, wearing a placard that said, "I'm a weatherman," stepped to the podium, the intercom clicked on to announce six cars in the parking lot with their lights on. Rachael stood at the podium miserably, the reading of license numbers delaying her public speaking moment.

After the interminable announcement ended, Patty slid around the desks until she stood behind Bobby. Bobby wore a perfume bottles necklace. If she stayed by him, she figured, he'd be less likely to showcase his talent and disrupt the class again. Orson looked down at his notebook. Patty couldn't tell if he were prepared or not. She chewed on her lower lip.

Like Bobby, most kids wore outfits to indicate a future career. Career Dress up Day seemed to be a student senate activity that involved a student majority for a change. Not surprisingly, Orson had chosen not to participate.

"Go ahead, Rachael," she said.

Rachael spent a few minutes explaining a hand-puppet version of the battle between Romeo and Paris. On the chalk board she drew a puppet theater and showed where the actors would hide. When she finished, she erased the board.

"Thank you, Rachael. Now we'll hear from Alice." Alice, who could set a coin spinning endlessly on her desk, marched to the podium, wearing a banker's suit.

Student by student, each presented a project to show their interest in the play, and they came closer and closer to Orson's demonstration. He never looked up. Patty couldn't sense his emotions from this distance. She gambled keeping Bobby under control was more important than finding out what Orson was feeling.

Finally, Orson's turn came. Just as Patty opened her mouth to call on him, the intercom clicked on again. Vice Principal Drabbe lectured the school for a few minutes about the carelessness of not turning off car lights because it interrupted the school day to find the cars' owners. The classroom of freshmen, not a driver in the bunch, fidgeted through the droning voice.

Patty waited a few seconds after Drabbe clicked off, took a deep breath, and called on Orson.

He didn't move.

The class waited. Patty knew an unwritten time limit for delay could pass. A short wait was acceptable, but at some point, the class would become restive and she would have to call on him again. She didn't want to do that. She wanted his presentation to be normal, to be like the others, not different or weird.

She cleared her throat. Some kids looked at her. She started to speak, and Orson stood. Patty's teeth clicked, she shut her mouth so sharply. Orson took his notebook to the podium.

Some presentations had gone well so far. Some had not. During Paul's discussion why a scale model of the Globe made from sugar cubes and popsickle sticks would teach him more about Shakespearean theater, the class's boredom was obvious, and they flat out laughed at Zach when he suggested the class reenact the honeymoon scene with all male actors since, "It would be more authentic to Elizabethan drama."

Orson arranged his notebook on the podium. He said something, but Patty couldn't hear it. William smirked and leaned over to comment to Fran.

"Could you speak a little louder, Orson?" said Patty.

He nodded and started again with more force. "Does the play's ending bother any of you?" he said. He put his hands behind his back and stepped away from the podium.

Nobody spoke. Patty clenched her hands. Please let someone be civil, she thought. Please, please, oh god, please.

Orson didn't move, and the silence stretched. Outlast them, Patty thought. A professor last year had taught her, "Ask the question. Then let them be uncomfortable. You're not going anywhere."

Wait them out, she thought.

Then Jen said, "The ending sucks."

Patty breathed a silent thank you.

"Sure," said Charles, "the ending is lame. It's a chick-flick trip."

Natalie shot back. "No, it has to end that way. It's a tragedy. And I'll have you know, Charles, there's no chicks in here unless you're a cock."

Before Patty could speak, Orson said, "Exactly. My project deals with how *Romeo and Juliet* is put together. I'm rewriting it so it will be a comedy."

His pronouncement hung in the air. Patty tried to read everyone's emotions, but none were clear. Leslie raised her hand. No one else spoke. Orson looked at Patty for direction, and Patty tilted her head toward the raised hand to indicate it was his call.

"Yes," he said. Patty thought his voice pleasant. Much deeper than his size indicated it might be. She thought it could be a compelling voice.

Leslie put her hand down. "I think that's a cool idea. How are you going to do it?"

Orson smiled, his teeth even and bright. Patty had never seen him smile. "It starts this way." He turned to the board. "First, Mercutio and Tybalt are secret friends. The fight is staged to trick Romeo into giving up his love for Juliet. They figured when he saw what trouble it caused, he'd drop her and go back to Rosaline."

"Wow," said Gloria. "That *is* cool. How about the killing of Tybalt?"

Orson outlined the plot changes on the board. Class members offered suggestions, and he incorporated them into the outline. The board filled with names and arrows.

Katy said, "So the nurse secretly loves the friar, and he's defrocked so they can get together at the end?"

Orson wrote and talked at the same time, laughing. "Yes, that would work, and Paris falls in love with Rosaline."

Joy filled Patty. The class interacted in that magic way that happens so rarely. Like a perpetual motion machine, it produced more energy than she'd put in. Hands went up. Their suggestions overlapped and the babble was happy and unrestrained. She wished she could hold the moment forever.

Then Jen pulled on Patty's sleeve. "Ms. Epson," she said. "Can you see?"

At first she didn't, but the class fell silent as Orson continued writing on the board and talking about what else had to change. He looked out at them. No one spoke, and they stared, like Patty, with their jaws a little dropped.

"What?" he said, and for a second a hint of black cloud swirled around him.

"That is *really* cool," someone said.

"What?" Orson asked again, and then he turned to look at the board.

All the words he'd written glowed. The names and arrows, boxes and lines, lit in pulsing color, revolving through the spectrum. Reds dissolved into oranges and yellows. Blues shifted into green, then indigo and violet. It was hypnotic and so unexpected.

Jen said, "Oh, Orson, you got your talent."

Orson looked from the board to the chalk in his hand like a magician's wand, and light from the board glowed off his face. He met Patty's eyes and said in wonder, "I think I know what I want to be, Ms. Epson. I think I know."

She could see the teacher in him.

The room flooded with the odor of freshly cut flowers.

Smiling at Orson, Patty touched Bobby's shoulder. "Thank you, Bobby. That's very nice. Very appropriate."

And she quit worrying about her evaluation meeting with Mr. Drabbe.

# Home

Lots of times when I walk in the high school like yesterday, when the monster gave me the death threat, I pretend I'm anti-matter, and the rest of everything is matter. I can't touch anything or the explosion would make Hiroshima seem like a stifled sneeze. No one can help me; I'm totally on my own. Kids push by me on both sides, their faces intent, eyes fish-blank and staring, and I'm sweating, leaning left, pausing, avoiding a contact here, the brush of a sleeve there. The fate of the entire school rests in my ability to slip through the hallway. I stay in the middle of the flow, away from the turbulent areas next to the lockers or where the opposing streams of traffic slide by. Nothing can graze me. It's rough: slow down, speed up, stay hyper-aware of people's positions. The cross hall that leads left to the offices and the gym to the right, messes up the traffic pattern, but I negotiate through without a tag. A letter jacket dangling a cheerleader and leading a pack of sycophants blocks the way, and I fade into a calm spot by an athletic awards case until they move on.

Two boys, Freshmen probably, in matching "No Fear" t-shirts, wearing visors turned upside down and backwards are shoving at each other in front of me, mouths moving. I don't really listen; I mean, hall-noise is pure white if you don't focus on it, so I see their lips flapping, and they're goosing each other.

Of course, my game's impossible to win, even though high school kids instinctively don't like to touch. I could walk normally through a crowded hall, and nobody would contact me most the time; but accidents happen, you know: people run into each other, and when one of the freshmen turns, he elbows me in the chest. Boom! In my mind we're all dead; the anti-matter/matter event border tearing protons, neutrons and electrons apart, converting mass to energy in a cataclysmic spasm, and I see the shock wave in slow motion blazing through the hall, vaporizing kid after kid, not even knocking them over; just atomizing them. Then my imaginary camera peels away from the school and wide-angles from above, retreating fast as the building turns into a tiny sun, washing the entire valley in acetylene-bright light. Only the surrounding hills that direct the blast up into the sky saves the nearby towns, and a week later, the magma at the bottom of the blast crater still seethes and bubbles.

All because some freshman elbows me in the chest.

So we're all dead, and there's no point in starting over again, when I see two things at once; the first is a skinny Side-by-Side kid trying to get his walker turned around. Side-by-Side's this program at the school to "mainstream" students who most likely would be in institutions otherwise. He's got himself up against a wall and he's trying to turn that way, but every time he jerks the aluminum tubes around, he smacks into the bricks. I don't know why he can't go to his left. The Side-by-Side kids have all kinds of problems that way. I mean, some are blind *and* have seizures, or are both paraplegic *and* fetal alcohol syndrome, and most of them look different. Life or the womb wasn't kind to them, but they're a part of the school. Generally I don't see them in the halls with the rest of the students Most "regular" students probably aren't even aware that the Side-by-Side kids exist. They pass before or after the bell. They have their own buses. Since I'm non-traditional myself, I know about them.

So this Side-by-Side kid is clanging his walker against the wall, whimpering to himself, and everyone else is passing by him as if he's not even alive or something, and at the same time I see him, I see the monster coming toward me from the science wing.

First of all, it's big. No denying that. Its head brushes the ceiling, and these are ten-footers. Second of all, nobody else seems to notice it. High school students don't notice much, I'll grant you that. I mean, they don't pay any attention to me most of the time, and I think that's pretty odd. I would pay attention to me, if you get my drift. But they're ignoring this monster, who looks like the Pillsbury Dough Boy crossed with Klaatu's silvery robot from *The Day the Earth Stood Still*. It's not the first time I've seen a monster, so I kind of track him out of the corner of my eye while helping the Side-by-Side kid.

"You've got to back up, buddy," I say. He looks at me; there's drool on his chin, but his eyes are deep brown and lively. He slams the walker into the bricks again with an aluminum clang and makes a frustrated whine from the back of his throat. "The wall's not going anywhere, champ," I say.

Meanwhile the monster's getting closer. As I said, they're no novelty to me. During seventh grade, when I switched foster families three times in six months, I did a lot of drugs, mostly home grown or harvested, like moonweed and the other natural pharmaceuticals that grow in the flats and canyons south of town. At first I did them to *get rid* of monsters:

stupid things that woke me at night in unfamiliar beds, fear-drenched and shaking, or what I think of as my amnesia dreams: of a life I've lost and can't quite remember—long, heart rendingly odd visions of too tall mountains and reddish skies that left me sobbing and drained, but the drugs brought their own multi-tentacled things to life, and I laid off them after a while. Flash backs hit me periodically though; a pterodactyl above the school bus or shining teeth glinting from behind a stack of books at the library doesn't surprise me all that much. Still, this monster seemed particularly persistent, walking against the flow of kids who moved around it without acknowledging its presence.

I get this tingle in the back of my neck, and it suddenly seems really important to get the kid off the wall and sprint away from here. This isn't your typical paranoid panic—I get those too; the dough boy robot's definitely coming toward me. I get behind the Side-by-Side kid and grab the left side of the walker; it's slick with his sweat, and I pull him gently backward, away from the bricks. He shuffles his feet around and completes his right hand turn, but now he's going against the traffic; kids' faces look panicked as they realize that the Side-by-Side kid isn't going to stop coming forward. They dance around him, pressured by the crowd behind them in the eternal rush to beat the tardy bell.

"Coming through," I yell. "Cut a path!" Now we're heading away from the monster, but he's gaining. I don't get it. Most of the time my hallucinations reside in my peripheral vision, and a good hard look banishes them. This one, however, takes a straight on stare and keeps coming. People detour around too, not responding to it directly; a nerdy girl in a pink sweater actually stops in front of it because it's right in her way, pushes her glasses up on her nose, fakes right then goes around it on the left, but she doesn't seem to have really seen it. It's as if she just got it in her head that she wanted to go one way, then changed her mind and went the other. Traffic's lightening up now this late in the passing period.

The Side-by-Side kid's into his rhythm: shuffle-shuffle-lift-and-klunk, and we're coming up to his room. He swings the walker to his right and heads for the door. The bell rings. Magically, the halls have emptied. He stops just before entering and twists back (to his right, of course) toward me, his chin slick with drool, his head tilted to the side; he gurgles something.

"What?" I say. I can feel the monster approaching, maybe twenty feet away. I'm itching to run.

He gurgles again, as if he's trying to push his voice through wet leaves, then it comes out clearly, "Thanks, K." His face grimaces. Maybe it was a smile. I don't know. He shuffle-klunks into the room, and I'm stunned, the monster forgotten for a second. He knew my name! No one in the hallway ever calls me by name. In classes sometimes, when I go, I hear it, mostly by the teachers who don't know where my nick-name came from and call me that without trying to be cruel.

"Thanks, K," the boy had said. The empty hallway echoes with his voice. I hear it bouncing off the lockers behind me. It is the first time I feel good about being in that school.

Then the monster taps me on the shoulder. Its touch is warm and hard. Tap, tap. I turn. Up close, I can see my own reflection, wavy and distorted in its silver skin. I look up; its head is tilted down, as if it is studying me, but it doesn't have any eyes, no features at all; sort of like what you would get if you carved a robot monster out of silver soap, then showered with it a couple of times: no seams, no sharp edges, the short neck flowing smoothly from the rounded shoulders then widening into the Christmas ornament head, and it's suddenly clear that my monster is a robot or something in a silver suit, but I can't see past the mirrored face plate.

Then, the death threat. It says, "Pack your things." The voice is real, I mean, it isn't telepathy stuff, and it sounds like a pipe organ, high in register but more metal than organic. My flashbacks have never spoken to me before.

I freeze for a second. What can I do? A ten foot silver robot that nobody else can see has a hand on my shoulder and has told me to pack my things. It might as well have said, "Kiss your ass goodbye," or "Make peace with your maker." And, of course, the words, "Pack your things;" this is a blast from the past. How many times have I heard that before? It's straight out of memory, not that a monster had said it, but in one way or another, every school and foster home I've ever been in gave me the same message. Here though...I mean it's ten-feet tall...the words sound much darker. All the little hairs on the back of my neck are dancing.

I back up, and its hand slips off me. "No," I say. It's not clever repartee, but I'm a little shook. It speaks again and says, "I've come..."

"Screw you," I yell, twirling away from it and sprinting down the hall. My feet make slap-slap sounds all the way to the double doors out of the building and I never look back.

It is the last period of the day, so skipping out doesn't sound too bad to me. Besides, Geography has never been my favorite class. Long, boring lectures about Euro-Asian trade alliances and then pop quizzes on the agri-products of the rain forests. I've looked at the globe on the teacher's desk, and thought that if I were an alien I wouldn't land there.

I jog down the street toward my house. It's ninety degrees out; the sun's toasty warm on top of my head. The air's got that flat, early September anticipation in it, as if it's tired of being summer but not quite ready to give up to Fall. I like it hot, so bouncing away on the road's shoulder, sweat already pouring off my face feels good. Already the tightness in my gut, the fear in the hallway is fading, and I'm half convinced that nothing happened there. Ten foot tall robots, after all; even I have a tough time swallowing that.

And I'm kind of happy until I see this boy walking toward me on my side of the road. He's a middle-school kid—they get out before the high school does; he's holding his skateboard behind his back crossways with his arms locked around each end. It gives him a Battan Death March pose, plodding in the shoulder's dust. Across the road and a little in front of him walking in the same direction is this girl, about the same age, lost in thought, eyes focused on the ground. She's slender, wearing a lot of black, her books clenched to her chest. The boy's staring at her. I slow down. His look is clearly one of yearning. He wants her. A semi rumbles by between them. He doesn't blink or glance away. I pass on his left, only a couple of feet away; he never sees me. All his attention is locked on the girl; his face is tragic.

Suddenly, I'm by, and the guy's expression lingers in my mind, and I start crying. The whole thing's so sad and stupid—me stumbling down the road, tears mixing with sweat as I run. Nobody understands me when I talk about stuff like this. I mean, I've tried, but they give me looks as if I'm a dweeb and wander off. Here's this kid, following this girl he's probably wanted to talk to since fifth grade, and she doesn't even know he's alive. The tragedy is in the yearning; that's where I come in. I see in his face everything that I'm all about, constantly wanting to be a part of the world that doesn't know I'm there. It's my essential being: isolation. I told this to a counselor Social Services tied me into last year. After scribbling a note on a tiny pad she'd balanced on her knee, she said, "Have you tried joining a club, K?"

Want to hear a joke? It starts, "I'm from Social Services, and I'm here to help."

Which reminds me of my name. In second grade, I pretended to be a praying mantis for six days. I'd rotate my head to look at people, but I wouldn't move my shoulders or shift around; I kept my hands close to my chest, fingers out and limp. If I wanted something, like a pencil or a book, I'd stare at if for a few minutes, swaying a little side to side, then I'd pounce. It was a lot of fun, but after I'd been doing it for a while, Dan Clurge, who spoke with a thick, Southern accent, called me a "space kay-det." The "K" part stuck, and I got used to it after a while. When I change foster families, I like to take on their last name, so right now I'm K Coder, but I've been a host of others too. My favorite was K Beebee; that lasted seven months and my signature looked like a cattle brand: KBB.

I kill some time at the park, pitching rocks into the pond. That way it'll look as if I didn't leave school early. When I get to the foster house, I climb in the bedroom window so I won't have to talk to my foster mother, but she hears me anyway and yells, "It wouldn't kill you to use the back door, you know."

I don't say anything. She's thirty; her husband drives long haul routes and is gone most of the time, and she raises three kids of her own; they keep her hopping enough without dealing with me. When I'd first got there a few weeks ago with everything I own in a duffle bag dangling from my shoulder, she gave me the once over; I could tell she was mentally inventorying me. The hair probably bothered her: I'd shagged it out, dyed it henna-red and braided four tight strands that fell across my face. I'd shave it off—really I would: hair feels weird to me—but henna-red is in. I thought maybe the new age crowd might take me on, or the skate-boarders; they seem the most open minded, but they didn't as always. Then my clothes didn't do anything for her either: flannel jacket, no buttons, no shirt underneath; an old pair of gray sweats I'd chopped at the knees, and blue running shoes, no socks. She shook her head and said, "What planet are you from?"

I wonder myself.

The evening comes. I stay in the room, watching the sun set all flaming and glorious but I'm still thinking about that kid walking down the street. By the time the first stars come out I've come to no conclusions. I'm wondering if I can sneak into the kitchen to get something to eat without anyone seeing me when my foster mother walks in. She doesn't say hi or anything.

"The school called and said you ditched your last class."

I can tell she's mad, but she's holding it. Her hands fist at her hips, clenching a bit of her skirt on both sides. She's probably a pretty woman if she didn't look so tired all the time: nice, high cheek bones. "We lose your support check from the government if you're dropped from the school, and I can't have that. You either straighten up and fly right or get your butt out of here. Is that clear?"

I don't know what to say to that because just as I open my mouth the silver monster pokes its head up in the window behind her. I figure it must be bending over or on its knees since the window's not that high. After a few seconds, my foster mother's rhetorical question hanging in the air, me not replying and probably looking like an idiot since I'm staring past her, she "humphs" disgustedly and stomps out of the room, slamming the door behind her that pops right back open because the latch is broke.

"Pack your things," it says in its pipe organ voice. "I've come to take you home." And I'm out of the room, heart pounding through the top of my head, dashing by my foster mother who's still walking down the hallway, and I don't stop running until I'm at the edge of town.

What does that mean: "I've come to take you home"? Is it like what the airlines call "Your final destination"? The happy hunting grounds? I don't like the sounds of it, whatever it means. Plus, it's a lyric from a Peter Gabriel song. My unconsciousness isn't dredging too deep to give me this nightmare.

Past the last street lights, the asphalt turns into fine gravel, ending up at the "Odd-Fellows" cemetery, where at the turn of the century they buried Jews, "citizens of color," and indigents. It's my favorite place even though it seems ghoulish considering that a hallucination is threatening to put me here permanently. A breeze picks up the smell of fresh cut grass from the Catholic cemetery across the road. Here, long weeds brush the tombstones.

I'm breathing hard, resting my back against Amelia Nurenberg's stone, thinking about what I'm going to do. See, I can live with a lot of stuff: kids who don't like me, teachers who only keep me in class because they have to, foster families one right after another. Those kinds of things bother me, but they're no biggie. Harder to explain annoyances get to me more: like feeling like my body doesn't fit me, or that sounds are too sharp, or that music rhythms are always off, or that none of the things I'm supposed to care about matter a fig and all the things I do care about nobody understands.

I'm at a break point, though, when a hallucination won't go away. Something's got to change. Not the world, certainly. It's got all this weight on its side. I'm outnumbered, so it's got to be me. I snap a long strand of weed off the grave mound and put it between my teeth. The taste is sharp, like almond extract, and there's a kind of anesthetic effect because my lips go a little tingly. How can I change? Of course, that's the problem. Nobody wants to be insane. Nobody wants to be unhappy. But if I did change, if I could even do it, what would I become? Another of those blank-eyed students in the hall who can't see when a Side-by-Side kid needs some help? And what really gets me is what if *they* all have some inner block, like that kid who couldn't go left, except that theirs is psychological; that they all have some mental thing that they fetch up to in their head just as solid as that brick wall, and within their skulls there's this metal clanging going on all the time that they can't even hear anymore because they've learned to ignore it? Would I even want to be like that?

So I'm leaning on a gravestone, listening to the hiss of weeds and the nice, cool silence of the moon and stars, and all my options look untenable. Still, the monster is pushing the issue. It's a new variable in the equation. I don't know what it means, but things can't stay the same.

Then I see the monster coming toward me from the edge of the cemetery, bathed in moonlight, walking silently between the stones; it's like a ghost. It couldn't have found me; it must have a homing device or something. Hiding's not an option. I'm trying not to breathe too loud, but I hear myself just the same: shaky and clear in the night air. I have this vision of it reaching me, rending me limb from limb, and in my fear I almost laugh because it suddenly occurs to me that the grim reaper is supposed to be darkly cloaked, carrying a scythe; not ten feet tall, silver and fat.

I hadn't thought of this before, but in the hallway it touched me. A hallucination that doesn't go away when you stare straight at it, that other people go around instead of through, that talks, doesn't change, and takes a reasonable amount of time to go from place to place isn't a hallucination at all. It reminds me of what somebody told me once: "If it swims like a duck, walks like a duck and quacks like a duck, it's a duck." The monster's real.

I can't stay, so I run, and the only place I have is the foster house, so I sneak in again and hide under the blankets like a little kid, convinced the whole time that the monster followed me back and is staring at me all night through that window that's too small for it to go through, waiting to say, "Pack your things. I've come to take you home."

In the morning, when I awake, the monster isn't at the window, but my foster mother sits on the edge of the bed as if she's been there forever waiting for me to wake up. I pull up my blankets under my chin, not all that surprised to see her. The room's not mine, after all, and I've had this kind of speech before. I could write her lines for her.

She starts with a sigh, her hands together in her lap, not looking at me. "I phoned my husband last night," she says. "And we talked about it for a long time." She twists her hands around, as if she's washing them. Her nails are neatly trimmed. No polish. "This isn't working out the way we hoped...you staying with us." She sighs again, and I think she's on the edge of crying. "It's not that we don't like you, or that you're a bad boy, really, but we think you might fit in better with another family."

I *have* heard it before, but I still feel small. No different than when I was five or six or seven. I'm thinking, if this were a movie script, I'd reach out and hug her and call her mom and all would be forgiven, or I'd get angry and yell names, but I don't really know her. She doesn't know me. It's just awkward.

"It's okay," I say.

She sits for another minute, never looks at me, and with a final sigh, stands and leaves the room.

I don't want to cause her any problems. It's not her fault, so I put the clothes I brought with me into my duffle bag along with a couple of books that I've carried around for years, and head for school. I figure that I'll go to Social Services after classes and talk to them about a new placement. Most of the time they move pretty fast on foster parent's requests, since Social Services doesn't want to lose them as residence sites, and I figure that I could be in a new place tonight.

Jogging's tough carrying a bag, so I walk. Everything looks empty. The cottonwoods along the way seem to be barely hanging onto their leaves, even though they haven't started turning color yet. The sound of tires on the road sounds muffled and dead. I don't hear a single bird the whole way.

Then I'm not in my first class for five minutes before I get a note to come to the assistant principal's office, and ten minutes after that, I'm expelled for too many unexcused absences.

So this all sounds pretty tragic, right? I'm sitting outside of the school by the bus loop, my duffle bag between my legs; these tears are just rolling down my cheeks, and I don't care. School's stupid. I never fit in there, and it shouldn't be a big deal that the foster family wants me to move on, but, still, I'm crying, feeling as if the whole world has a plan for itself, and I'm not part of it. I'm a minority of one, an alien, a special interest group that no one's interested in. My whole life's spinning in my head, and I'm half thinking that if I could throw up I might feel a little better.

It seems like a long time, but it wasn't, because I stop sniffling when, like yesterday, two things happen at once: first, a gleam out on the football field catches my eye. It's the silver monster, and this time it's not moving; he's just standing there facing my direction. And he's not alone either; a smaller version stands behind him, and a tiny one, like maybe four feet tall is running around the smaller one's feet. It's truly an arresting sight. I almost have to laugh.

Then the last bus of the day pulls up to the stop; it's the Side-by-Side program bus. Some of the kids come out the regular door by themselves; some need assistance, while a wheelchair lift in the back is unloading some others. I've watched this other days. The process can take ten minutes.

So I'm watching the bus unload, and I'm watching the monsters. In the clear light of the morning, standing in the middle of the short-cropped green of the football field, the largest robot looks a lot less threatening, almost pretty. I've lost the hollow spot already; whatever happens is going to happen. When something ends, something else begins. Once again, I'm on the edge of a new chapter in my life.

Then, the guy that I aided yesterday gets out of the bus. A teacher helps him down and holds him under one arm while the driver hands out the walker. The kid concentrates mightily getting his hands placed right, and I realize that he must stay up in that walker mostly by force of will because his legs look useless. I wonder why he doesn't use a wheelchair, but I admire the effort. It takes him two or three tries to get moving. He leans back to get the walker off the ground, then kind of falls forward to move the walker a few inches. It's an amazing display.

He spots me, jerks the walker to his right, and starts my direction, a big grin on his face. His muscles bunch under his shirt; he lifts and comes forward. Shuffle-shuffle. All his motions are focused, intense, irresistible, and I realize, nothing will stop him. If he miscalculates, he'll turn a 360 to get back on track. If he falls down, he'll figure a way to get up. I think he knows who he is. He and his walker work together to get him where ever he's going, and it doesn't matter to him that no one in the halls knows him. He's moving in his own way, and that's enough.

That's enough, I think; then I do laugh, because it's not. I admire him because he *looks* so independent, but he's not. Teachers help him, his parents help him; heck, even I helped him. And that's what I was trying to do, bang my own walker against a wall and not ask for help from anybody. You can't do it on your own. You've got to have help or you'll go crazy. Anyone could tell you that.

He reaches me. He strains in his throat for a second, then says, "Hi, K."

It's beautiful. I've put it all together. The bus gleams bright yellow in this world's sun. *This* world's sun, not mine. Mine is some place else; it has to be. Behind the bus, the cottonwoods seem perkier, more alive and ready to soak up the rays. The boy's face shines in the light of his happiness. He got to me. He said hi. He found someone who would help, and it was me.

I'm not sure what to say to him, but I know what I've got to do. I've got to find my help. I've got to go where I belong.

I drape my duffle bag over the front of his walker. The silver monster had said, "Pack your things." Out in the football field, he waits. I'm going to it. Hidden in the forest, or maybe hovering above must be his space ship. I'll bet they're from some place like my dreams, where the mountains are too tall and the sky a dusky shade of red. My rescue has finally arrived.

"You can keep my things," I say. "They've come to take me home."

# Nor a Lender Be

On a park bench near the swings, the old man in an overcoat eyes the children. He's positioned himself carefully away from the parents who are talking amiably on a set of benches on the other side of the playground equipment. Near him, a pair of boys dressed in matching blue jumpers take turns going down the slide. The old man studies them for a while. They're maybe five and four, he decides, very sweet; they smile often; the same shade of blonde hair curls out from beneath their caps.

On the teeter-totters, a handful of older kids, around nine or ten years old, rise then fall in rhythm. They laugh in unison at some joke. Beyond them on the grass, a couple of teens throw a football back and forth. The old man sighs and looks at his hands. Liver spots mar the knuckles and make indecipherable patterns on their backs. He imagines things crawling under his skin, moving beneath the loose parchment of his flesh. He resists the urge to scratch his fingers. When he raises his left hand from his leg, it trembles slightly.

Underneath the slide, a little girl sits against a support pole, drawing patterns in the gravel. She's maybe eight, the old man guesses. Her blonde hair matches the boys going up the ladder. Her lips are thin and serious. She concentrates on what she's drawing, erasing a part of it and starting again. When she finally looks up, as if sensing she is being watched, her eyes are dark brown.

"Hi," she says, not lifting her finger from the spot on her drawing.

The old man glances at the parents on the other side. They're facing each other, chatting. Nobody seems to notice him or the child. He gestures to her—a come closer wave.

"Hey," he says. "Hey, little girl. Do you want to know a secret?"

She looks at her work for a moment, makes a final line in the gravel, then gets up, brushes the back of her dress and says, "Do you know one?"

"Sure," he says. "A good one. Come a little closer so I can tell you." He keeps his hands on his legs so she won't see the trembling. The trembling might frighten her. If she knew about the things under his skin, it might frighten her. If she knew what swam behind his eyes, it would drive her off.

*T*he two observers, a black-haired woman in a gray pantsuit, and a man, sporting old-fashioned glasses, jeans and neatly pressed sport shirt had come into class at the beginning, taken seats in the rear, then not moved other than to whisper quietly to each other during William's lesson on *Hamlet*.

William paid them little attention. Visitors came to his class regularly: parents who'd just enrolled their kids, still suspicious of a live teacher instead of a computer DeskTop unit; media people with tiny cameras who'd film for their programs ("Retro-Teaching Survives in Colorado" was the title of a piece a week earlier); board of education members, each with their own agenda, etc. They'd make notes about the semicircular desk arrangement, how much William talked, how often students responded. The minute details seemed to fascinate them. Sometimes old folk came in to wallow in nostalgia, to remember when all schools used to be like this.

William concentrated on the class of fifteen students; they were playing a quote game.

"So," said William, "If I were your boyfriend and you wanted to dump me, what might you say?"

Shelia, a sixteen year old with a splash of freckles across her cheeks and nose nervously raised her hand. "My Lord, I have remembrances of yours that I have longed to deliver?" She paused, pantomimed handing him something, then smiled when William took it. Her fingertips brushed his palms. She said, "I'd tell you that if I returned your ring or something."

William nodded again, leaning toward her. "Yes, Shelia. Exactly. But what if I denied it hurt me? What if I were a creep and said to you, 'No, not I. I never gave you ought'?" He said it gruffly, brusquely as if he really was irritated at her, as if he despised the idea of her.

"My honored Lord," she said, flushing. "You know right well you did. And with them words of so sweet breath composed as made the things more rich." She sighed. "I love that part."

William wandered around the room. The students watched him; he could feel their eyes—their attention—centered on him. It was always this way: the interaction, the game with the things he loved and the class, like opening a great oak door between them and the material, and he remembered again the first time he'd really understood Hamlet, facing the ghost on the stage, talking into the darkness, "King, Father, royal Dane. Oh, answer me! Let me not burst in ignorance."

William shivered. Literature struck him so immediately. He could feel it in the air, shimmering out of the texts on their desks. He said, "What if I were angry with someone and wanted to call him a name? Can any of you give me an insult?"

Jason, a skinny, pale boy said, "Bloody, bawdy villain! Remorseless, treacherous, lecherous, kindless villain!"

"Ouch," said William, grinning, as he stuck an imaginary dagger in his chest. Several students laughed.

Just as strong in room as the presence of Shakespeare were the kids, all of them awake for a moment in this play. William felt like a friendly conductor, punching their tickets on the Hamlet express. They'd boarded as they always did—a bit full of the world, distracted and fragmented, but the rocking of the iambic rails had lulled them into receptiveness. William had played Polonius for them at the beginning of class. He'd said, "I do know, when the blood burns, how prodigal the soul lends the tongue vows."

They'd been caught. By the time he'd gone back to "Neither a borrower nor a lender be," they'd dropped every concern they'd brought to class. It was just them and Shakespeare and William playing three-cornered catch. He closed his eyes to feel it washing over him, and he almost forgot for a moment what they had been doing until Rupert, a dark-eyed boy, cleared his throat before speaking. "What if I said that you were an old man whose face was wrinkled; your eyes purged thick amber and plumtree gum, and that you have a plentiful lack of wit?"

"I'd say, 'Though this be madness, yet there is method in it.'"

Red-haired Tracy said, "Do you think Hamlet was mad?"

Dirk, who sat behind her tapped her on the shoulder. "'I am but mad north-north-west. When the wind is southerly, I know a hawk from a handsaw.' Hamlet knew what he was doing."

Five hands shot up.

"In quotes only," said William.

A bell rang, ending class, and several students groaned in disappointment. They gathered books and headed to the door.

"Good night, sweet prince," said Rupert as he left. Jason prodded him and said, "Ah, ha. I knew it. Women delight you not."

Rupert's voice drifted into the classroom from the hall, "What a piece of work is a man. How noble in reason, how infinite in faculties . . ."

William chuckled and turned to his desk.

"How impressive," said the woman in the pantsuit. William jumped; he'd forgotten about his visitors. The woman rose and her companion followed her, standing slightly behind her to one side. "Victoria Baseman," she said, extending a hand. "Of the Reinhart Group. This is my intern, Isaac. We'd like to talk to you about what you're doing here." She looked around the room. Student art work covered most of the walls: painstakingly hand-drawn renditions of The Globe Theater, examples of Elizabethan dress, and scenes from *Hamlet*. "The students appear to enjoy learning." Isaac, who might have been twenty and easily ten years Victoria's junior, took notes.

"That was...amazing. I was moved," said Isaac. Victoria shot him an annoyed frown.

William pushed the student's papers into a pile, trying to appear calm. The Reinhart group had swallowed Disney a decade ago, and had made massive strides into education in the last few years. Half the corporation schools in the country relied on Reinhart funding in one way or another, and they were one of the few companies who made money in the field since the privatization of schools thirty years earlier. "They're a good class. It's easier when they're motivated."

The woman consulted a data reader in her hand. "Looks like *all* your classes are motivated. Best test scores in the country."

"It's the school," said William. "The curriculum works."

Victoria snorted derisively. "False modesty. You've changed schools three times with a different curriculum each time. Your students excel when you're there. They're average when you're not. It's not the curriculum; it's you."

"I just teach them one day at the time. I've been blessed with good kids."

"The Reinhart Group thinks it's more than that. We've done extensive studies of student behavior—your students—and we've made interesting conclusions. Because of them, we'd like to make you a proposition." She sat on the edge of his desk.

"I'm happy here," said William. "I like the area." He pushed essays into his briefcase. "They pay me well."

Victoria put her data reader into her jacket. "Fifty years ago, you wouldn't have been so lucky." She turned to Isaac. "Fifty years ago teachers weren't paid by their successes. Good teachers, bad teachers, it didn't matter. They were paid the same."

"That seems silly," Isaac offered quietly, "Doesn't it? Why would anyone work hard?"

"Surprisingly, many of them did anyway. Teaching's more of an avocation than a vocation, wouldn't you say, William?"

William nodded. He wondered what she was leading to.

She continued, "But the schools weren't very good, just the same. When public schools collapsed and the corporations took over, good teachers were bid for. Bad teachers got better or quit. Generally education improved, and education became big business."

"Yes," offered William. "But there are still failings—whole groups of kids who are under served."

"Of course," Victoria said. "The corporate model has problems too. Applying management principles to classrooms hasn't made them all that much better, at least not as good as they need to be, despite the different approaches."

Isaac said, "You mean like individualized, home study."

"Yes, everything done at home through computers. No classrooms. No group contact. Interesting experiment," said Victoria. "An approach the Reinhart Group invests heavily in, but getting rid of the schools as structures hasn't done it. No, the problem is that every approach emphasizes curriculum."

Isaac looked puzzled, "Naturally. Curriculum and technique can be duplicated. It can be marketed. What else is there?"

"The teacher," said William.

Victoria nodded her approval. "Yes, the teacher. So we went big into teacher recruitment and training. That's why Reinhart is the major player in education. But it's time to make the next jump. It's time to get rid of the corporate model that relies on thinking of curriculum as product. The product model is dead."

Isaac said, "But what can replace it?"

"Yes, what?" said William.

"The pro-sports model is our new direction."

William sat on the edge of his desk. He'd read of something along these lines in the latest journals.

He said, "It's elitist, isn't it? Sell the superstar teacher to the high bidders? I'm not interested in teaching to a half-dozen rich kids."

"Of course not," she said smoothly. "We know you've turned down similar offers. No, we're ready to take the next, logical step. The pro-sport model of education is like a pro-sports team. We need a franchise player, though, a Babe Ruth. Someone who is so much obviously better that success rests on that person's shoulder."

"How's that different? There's only one of me."

Victoria smiled, and William realized she'd led him to this question. He admired the technique; it seemed so Socratic.

"That's our new direction. We want you to be the franchise player, but not like those pro stars. You are a superstar teacher, the maestro of the blackboard. No one is any better. You're the best. But there's no profit in selling you *individually*. We can't make enough. We don't want to buy you; we want to buy your style. Then we can franchise it."

Isaac said, "And we're willing to pay you really, really well."

*D*o you know the story of Alice?" the old man asks. He leans close so his voice won't carry.

The little girl scrunches her hands in her lap. She doesn't appear uncomfortable, just interested in how her skirt wrinkles when she plays with it. "I don't know an Alice," she says.

The old man looks at the parents across the play area. They're still animated in discussion, not paying attention to anything beyond their talk. He doesn't see any police officers. A breeze rustles the willow behind them. He says, "Alice is a little girl, just about your age, and her story begins with a rabbit. Do you know what a rabbit is?"

"I've been to a zoo," she says. "I saw a cat and a porcupine there too."

"Of course you have," says the old man. "I knew you were a bright little girl."

"So, what about Alice?" she says.

"And inquisitive too. Oh, you're a bright one for sure." He settles back in the bench; he touches her shoulder gently. "Well, the rabbit is late to begin with, and he has a pocket watch. Why do you think he might have a pocket watch?"

"The rabbit has pockets?" The little girl covers her mouth and giggles at the idea.

"He's a special rabbit. Do you want to know all about him?"

"Oh, yes," she says. "My dad has a pocket watch too. It's on a big chain, but it's a lot more than a watch. He says it's his little assistant, and it's really expensive. He downloads it all the time, and I can't play with it. Tell me why the rabbit has one."

The old man checks the parents once again, slides toward her so their hips nearly touch and begins the story. Within a minute, he's forgotten about the crawling under his skin, the extra presence behind his eyes—he's into the story, and he's into her being into the story.

*W*hat sold William was Victoria's picture of the product: "Imagine your successes happening with students all across the globe. More and more kids in love with education, with learning, helped there by our simulacrums of you."

By this time they were sitting in the bar down the street from the school. Victoria had bought drinks for them all, and they'd talked about education for a couple of hours. The lights hung low and dim over the tables. Victoria's eyes glistened with interest, and her face glowed. After a while, William found her to be totally sympathetic to his views. "Teaching's about reaching," he'd said. "You have to touch the student with the material and your enthusiasm, or nothing happens."

She'd nodded encouragingly and ordered another round. Isaac took notes and moved empty glasses out of their way. "So how do you do it," Isaac asked. "Are you a stimulus-response man? Do you teach 'whole language'? Or are you into one of the more traditional, back to basics modes?"

William leaned back in his chair and crossed his hands on his stomach. Over the years he'd developed a slight paunch, but it didn't worry him; it made him feel comfortable, like Pooh Bear or Bilbo Baggins. It was the way he imagined a forty-year-old confirmed bachelor should look. He said, "When I first started teaching, I played around with lots of theory, but I don't think much about it anymore. I guess I'd have to say I'm pretty unconscious about technique. The kids are there; the material is there. I teach."

Victoria said, "Like Mickey Mantle."

"Scuse me?" said William. He nearly missed the table with his elbow when he straightened up, and he realized he'd drank a bit too much.

"Mickey Mantle was a great player. Maybe one of the best hitters ever but not much of an intellect. One day he was giving a batting demonstration for a bunch of little leaguers, and he was trying to explain to them about foot placement and how to hold the hands and where the elbows should go, and the longer he talked the more tongue tied he became and the more frustrated. Finally he couldn't stand it any more and said to the bunch of little kids, 'Ah, hell. Just hit like this,' and he tossed a ball into the air and belted it over the fence. He couldn't explain it, but he could do it."

"Maybe I'll be no good for you then," said William. His face sagged with sadness and the bar darkened. He'd begun to think of Victoria and Isaac as friends. They liked education. They understood the passion of teaching. They liked him, and he wasn't going to be able to tell them how he did it. The money didn't matter. Victoria had painted a vision of thousands of students in love with literature. He imagined them lining up for play tickets, a new audience for Shakespeare and the rest, and now they were turning away all because he couldn't tell these nice people how he taught. "I don't have a method," he said, looking into the depths of his drink.

Victoria put a hand on his wrist. Her fingers felt cool and delightful, and William began to think of her like Shakespeare's dark-haired mystery woman who was a part of the sonnets. "You don't have to. That's the beauty. We can study your teaching while you're in the classroom. We can capture it and can it and reproduce it. All you need to do is what you've always done, which is to teach. We're not buying a technique. You could teach a technique, but no one could do what you do. What we want is for you to sell us your style."

A half-hour later, Isaac pulled a sheaf of contracts from his briefcase, and William signed them all.

Victoria said, "You're a rich man, William. You'll never have to work again, but you'll be reaching thousands. What a legacy. What a legacy."

Their knees touched under the table. William was sure that it was an accident, but he was thrilled just the same.

He didn't remember the ride home.

A week later, the technicians were waiting for William when he entered his classroom. They were white-suited and entirely business like. He could barely tell them apart as they placed dozens of silver dollar-sized disks on the walls and ceiling.

"They're transceivers, William." Victoria said. She wore white like the rest, and her black hair spilled over her shoulders. "We'll be recording everything you and the students do while our computers build a model of your responses to student cues. Our programmers tell me that this part of the process will last three months."

William scanned the room. The disks matched the wall's colors, and he could tell that they'd be easy to overlook.

"That doesn't seem like it'd give you enough, though. A bunch of vid of a teacher won't give you everything the teacher does. So much of it's internal." He was only half paying attention. Today he'd be starting with a new group of students, and his lesson plans filled his mind. Beginnings were so much fun, he thought. Starting them off right was part of the secret.

Victoria half sat on the edge of his desk. William liked the pose; it made her look long and sultry. It was distracting. He imagined writing her a sonnet.

"So how are we going to get more?" she said.

William recognized the strategy. She'd used it earlier on him. "You're being Socratic again."

She smiled.

He said, "All right, do the disks do more than vid?"

"Good question. Yes they do. What else do you think we need to capture your style?"

He turned the problem over for a bit before saying thoughtfully, "Teaching is mostly responding to the audience. What works great one time might crash and burn the next. So you've got to get inside my head, somehow. You need to see the students the way I see them, or it will be useless."

"You come to the point readily. So how are we going to get inside you?"

Something he'd signed on one of the contracts surfaced in his memory; most of the evening was lost to him now in a blur of pleasant drink and conversation. "A new technique, you said, I think. Some way to, umm, more closely monitor the environment."

"Your environment, to be exact," said Victoria. "We need to monitor you, so we've designed some very special nanotech to do the job. You'll need to be injected, of course, and it will be a few days before we have everything adjusted, but by this time next week, we will be getting a complete picture of the students and the classroom as you experience them. Not just visuals, but touch, smell, taste—all of it. All the subtle cues you use to teach from and how you respond to them."

Behind her, one of the technicians was preparing a hypodermic. She drew what looked to be a couple of cc's from a small bottle of cloudy, white liquid.

Victoria said, "It's really no different from what the doctor might give you to clear cholesterol from your system, or to hunt down cancer cells. Only these will attach along your nerve pathways. Totally painless, naturally. You won't even know they're there, but they'll broadcast to the transceivers while the computers build the model of your behavior. In three months, we'll have everything we need."

"That's sophisticated stuff." William bared his upper arm to receive the shot.

"It's proprietary. We'll have to keep you under surveillance outside of the school. Industrial espionage, you know. Afterwards, we'll neutralize it and you'll be free of our interference in your life. It's a small price to pay for the price we're paying you." Victoria patted him on the arm. "There. All done now. We'll clear out before your students arrive."

The technician said, "You might run a slight fever for twenty-four hours. The mechanisms will be duplicating and some people react to that."

William's arm felt warm at the injection site. It spread up his arm into his shoulder. Not unpleasant, but a little creepy, he decided. He felt as if he were being invaded, not like nanotech in the doctor's office, which didn't seem any different from medicine, but like his system was filling with spies. He decided he didn't like the idea of tiny transmitters seeing what he saw. It made his eyes itch to think of it, but he stayed calm. It's a silly reaction, he thought. Nothing will go wrong.

The police officer approaches the old man and his young companion on the bench while the old man recites the Lobster Quadrille for the third time. "Will you, won't you, will you, won't you, will you join the dance," he says to the girl. She looks up at him and smiles.

"I wish I could join the dance," she says.

The old man glances at the officer, who stands in front of them, his arms crossed at the chest.

The old man whispers to the girl, "Remember, the further off from England, the nearer is to France."

She recites back to him, "What matters it how far we go? There is another shore, you know, upon the other side." She claps her hands and laughs.

"Good girl," he says.

The officer clears his throat. "You're doing it again, William, aren't you?"

"What?" says the old man. "I'm just being myself."

"That's the crime," says the officer. "You're not going to make me cuff you this time, are you?"

William closes his eyes. He believes he can feel the nanotech moving around behind them, quietly capturing everything he does, still broadcasting the essence of himself to unseen transceivers. They're under his skin. They're coating his heart. "No," he says. "Not this time."

He stands and says to the little girl, "The book is called *Alice in Wonderland*. You can look it up if you want to know the rest of it. There are other books there too, like Shakespeare. Books for when you're a big girl. Make sure you read *Hamlet* when you're older. You'll like it."

"Thanks, mister," she says. "I will. Thanks a lot."


Within a week, William had nearly forgotten about the disks. He almost never looked for them. The students didn't mention them. He was into the ebb and flow of the class. As always, the kids started off as ciphers, completely unknown and blank. Some had gone through dozens of educational strategies before arriving in his room. All had been on a waiting list for at least a year. They won their spot by lottery. He was highly paid. His school marketed him and the other teachers on the staff through international advertising; like all other schools, they competed for the students, offering a program of study and a tradition of results.

William didn't care. He'd teach in a barn. He'd teach at a bus stop. Every concern dissolved in the face of students and the material. He was in his medium. He thought about sports superstars; did they play for the money? How could they? At the top of the sport, with no human peer, they had to play for love. That old basketball legend, Michael Jordan, going for the hoop, flew for the love of the game. William had heard stories that late at night Jordan used to strap on old tennies and head for the neighborhood civic center in Chicago to play pick-up ball. Some of the press knew it, but no one ever put it in the paper. At two in the morning he'd be setting picks and flicking passes to street players who came in to run hoops instead of hanging with the gangs. Jordan just loved to play.

So William ignored the disks. He moved from desk to desk. He set up small group discussions. A tap on the shoulder here, a well-timed smile there, and always the shades of literati that he brought back to life for the students: Shakespeare, Homer, Dickenson, Bronte, Carroll and Twain.

The only disturbance in the beauty of the lessons happened in the quiet times in class. He'd be sitting at his desk, watching the students read, and he'd feel a shift under his skin, a subtle sliding like the slipping of a sheet of paper from the middle of a stack. Or a sudden irritation behind his eyes. He imagined nanotechs with legs, running from one nerve ending to the next, leaving tiny footprints on the back of his retina. Even at home, without the disks, he felt observed. They were with him, and they never went away.

William took hot showers. He scratched his skin sometimes until it was raw, then he'd scold himself for the silliness of it. At the microscopic level the nanotech operated in, he could never really feel them. They weren't doing anything. Still, he went through several bottles of calamine. In the quiet times of class, he'd sometimes feel like a fly in a web, and every disk held the end of one string. He squirmed slowly in the middle, connected by the radiant lines of the disks.

At the end of three months, Victoria and Isaac sat in the back of his room again. Except for technicians who came in occasionally to reset the disks, William had seen nothing of the Reinhart Group.

Victoria looked better than ever. She'd crossed her legs at the ankles, and William was keenly aware of her posture, the turn of her hand on the table, the tilt of her head, the half smile he imagined lifting the corners of her mouth when they met eyes.

"Bravo," she said, after he'd dismissed class and the last student had left. "A truly outstanding performance of the teacherly arts."

William blushed. "They were a good group."

Isaac said, "You have no idea."

Something in the way his comment sounded caught his attention. "What do you mean by that?"

Isaac cleared his throat nervously.

"Oh, it won't matter now," said Victoria. "Go ahead and tell him. It was partly your concept anyway."

Isaac held his clipboard to his chest. "We would have told you earlier, but we were afraid it would disturb your style. Maybe it wouldn't. You did fine with all the scrutiny any way, but this wasn't your normal batch of students."

"Not at all," said Victoria. William glanced between the two of them, confused.

Isaac continued, "We hand picked this class for a wide range of learning styles. Several of them were classic, reluctant learners. A couple were ultra-high achievers. We tried to mix them up as much as possible. We needed your reaction to all kinds of students, so this way we guaranteed it."

Victoria signaled to someone outside the door, and a group of technicians swarmed in and began removing the disks from the walls and ceiling. She said, "The students were nanotech primed also, the way you were. We recorded their perceptions of the class too. It truly was remarkable. Do you know that you respond to bored or drifting students *before* they know they're bored? I was stunned. It has been a phenomenal display."

"Oh, yes. About that. When will you...you know...remove them?" William resisted the urge to scratch his forearm. Even thinking about the germ-sized observers made him itchy.

"Right now, naturally." Victoria tilted her head to one of the techs, who immediately began preparing a syringe. "They would break down on their own in the next few weeks, but this will make sure that none of our competitors get hold of them."

"I wouldn't go to any of them." William drew himself up and straightened his tie. "It would be dishonorable."

Victoria stepped aside so the tech could get to William's arm.

"We're not worried about *you*, William. But our competition might not be so pure in spirit. You'd probably wake up in an alley with a tremendous bump on your head and a bruise on some vein from a sloppy shop-doc who just wanted your blood."

This shot hurt going in, but there was no warmth in his arm or shoulder like the first time.

The last tech cleared the room in a few minutes, and only Victoria, Isaac and William remained. Victoria shook his hand.

"Don't spend all your earnings in the same place, William. I doubt you could. It's been a pleasure working with you." She waved to Isaac, and he rose to leave.

William's throat suddenly felt dry, and he swallowed a couple of times. "You mean, that's it? We're all done?"

Victoria turned back to him. "That's it. But your contribution has been invaluable." She laughed. "Don't tell the accountants that I said that."

"I thought." William cleared his throat. "I thought we could talk over the project some more. Maybe during dinner." He coughed. "Or something," he finished lamely.

"Oh, William," she said. In the pause that followed, William felt like he was abruptly unanchored in his own room. The shot coursed through his veins, and it seemed he could feel the company's nanotechs being neutralized within his blood: a million deaths happening inside him at once. He realized he'd made a terrible mistake.

"You really are precious," she said.


The first time he wasn't arrested.

William had prepared for his next class as he always had, rereading, writing new notes, preparing new plans. He was excited about vid that he'd shot a month earlier in the recreated Globe theater in South Hampton. The New King's Men had played *Comedy of Errors, Henry the Fifth, As You Like It, The Winter's Tale* and *Hamlet.* But as he bustled about his room, putting up posters (beautiful, brand new art prints that his Reinhart money paid for), rearranging desks and rehearsing his introductory lecture for the next day, he felt distracted. He'd stop to itch the top of his hand or to rub his eyes occasionally. Even though a check-up the day after the cleansing injection confirmed it, he imagined that not all the nanotechs were gone. It was a crawly sensation, alien-like and disturbing.

As he reached behind his ear to rub a bothersome spot, an official looking man in a gray suit knocked on his open door. After a brief introduction, mostly to assure the man that William was who was named in the papers he carried, the man served William with an injunction. Most of the multi-sheeted document was legal gobbley-gook, but the essential part was clear: "Because of considerable financial and competitive risk, and whereas The Reinhart Group did in good faith purchase the style, mannerisms, content and appearance of the aforementioned party, he shall be forever forbidden from using the same said style, mannerisms, content or appearance."

"Essentially," the gray-suited man said, "You are no longer allowed to teach."

"They can't do that," said William, sputtering.

The next day, however, he found that they could. The school's administration called his students and rescheduled them with other teachers. His classroom was given to someone else and his posters returned to him along with a note asking for his resignation. The principal, a woman of indeterminate age and colorless hair was very apologetic. "It's a copyright issue," she explained sympathetically. "They own the copyright to your style, and if we allowed you to teach, we'd be fined or face possible criminal charges." She offered him a handkerchief to wipe his eyes. "It's all very clear in your contract. You read the contract, didn't you?"

William shook his head.

"Oh, that's too bad. Well, you have plenty of money. You'll never need to teach again. You can enjoy your retirement. Travel. Read. Things could be much worse." She offered her hand, and numbly William shook it.

"They can't do this," he said again. His voice rose. "I'll take them to court. You can't confiscate a person's style!"


*I*t took two years, and all the money that Reinhart had paid him, but he found out once again that they could.

Sitting in a book lined office, William's lawyer, a scruffy looking man who appeared perpetually unshaven but who was an old veteran of copyright law battles, and the absolute best man in the business, explained it to William their first conference. "The precedent is long established, but the most famous example is The Lone Ranger."

William said, "I'm not familiar with him." None of the books on the office shelves were literary. All were legal titles. Earlier when he'd tried to take one down, he'd found that they were merely decorative. The lawyer's computer stored the centuries of copyright law, rulings and precedents that the case would be argued from.

The lawyer said, "In the middle of the last century there was a television show called *The Lone Ranger*. When it went off the air, the actor who played the lead character couldn't find steady work, and he began doing promotional gigs as the Lone Ranger. He'd wear the costume and show up at the opening of used car lots and shopping centers. The studio successfully prevented him from appearing in costume because they owned the character, they argued, not the actor." The lawyer stroked the stubble on his chin. "It's a sad case, really. I think about that guy sometimes, these old Lone Ranger costumes hanging in his closet, and instead of being a hero like he was in the show's heyday, he's just a broken down has been who couldn't even pick up a few bucks for appearing at the ribbon cutting ceremony for a fast food place."

"That's bleak," said William.

Surprisingly, at the trial, Isaac offered to testify on William's behalf. When it became clear that William could not beat the contract on its own merits, the lawyer tried to argue that William was drunk when he signed it. Isaac corroborated the drinking, but Victoria testified that William drank very little. On the stand she appeared imperious, unfriendly and very believable. The day after Isaac's day in court, he quit Reinhart and joined William's defense.

"I sat in your class that day and learned to love Shakespeare," said Isaac in way of explanation.

"But your job, Isaac," said William. "You didn't need to do that."

Isaac looked thoughtful, then furrowed his brow in concentration as he recalled, "Whither wilt thou lead me? Speak. I'll go no further."

Despite himself, William smiled. "Mark me."

"I will."

William said, "My next line is 'My hour is almost come when I to sulphurous and tormenting flames must render up myself.' I hope it doesn't come to that."

"Alas," said Isaac. "Poor ghost."


*B*ut it did come to that.

They arrested William the first time for teaching *Through the Looking Glass* under an assumed name at a small, family school in Mississippi. He had no money for the fine and served ninety days instead. Reinhart lawyers successfully argued William should be isolated from other prisoners.

A year-and-a-half later, they caught him guest-lecturing on sonnet structure in a friend's classroom on the east coast. Ninety days again and a restraining order requiring him to stay one-hundred feet from school-aged children. William learned that Isaac had formed a small lobbying group and was trying to change the copyright laws.

A third violation earned him a monitoring ankle bracelet. A sympathetic former student removed it, which was supposed to be impossible, and the student wore it for two months while William taught night classes in Shakespeare through a city-run continuing education program. Three violations put William into the scoff-law category, and he served four years.

By the time he was sixty-four, William had spent more than half of the previous twenty years in jail, always in isolation. Teaching kids in the park had become his favorite technique. Cops knew who he was, and he'd developed a kind of infamy with them. Most of the time they chased him off. Occasionally someone new on the force or a grumpy veteran would haul him in, book him and hold him overnight. Victoria ascended to the

Reinhart presidency and seemed to have long forgotten her project from years past, but the meticulous wheels of the company's legal division ground exceedingly fine and continued to prosecute him whenever he was arrested.

He'd sold his books long ago, and he couldn't afford net charges for computer access, so his reading was limited to the public library. Not that it mattered. Most of the works he loved, he'd memorized.

The only result of Isaac's years of work on William's behalf was finally a suspension of the isolation order in jail as cruel and unusual punishment, but the problems with the law never stopped.

So, there is no surprise in him when he stands and says to the little girl, "The book is called *Alice in Wonderland*. You can look it up if you want to know the rest of it. There are other books there too, like Shakespeare. Books for when you're a big girl. Make sure you read *Hamlet* when you're older. You'll like it."

"Thanks, mister," she says. "I will. Thanks a lot."

The script of what is said to him at the police station seems as familiar to William as any play. He knows his part within it.

He pulls his overcoat close to him as they lead him to his cell. Modern as the prison is, with its soft white walls and acoustic ceiling, it makes him cold, and when he's cold, the ghostly writhing of long gone nanotech bothers him most.

The officer is curt, businesslike. "We have to double you up with someone tonight. A delusional kid. Shouldn't bother you." He opened the cell door. A boy, no more than twenty sits on one of the fold-down beds, his back to the wall, legs drawn up, a shock of black hair hiding his eyes. He doesn't look when William takes his place on the other bed. The cell is narrow; William's knees nearly touch the gray blanket on the young man's mattress.

Even though the cells are soundproofed, a soft clatter of noises from up and down the hall reaches William. Somewhere, someone sings. Water gurgles in the wall. For a long time, William listens while thinking of lost classrooms, students shining from within, their own light coming through, reaching for him in his darkness. Memories are vivid and sad within him. He thinks of that last class before he'd signed the contract. If he'd only known, he would have done more with them, he thinks. He would have slept less, thought deeper about each lesson, concentrated harder on individual problems, made a bigger difference. They will always be the "last" class, he thinks. There will never be another. I will never close a door again and turn to face the faces that wait for me to launch their adventures.

"Why do you keep scratching?" says the young man.

William flinches. The voice sounded loud in the tiny room. He stops his hands. "I didn't realize I was. Sorry."

The man's eyes are still hidden behind his hair. "You're pretty old to be in here, aren't you?" He doesn't wait for an answer. "Pretty small room for two people if you ask me."

"I could be bounded in a nutshell and count myself a king of infinite space—were it not that I have bad dreams," says William.

"What's that?" says the young man.

William folds the blanket at the end of his bed into a pillow and rests his head. "Nothing. A bit from a play. You're pretty young. I suppose I could ask the same question. What are you doing here, if you don't mind my asking?"

The man laughs nervously. "I killed my uncle." He pauses as if waiting for William to comment. "Really, I did. Or at least I think he's dead. I hope so."

William closes his eyes. The bed isn't too uncomfortable: a lump under his hip that feels like it will bother him if he stays on it too long, but otherwise not bad. "You want to talk about it?" William asks, half hoping the man will not.

"He deserved it," says the young man. "Nobody would behave any differently in my situation. See, he married my mother."

William opened one eye and looked at the man. "Really?"

"Yeah. He married her, and I think he killed my dad to get him out of the way."

With some effort, William sat up. "Really?"

"My lawyer says that he can get me off, though. He says I'm crazy. See, I told him that my dad's ghost told me what to do."

"Did he?" William's voice cracks, and the walls of the cell begin to vanish. Everything focuses on the young man sitting with his knees up, hiding behind his hair.

"But you know what's really crazy?" The man leans forward and whispers, "I did talk to my dad's ghost." The man falls back against the wall. "Now that's a story you don't hear every day," he says. "That's one for the books."

William rubs his hand across his chest as if straightening a tie. He looks around him. The cell doesn't seem that small anymore. He pictures some posters on the wall, maybe the Globe Theater. Perhaps a playbill or two. "That is an interesting story," he says. "Maybe I can tell one too. It might mean something to you. What do you think?"

The young man shakes the hair out of his eyes. They are bright blue and young, very young. They look like a student's eyes.

"Sure," he says. "I have plenty of time."

"Have you ever heard," says William, "neither a borrower nor a lender be? This is the story that it came from, and it starts with three guys talking about the ghost of a dead king. The king's name is Hamlet, and it's about his son of the same name."

They talk all night, and when Isaac comes in the morning to bail him out, William refuses to go.

# Happy Ending

The bullet stirred from its bed of bone in the back of the skull, then leapt through the bloody tunnel of brain tissue behind it. Neurons closed on neurons, and severed capillaries reknit and healed as the bullet flashed through the brain, out the hole in the roof of the mouth, past shattered teeth—whose fragile fragments came home again to perfect, flawless form—and flew down the gun barrel to nest tightly in the now unexploded casing.

Against his lips, the barrel pressed heavily and tasted of oil.

Bob took the gun away from his mouth, rested it in his lap and opened his eyes. Tears crept up his cheek, as he turned his gaze away from the gun and to the window of his study where autumn leaves streamed past, their tattered glory afire in the evening sun. He couldn't see the elm or willows, just the leaves dancing by, and a fanciful thought returned to him: if you can't see the source, who can tell if leaves are falling to the ground or jumping back to the limbs? And what does it matter? The leaves are in the air. They don't know their direction. Karl was right.

I'm twenty-four, he thought, and he felt old, used up and gray. Beneath the pale, unlined skin on the top of his hand, he could sense wrinkles and liver spots. His knuckles waited to bulge, to become arthritic. I'm old, he thought. I've grown old.

Leaves tumbled across the window in shades of gold and red for a long time before he put the gun back in the desk drawer, and picked up the phone.

It droned in his ear like a death knell for a minute, then clicked. "You're no hero," unsaid Mrs. Downs in his ear. "You had a responsibility."

Bob replied, "It was just a lesson. A discussion of story theory. How could I know he identified so strongly?"

"The boy believed in you. You walked on water." Her voice stayed flat and cold. Nothing remained in it. No hope. No anger. She could have been reciting a laundry list. "He wanted to be a writer like you."

"Karl made choices. I believe if he had lived he could have done anything. Karl had great potential." Bob remembered their first days together. Karl sat in the back of the room, writing in his tight, black scribble every word Bob said. Karl *always* wrote no matter what else was going on in the room, his dark eyes occasionally looking furtively away from his legal pad. He'd shown a story to Bob after the first week of the creative writing class. It was a 1,000 word time travel piece called "Rats Live on No Evil Star."

Later, Bob gave him a copy of Hawking's *A Brief History of Time*, so he could see what modern physists thought of time.

Karl had handed him the story reluctantly, frightened. Bob knew he'd signed up for the class because Bob had published. "Here," he'd said. "It's no good."

Mrs. Down's said, "Nothing you do today can make a difference. I know who my boy was before. I know who you are now."

Bob held the phone tightly against his ear. He could almost feel her presence. She stood in the room with him, her lips only centimeters away. "You have to blame me, I know. My name was in the note, but I didn't see it coming. It's too much...it's way too much to ask for forgiveness, but I hope you understand."

"Why did you call?" Mrs. Downs didn't sound surprised at all.

"Mrs. Downs, I'm Bob Wells," Bob said, his voice squeezed tight and scratchy. "Karl's teacher."

Bob dialed.

Bob put the phone down gently, fearfully and full of guilt. On the desk in front of him lay three pieces of paper: a form rejection from HarperPrism telling him his novel was being returned; a formal request from the school board for his resignation, and a note to him from Karl that had been folded into the back of the book. Hawking's book, Karl had returned to him, held down the notes.

E verywhere Bob looked within himself he could see nothing but darkness: no way out.

Gazing blankly at the letter on the floor, he thought of all the time in class lecturing from his position as a soon to be published novelist; all the conferences with students who signed up for his courses on the weight of his reputation, and it pushed upon him with the bulk of a terrible lie. He remembered looking at students' stories, his red pen in hand, marking in the margin, *Unbelievable dialogue, What's the conflict?*, or *Why should the reader care?* And as he marked, he thought about how important his words would be on their papers. This came from *the* Bob Wells, they would think. He was my Creative Writing teacher in high school.

He held his hand out, and Karl's note fluttered from the floor back to his hand. Bob's eye held to the last words that he had written on the paper—the words that he had written that ignored so much of what Karl said, that refused to read between the lines. They were, "This is an unlikely idea for a story, Karl. Trash it and work on something more believable."

Above that, Karl's note read,

*Mr. Wells,*

*I know you don't think I can make it as a writer, but I've thought a lot about what you said about how stories are structured. I still think you are wrong about that, just as you are wrong about failing me. A story ought to work the way the universe works. According to Hawking, the universe tends toward* disorder, *not order. Cups don't leap off the linoleum and reassemble on table tops; they fall and shatter. Chaos is the rule, and that's the way we perceive it. So fiction that makes "order out of the chaos of life," as you put it, runs counter to the direction of the universe.*

*If I lived my life according to your description of stories, jumping off a cliff shouldn't kill me. The disorder of my corpse at the bottom should undo itself and I'd fly to the top alive.*

*I think I can prove it. I can write a story that will get an "A." Kind of a performance story. I'm a good writer. It will be a story about a cliff and how the real direction of a story should be disorder and mystery, not order and understanding.*
            *Sincerely,*
            *Karl Downs*

Bob put the note back into the book, and returned it to his desk. He retreated to a corner of the room and sat in it, his back squeezed by the conjunction of the walls.

After a while, he stood, then backed out of the room, his head hanging, his hands like rags dangling from his arms.

Walking through the campus, he barely noticed the students passing around him. Their conversations stopped as he approached.

"That's him," Bob heard one say behind him; then the boys walked by silently, their eyes darting at Bob and switching away. Facing each other, the distance between them grew, until he saw them talking with animated pleasure.

In the principal's office, the silence lingered and vibrated like a discordant note.

"Thank you," said Bob, finally, knowing that it wasn't appropriate, but what else could he say?

"We think it best if you resigned immediately," the principal said as she closed his file.

Bob shook his head as if he were trying to wake from a dream—one of those nightmares where he knew what was going to happen but where he could do nothing to stop it. "What are you suggesting?"

"We're going to have to make a change. The Advanced Class in Creative Writing won't be offered again. It was a mistake to put you in charge of it. Karl shouldn't have been there."

"He had talent, but the boy was troubled. I didn't know," Bob said in surrender, putting hardly any voice behind the words, nearly whispering them.

The principal, a woman five years older than Bob, unfolded the photocopy of the suicide note. She appeared to mull over the lines, and Bob tried to think of anything to say. He thought, they're blaming me! And when he looked inside, he saw that they were right. The knowledge spun up to him darkly.

"The school board," she said, "Has seen this. They met last night just to talk about this. It's bad, Bob. Your name is all over it, and we talked to kids in your class. They confirmed much of what Karl says here. They said you badgered him. Their words. One said you ridiculed Karl. Another said you singled him out."

Numbness dominated his face. He wanted to reach up and touch his cheeks to see if they were real. His shirt felt too tight; he could hardly breathe within it. "Karl wrote notes all the time."

"They found this from Karl," she said, holding a sheet of paper. "In his coat pocket. You know, he left his coat on the rail? It was neatly folded there. Did you know he took his shoes and socks off? Why would he do that? Fifteen years old, and he dives off a cliff, but he takes his shoes and socks off."

"I don't understand it either," Bob said. The whole conversation might as well be taking place in an echo chamber, he thought. It seemed so unreal; so much like it all was unwinding around him.

"Why did it happen, Bob?" The principal sat back in her chair. Bob could tell she'd already made up her mind.

B ob surveyed the empty class room. Marcia Binder, who loved Bob best after Karl, had left a pile of crumpled paper on her desk. He could see his own comments written on one of them; it was a feedback sheet on her last story. "Good job," it read. "With a little more work, this will really shine." She'd beamed when she'd read it the day before, and the color had risen in her cheeks when she'd thanked him after class. She has a crush on me, he'd thought, as she smiled shyly, holding her books close to her chest.

The doors opened and students backed in, pointedly not looking at Bob as they took their seats. Outside in the hall, the end of class bell rang, and the angry mutter among them rose like a muddy creek.

"It's a variation on the old Chinese blessing," Bob said desperately, aware that he'd lost them completely. "May you always have interesting material."

No one raised their hands. None of them wrote anything he was saying into their notebooks.

"There's a story about William Faulkner that he was at his father's deathbed when the old man passed on. Faulkner was supposed to have gone to a mirror and looked into his own face so that later he could write an accurate description of what a man whose father just died looked like. I'm not saying we should view Karl's death as a source for fiction, but we have gone through something here, and that something will effect us and our writing. We're more plugged into the reality of the human drama."

None of their faces offered support. Nothing is colder than high school students who think of you as the enemy, thought Bob. Marcia's lips were thin, white lines; her hands were locked firmly on top of her desk. She looked at him without blinking.

Bob realized that they couldn't get past it. Karl's empty desk vibrated like a terrible black hole, sucking all his words to it, all of his energy in, and it returned nothing.

After forty-five minutes of lecture, Bob gave up. The lesson wasn't going to work. They were more than silent; it was if they were seething in their seats.

He tried to move on, to follow his lesson plan. Yesterday had been a review of building scenes. "A scene is like a tiny story in itself," he'd said. "The beginning will be related to the end. Whatever action you start with will complete the scene; whatever emotion you provoke will be a part of its structure. It'll change the story and move it, so despair moves toward hope, or victimization to control. Everything in the scene contributes to the story, but the scene is a story too."

Today he was to discuss techniques in description. The farther he went though the more obvious it was. They hated him.

He waited for a question. The material was abstract. Generally the students couldn't follow him when he went into fiction theory, but he'd present it anyway until someone asked him for an example. No one said a word.

He started class with "Order in a description is discovery. The reader discovers what is there in the order you present it, as if you are holding the reader's head and directing his attention. Presenting the information in a different order gives the reader a different perspective, and it can change the whole story. Order is everything."

The tardy bell rang. Facing their desks, the students backed out of the room.

Karl's death came with him into the empty class room, and the note from HarperPrism telling him that his novel "...does not fit our current publishing needs," still reverberated. The two seemed linked. As he prepared his lecture for the day, though, he felt the old confidence returning. In my room, I'm king, he thought. They can beat you down, but they can't kill you. Dozens of publishers rejected John Grisham.

Yesterday's ugliness could be washed away. They could start fresh. He waited almost eagerly for the students to come to class.

*T*he radio unannounced the news of Karl's death while Bob filled his breakfast bowl, spoon after spoon.

*I*t's probably no good either," said Bob, venom dripping from each word. Karl handed Bob a twenty-page manuscript. "Here's my semester project. I finished early." he said. "But, you won't get it, I'll bet."

Stunned, the rest of the class watched. Bob knew he was out of control, but the anger rolled up within him. The class would be so much better without this imbecile, thought Bob. This is *Advanced* Creative Writing, and they're taking it because I'm a *real* writer, not one of those lit fools that make up the rest of the department.

"You can't be a writer if you won't learn!" Bob's voice boomed in the room, overwhelming Karl finally. The boy shrank within himself, as if he suddenly understood that their battle was no mock game but a serious war. He reacted as if he just realized his teacher hated him. Karl's neck nearly disappeared as his shoulders rose to his ears.

Bob shouted, "You have a crummy attitude!"

HarperPrism's rejection buzzed around in Bob's thoughts like a malevolent horsefly. He couldn't concentrate on Karl, who glowered in the seat beside him. The arrogance of this kid, thought Bob. What does *he* know about fiction? Who does he think he is telling *me* what makes a story work?

"You told us that a reader doesn't remember a story chronologically," said Karl. "You said that the story is like a memory—that the reader has access to all of the story at once after he's read it—so it shouldn't matter what order it's told in. Time in the mind flows both ways, which is what Hawking said. *You* said that a writer revises the first word of a story knowing the last word, and that a writer writes from the end. My story does that."

Bob gave up on lecturing to the whole class. Only Karl existed. Only Karl needed to hear this. Only Karl challenged Bob's knowledge of writing. How could he? Bob thought. I'm published. I have put in the lonely hours and hours writing until my brain loosened up, and the muses came down and touched me.

"You have an 'F' on this, young man, not only because the story is three sentences long, but because it demonstrates no understanding of the order in which a story must be told. You have started with the end and moved to the beginning. The whole story, and I quote, is 'He died. He struggled. He was born.' No matter how you revise this, it will never be a story. It's backwards."

Karl scrambled through his notes. "Last week," he said, reading from his cramped handwriting on the yellow legal pad, "you told us that a story has 'profluence.' You said that was 'movement.' You also told us that stories are about reversals. 'Whatever condition begins the story must be changed by the end.' My story fulfills those requirements."

"You have purposely ignored every piece of advice I've offered about creating readable fiction. What hurts most here is that you have talent. You know your way around a sentence. There's a spark of imagination within you. But you waste it all in this tripe. Your 'story,' Karl, doesn't meet *any* of the requirements of narration."

Karl said, "It boils fiction to its essence. Stephen Hawking has told me more about the way the world works than you have. He says the arrow of time can point either way. We just perceive it the one way and not the other. The universe either moves toward the Big Bang or away from it, and that's reflected in stories."

The class giggled nervously. For a second, Bob realized he was playing to the crowd. "You don't make sense, Karl. My head aches just trying to follow your thoughts. I get twitchy thinking about it."

Karl said, "There's lots of ways of perceiving the world. Looking backwards ought to reveal themes we haven't explored the stodgy old way. I mean, for crying out loud. Plod, plod, plod. Once upon a time to they lived happily ever after. Don't you think it's more interesting to start with the result and see how it happened?"

Karl hunched forward in his seat, intense and fiery, his dark eyes lit up like Bob had never seen them.

"I know the rules," Karl said. "I've known them since Saturday morning cartoons. All of us..." He waved his arm to encompass the entire class. "...have heard a million stories."

Clenching his fists at his side, Bob said, "You can't break the rules until you know the rules."

He's mocking me, thought Bob.

"You've got to be willing to experiment," said Karl, laughing after he saw his grade. His legs sprawled out comfortably from under the desk, and he leaned back in his chair, relaxed. Bob remembered when Karl had been frightened to show him his first story. I've created a monster, thought Bob. I hinted he had talent, and now he doesn't believe he needs me anymore. Well, it's time to take Mr. Know-it-all down a notch.

All of them looked over their stories. Bob had written voluminous notes at the ends of each filled with suggestions about plot and pacing, description and conflict. He struggled with his face though. He felt sure they could read his expression and could see the HarperPrism rejection in it.

The class began innocently enough. Holding his disappointment inside like a sullen coal, Bob backed down the aisles between the desks, watching each student look over their grades eagerly, then handing their stories to him before assuming an expectant expression. Finally, he stood at the front of the class, holding their stories in a neat stack. At the bottom, because he sat in the last seat, waited Karl's story, a single page with little writing on it beside the red "F" in a big circle.

<br>

Still hungry; he hadn't eaten anything, Bob left for school. He knew they'd rejected it by the opening salutation; "Dear Contributor."

Trembling, he folded the letter neatly, slid it back into the envelope and unripped it closed. This is it, he thought. They've bought the novel. They have to. The editor was so gushing in her request to see the complete manuscript after he'd sent the sample chapters.

He'd told everyone in school, casually, just dropping it in at the end of conversations. "Oh," he'd said, "by the way, HarperPrism has my novel now." Invariably they'd ask when it would be in the stores. He'd shrug his shoulders ruefully. "Who can guess? You know how the publishing world is." He'd wink as if they both were knowledgeable conspirators.

In the left corner, the return address said HarperPrism Publishing.

Coming out of his house, with a bounce in his step, he backed to the mailbox and put the letter in it.

Lunch is an adventure, he thought. The mail comes at lunch, and who knows what magazine has mailed an acceptance. Maybe, even, some news of the novel.

*S*ettled comfortably into his chair now, Bob picked up Marcia Binder's story, which turned out to be a sweetly told romance between a talented high school student and her Art teacher. The ending scene took place in a subway station as the student left for college. She waits for him, hoping that he'll see her off, but he never comes. In the story, she'd not told the teacher of her love, and most of the story was of her struggling with her feelings. Bob paged back to the dream sequence in the middle—a graphically rendered fantasy of the student and teacher's consummation of the relationship. Taking Bob's advice to heart, she'd concentrated on senses other than sight and sound: the pressure of a fingertip, a suggestion of lemonade on the tongue, a thread of hair brushing a forehead, a hint of coppery excitement in the breath, and the rasp of a sheet sliding across skin. He wrote comments in the margin complimenting her on her use of sensory detail.

Five weeks had passed since HarperPrism asked to see the novel, and the joy of it buoyed him through the drudgery of grading, through the frustration of teaching to freshmen and the inanity of department politics. High hopes and Advanced Creative Writing pushed him through the day.

He moved on to the next student's work.

Bob neatly unwrote an "F" at the end of Karl's story, his pen tip rolling across the red line, sucking the ink back until the page was clean of any mark.

Closing his eyes, Bob thought I must have praised the boy too much. He needs to be shook up, for his own good. In the end, Karl will appreciate the lesson; he'll look back and recognize my guiding influence. Almost as good as "Bob Wells" on the cover of his own novel, Bob thought, would be the inscription inside his talented protégé's first book, "To my mentor, Bob Wells."

Bob knew he'd have to get Karl's attention some way; the grade wouldn't be enough. Why, the boy might even take the "F" as his own "Red Badge of Courage." Hadn't all the greats been misunderstood? Who recognized Poe in his lifetime? And Fitzgerald had ended his career in Hollywood scripting hack screen plays.

He tapped his forehead in disbelief. Karl's new story was only three sentences long! In a stack of students' stories, pristinely enclosed with clear, plastic covers and all ten pages or more, the single sheet of paper with Karl's name on it seemed like a joke. He read it twice.

The sun rose slowly and barely noticed in the west. Paper after paper he read until he came to Karl's.

Two weeks later, he read the first story on the stack.

*T*he bell rang, ending class. I couldn't be happier, thought Bob. In all of their many ways, they love me.

Students nodded their heads and copied the information into their notebooks. Karl wrote furiously, and Bob could see that inspiration had overtaken him. Careful to appear casual, Bob strolled by Karl's desk and saw his first paragraph was something gruesome—something about a suicide. Bob shuddered a little. It was the only gray spot in his otherwise wonderful day. Talk of suicide hit too close to home for him. It reminded him that he too thought about swerving into oncoming traffic. It's the curse, he thought, of the overly imaginative. Suicide always seems an option, a romantic, final gesture of retribution, sacrifice or defiance.

"Remember," he said finally, "If you try an experimental technique in your semester project, like a metafiction, be sure to give your readers enough clues to figure out what's going on. They should, for example, be able to tell who's telling the story and why."

The students were busy at their desks; even Marcia Binder seemed busy now, writing. She checked her notes, then returned to her story. She had really effected him, he realized. He passed a hand over his eyebrows, depositing a thin sheen of sweat.

Thankful, Bob backed away from Marcia's desk and sat next to the next student. "So, what's your plan for your project?" Bob said. He wiped his palms against his pants.

"Umm," Bob said to Marcia, "It sounds like a challenge. I'm sure you could handle it," and that sounded stupid to him. Every word had a possible double meaning. Finally he offered, "You're a good writer. Give it a try."

Marcia looked at him, her eyes gleaming and frank. Bob forced himself not to glance down. He was sure, now, that she'd loosened a button on her blouse since he'd sat next to her.

"So what do you think?" she said.

She leaned forward, the tips of her fingers nearly touching Bob's hand.

Marcia said, "I've been exploring May-September relationships. I thought my semester project could be something that continues that theme." She sounded nervous and excited, as if she were torn between fearfulness and something else. Bob couldn't decide what it was, and with her so close to him, nearly whispering, he had a hard time thinking about it. Maybe it was love—maybe lust. He remembered the first assignment she'd handed in, an autobiographical description of a date she'd had just a month earlier where a boy had tried to kiss her. She'd confessed in the story that she'd never kissed a boy before, and the prospect had scared her, but she hadn't been able to sleep that night. In the story, she felt the ghost pressure of the kiss that never happened on her lips all the next day.

He caught a whiff of her shampoo, a soft fruity smell like peaches and cream, but under that a hint of just her. It wasn't unpleasant. Definitely warm though and animal. He wondered if she had P.E. the hour before his class.

"What will your semester project be, Marcia?" said Bob. Her hair hung across the side of her face, partially hiding her eyes.

He couldn't help but notice Marcia at the end of her row, glancing at him as he moved from student to student. She was wearing a loose peasant blouse, the top button undone, and when she leaned forward to write, he caught a glimpse of lace in the swells of shadow. As professional as he wanted to be, he couldn't help but notice, and he wondered if she *wanted* him to see. She leaned a lot when he was around, coyly, like part of her didn't know she was doing it while another part did, like her subconscious controlled her posture.

"You'll be a hero, Mr. Wells," said Karl enthusiastically as Bob unleft his desk. "It'll be cool."

Flattered, but not sure how to handle the attention, Bob said, "That might not be a good thing to do. It could be embarrassing."

"See, if I base my semester project on people I know, then I've got a better chance to get the characterization right. Like I could tell the story in first person from your point of view."

"Why would you want to do that?" Bob looked around the room.

"I've been reading Hawking, like you suggested, and he's really given me some ideas, and the stuff you just said, too. I see now that you were right. Typical time travel stories are old hat, so I'm going to write a new kind. I mean, why should the character be the only one who gets to travel in time?" said Karl. "And you'll be the protagonist."

"What will your project be?" asked Bob. Karl straightened the stack of pages on his desk, all of them apparently like the top one, filled with his crabbed, black handwriting.

Bob started class with a short lecture on metafiction. "Some stories," he said, "turn the tools of fiction upon itself. It's like Ferris Bueller talking to the audience, or *The Never Ending Story*, which makes the movie goers a part of the story at the end. Any story that reminds the readers they are reading a story is a kind of metafiction."

The class greeted him with smiles. Their eagerness to learn seemed genuine. They loved him.

"Not yet," he said.

"Any news on the novel?" someone asked.

Bending down, he placed his pencil on the floor. He stood.

The pencil undropped into his hand.

He backed to the door and opened it. The door grew smaller and smaller as he walked away.

He was unbreathing. He was unthinking. The events unrolled behind him. Life was good and getting better, and the innocence of youth waited for him.

# Love

# Shark Attack: A Love Story

Willard was day dreaming about Elsa when the shark caught Benford, the new mail boy, directly in front of Willard's desk. Lost in his dream, Willard didn't look up from the stack of forms he was filling out mechanically. Bustle and commotion were standard fare at The First North American Trust Title Company, and the boy's silent waving of arms wasn't enough to distract Willard. Then the boy screeched.

Willard dropped his pen and instinctively pulled his feet off the aquamarine blue shag carpet. The shark, a small one if its head were an indication, probably five or six feet long, had Benford by the calf. He screeched again, then started slapping at the fish with a thick manila folder. Papers squirted from it into the air, spiraling about like sea gulls. The boy twisted in an effort to get loose and his pants tore along the seam. Willard saw a long stretch of white leg that ended at green boxer shorts.

"Help!" Benford said, his face an etching of pain and fear. He reached for Willard. Using his chair as a step, Willard climbed to the top of his desk, knelt on the desk pad and extended his hand to the boy.

"Grab on!" cried Willard, and their hands locked. For a second, he thought the shark had lost. Benford moved toward the desk, and his face beamed with hope. Then the shark regripped, shook back and forth angrily, sending ripples in the carpet that lapped against the other desks, and drug Benford under.

Benford's hand disappeared last, fingers still bent as if Willard had never let go. The carpet closed over him and the last papers drifted down to float on its now placid, blue nap. Then a dark swirl of red eddied at the spot, bloodying some of the pages. Within a few eye blinks, the color faded away and only the stained papers remained.

The attack lasted less than fifteen seconds.

Willard dropped his forehead to his hands.

When he had first seen a dorsal fin cutting through the carpet days earlier, he'd glanced around to see if anyone else noticed. Elsa, the prim title clerk he dreamed of in the desk beside his, didn't raise her head. A drooping of tight blond curls covered her eyes. Her cool looking, pale fingers moved efficiently to the next form and she began writing. The fin continued down the long rows of desks, avoiding a secretary carrying a stack of papers.

Later, he saw three fins circling the water cooler. They moved hypnotically around and around, and when Humphrey, the chief accountant, walked to the cooler for a drink, Willard bit down an urge to yell a warning. The fins widened their circle while the fat man filled and drank four tiny cupfuls of water. A bubble hiccupped in the large glass bottle each time.

No one else seemed to see them. He had attempted several times to tell Elsa. Once, he leaned toward her and almost spoke—the words were on his lips—but she glanced at him, her eyes bright, brown and shy, and he said nothing. He loved her eyes and the tiny wrinkles that radiated from their corners like she had spent time squinting at sunlight. Lifeguard eyes, he thought. Protective eyes.

In the year since she had joined the firm, he'd never had enough nerve to talk to her, and she had not spoken to him, even when he left funny little sticky notes on her computer screen like, "HELP! I'M DROWNING IN DOS!" She'd smile faintly in his direction, then pull the note free and tuck it into a desk drawer. He wanted desperately to talk to her now, to alert her.

A heavy slap next to his ear startled a scream out of him.

"What the hell are you doing, Willard?" bellowed Mr. Trusty, the office manager. He was wearing his favorite gray, pin-striped suit and an orange tie with the words, *Get your butt in gear*, printed over and over in black. "God damn it, Willard. You look like a seal crouched like that. Get off there right now." Mr. Trusty slapped the desk again.

"Yes, sir," said Willard, and he slid off the top into his chair. He braced his feet on a ledge in the desk so he wouldn't be touching the carpet.

"The deeds on the Hinson deal and the Arlington Estate have to be finished and at the bank tomorrow morning. I can't have you flipping out when there's work to be done. You'll stay late tonight."

The other workers began to clean their desks, putting folders into file cabinets and packing briefcases. It was quitting time. Mr. Trusty saw the papers strewn at his feet. His cold, gray eyes scanned the office. "Where is that little squid, Benford?" He kicked one of the pages. "Pick up this mess."

When Mr. Trusty turned and headed toward his office, Willard sucked in a sharp breath. The back of Mr. Trusty's jacket bulged slightly. Something between his shoulder blades pushed the jacket out, giving him a mild hunchback. Mr. Trusty grinned at another title agent a couple of desks away and said good night. His smile was full of teeth. Willard hadn't paid much attention to this before, but Mr. Trusty's face, when he smiled, was mostly shiny, white bone.

Other employees walked by Willard's desk. A couple nodded as they passed, but most didn't seem to see him. Their eyes were blank and, Willard realized with a rush, fish-like. Several of them had oddly bulging backs, and Willard wondered if this had always been the case and he'd never thought about it, or if the bulges were new. He watched one man, one he didn't know well—Quinton or Quigley—as he walked away. Before he reached the door, Quinton or Quigley placed his briefcase on a desk, bent down behind it, as if he were picking something off the carpet, and didn't reappear. A fin sliced between the desk legs and sank out of sight near the photocopy machine. Although the office was almost empty, briefcases rested on many desks.

Willard didn't know what to do, but he did know that nothing was going to get him onto the carpet now, not after what he'd seen.

He wished he was back in his bachelor's apartment with its comfortable chairs and neatly swept, beach brown, hardwood floors, where he'd sit at his kitchen table and work for hours constructing ships in bottles. Not ones from kits, but ones he made on his own from balsa stock that would go into antique wine bottles he'd buy at flea markets and garage sales. Using special glues and long tweezers, he'd place each pre-painted piece in its place, plank by plank, until finally he'd attach the tiny spools and pulleys and raise the toy sails. Willard imagined standing on their decks, the wind at his back, the solid thud of waves passing beneath the hull, the smell of birds and islands and exotic flowers in his nose, and beside him, Elsa, tanned and laughing and loving. Willard never sailed his ships alone in his dreams.

A fleet lined the living room on shelves he'd built specially for them, and track lighting illuminated his best ones like art work in museums. Only his landlord had seen the collection.

Now that it was after five, the office was mostly empty. The steady patter of computer keys, the ringing of phones and the shuffling of papers was replaced by the buzz from the florescent lights.

A soft sobbing attracted his attention. He turned. Elsa's hands hid her face and her shoulders trembled. She sobbed again.

"Elsa?" he said.

Her crying continued. "That poor boy," she said, finally. Her voice was low, and even though it was caught in a sob, melodious. "That poor, poor boy."

Willard almost leapt to his feet; then he remembered the carpet. "You saw!" he whispered in exultation.

She said, "It ate him right there." She dabbed a napkin under her eyes.

"How long have you seen?"

"Since the first, I guess." She pulled a book from a drawer in her desk. "I've been reading about them. They're just big eating machines, you know."

A tall, gray fin glided smoothly past Willard's desk. It slid through the carpet for twenty feet, then circled back. Another fin joined it, then a third and fourth. A glimpse of tail fin broached the carpet and a wide expanse of solid, dark back. By the size of the fin, Willard guessed the largest might be fifteen feet long.

"There are so many," said Elsa.

A weighty thud almost knocked Willard out of his chair. He braced his hand on the seat, and a fin scraped it. The knuckles shown white, then beads of blood welled through the skin. He scrambled to the desk top again. Elsa climbed to the top of her desk too.

"Why are they going after us?" asked Willard. "They never bothered us before."

Fins crossed back and forth in front of him. His chair rumbled away, snagged on the back of one of the larger fish. The shark turned in its path, shaking the chair off; then its broad head broke the surface, mouth agape, teeth glistening and it ate the chair, dragging it under in one bite.

"Feeding frenzy," said Elsa. "They're stirred up."

The carpet undulated from their passage. Strong, fishy smells filled the air, like seaweed baking in the sun.

"It must be the blood," said Willard. He pointed to the late Benford's papers on the floor, many darkly stained. A fin cruised through the middle of them, pushing some aside. "Maybe I can draw them off." He yanked some tissues out of a box and blotted blood off his knuckles. Squeezing, he coaxed a few more drops from each one, then wadded the tissues and threw them as far as he could. They fluttered down ten feet away.

He waited hopefully, but after two or three minutes, it was obvious that the sharks weren't interested.

"It's not enough," said Elsa. "We'll have to out-wait them."

They watched the sharks' activity. It seemed they'd settled into a waiting mode of their own. Generally their circles were counterclockwise, although one would break the pattern and dash through the blood-stained papers once in a while, and several times the flurry of fins and splashing showed they were still agitated.

After a long time, Willard said, "Why didn't you tell me you saw the sharks days ago?"

She scrunched her knees around to make herself more comfortable. "Until you tried to help..." She gestured at the papers on the floor. "I thought I was the only one. Why doesn't anyone else see them?"

Through the western facing windows, the sun neared the horizon. Desks and computers cast long shadows across the blue carpet. Willard shrugged. "Denial, I guess, or they're with them."

She said, "Why didn't you tell me?"

He blushed, then turned his head away to hide it. He was about to say, "Because I was shy," but a movement in the back of the office stopped him. He stood on his desk to see better. Coming toward them, a fin five feet tall wended its way between the desks. "I don't think we'll be able to out-wait them after all," he said. "We're really in trouble."

The wave from its passage tumbled telephones to the floor. Desks rose and fell in its wake.

"Uh oh," said Elsa as she dug through the top drawer of her desk. She sat up holding a nail file.

"That won't stop it," said Willard. He imagined the shark that could have a fin that size. It'd swallow him and the desk and still want more.

Elsa stabbed her hand. She winced and stabbed it again.

"What are you doing!" shouted Willard.

"We'll have to divert them." She looked around the top of her desk, her hand dripping freely. The fin moved ponderously by. "Dang," she said. "Don't look." She unbuttoned her blouse, took it off and smeared the blood into it. "It needs to be fresh and there has to be a lot."

"Better hurry," said Willard.

The fin started back. Elsa wadded the blood-soaked garment into a ball, thought for a second, dropped a paper weight into it, and tossed it fifty feet away.

"It'll take a minute for them to notice," she said, "if they do."

Their reaction, though, was almost immediate. Three fins broke from the pack and headed for the blouse. With majestic grandeur, the massive shark ignored their desks in favor of the fresh scent. At least for the moment, no sharks were near them.

Willard's desk was twelve feet from Elsa's. He studied the carpet between them for sign of a ripple or any hint of a shark waiting below.

"Better do it," said Elsa.

He took a deep breath, jumped on the floor and onto her desk. She grabbed his arm to steady him. The fins closed in on the blouse.

"That won't hold them long," Willard said. "Should we go desk to desk, or sprint for the door?"

She looked panicked, and he could see the memory of Benford surfacing in her eyes. She steadied herself and said evenly, "Desk to desk."

Fifteen desks later, they stood in the tiled hallway that led to the elevator. Willard propped his hands on his knees and breathed in loud gasps. Elsa said, "I've never seen one out here. Have you?"

He willed his breathing to slow down. "No, but I'll feel better when I get home."

He straightened himself. She clasped her bleeding hand next to her chest in a fist. A streak of blood marred one side of her pink camisole, and she was shivering.

"Maybe you could come with me," he said, "and I could bandage that." He could hear his heart in his ears. It was only the adrenaline from the rush to the door that gave him the nerve to be so bold.

She looked at him sternly. "Turn around," she said.

"Excuse me?"

"Turn around."

Confused, he did. She pressed her hand against his neck, then felt his backbone to his belt. He remembered the bulges under some of the employee's clothes, and he understood.

"You're a nice man," she said. "What kind of floors do you have?"

He laughed. "Hardwood."

"I'd be happy to go home with you."

As they walked away, they heard the crashing of office furniture. Frustrated, the sharks had begun to feed on each other.

# The Infodict

anji kept a spider on Marlyss constantly, and his Concierge prompted him with updates. As Sanji sold forty cases to the crosstown outlet, it scrolled her location when her car passed under a traffic vid at Divisadero and Pine.

At the moment, he was in his office, deep in his leather chair, feet up, but it wouldn't matter if was at home or at the park or on a flight; when the info flowed, he swam in it.

Earlier in the day he'd played back some of her phone calls. Last week she'd said, "I'd love to have dinner with you." He replayed it several times, her liquidy contralto. "I'd love to...I'd love to...I'd love to..."

Where's she going? Sanji called up her travel patterns for the last week, Mondays for the last month, and every 5th of the month for the year. Numbers rolled through the air between him and his desk, everything he'd gathered on her since they'd started dating a year ago. No match. He okayed the delivery, quick scanned for reservations she might have made or credit blips. Nothing. He red flagged the time for later analysis just as it reported her at the Divisadero and Lombard.

"You watching Marlyss again, bud?" said Raymond. "You're obsessive." Raymond sat on the edge of Sanji's desk. As usual his tie didn't match his shirt, and the suit coat should have been retired years ago. Rather than getting a hair implant, he had combed thin strands over the bald spot.

"Where's your specs? Don't you work here anymore?" Sanji minimized the Marlyss profiler, but kept the program running in the background. New numbers showing this afternoon's inventories, shipments and condition of the delivery fleet popped up. All in the green. He stood, smoothed the front of his jacket, checked his look in the mirror. Businessman perfect. Just the right part in the hair. A meticulous, trim appearance.

"I get buzzed if there's a problem." Raymond pointed to the flesh-colored button in his ear. "I'm just a P.R. flak. Non-essential paperwork only. Short of a complete emergency, my job could be done by a high school intern." He shrugged. "Let me take you to lunch."

Sanji's own earphone squeaked a high pitched, short-speak message about highway traffic and truck travel time. With a pressure on his desk handplate, Sanji alerted the drivers.

"I've got the expense account. I'll pay." Sanji put his desk on auto mode, which handled routine calls, rerouted e-mail and forwarded everything to the Concierge, a black, wallet-sized case attached to his belt.

Sanji checked the daily specials at Reefers's, a favorite spot for the business crowd, and ordered while they walked. "What do you want?" Above them thin clouds filtered the San Francisco afternoon, softly lighting apartment buildings and trees.

Raymond said, "Don't you ever turn that thing off? I thought I'd decide when we got there."

Sanji laughed. They wove through the lines in front of the fast food kiosks. "You're a positive Luddite. We can have the food waiting, cooked to our specification, eat and be out in fifteen minutes. Don't you know they hate customers like you?"

They turned down a long hill, each step jolting Sanji's specs as they flashed that Marlyss had used credit to park her car at a lot just off Divisadero and Marina Boulevard. Weather numbers scrolled up: sixty-five degrees, eighty-six percent humidity and gusty breezes off the bay. Probably cold as hell. A list of small restaurants and shops within walking distance appeared, all in historic San Francisco, most without vid security he could tap into. He checked her med monitors. Pulse over 100 and steady. Respiration elevated. She was walking. Blood sugar a little low. Probably going to lunch herself. But why downtown? Why the change of habit? Did it mean anything about their relationship? He wouldn't know where she was until she paid for something.

Sanji ran a quick check on her infosystems. As far as he could tell, she hadn't accessed any data about him since dinner last night. Did that mean she didn't care?

"Maybe I don't know what I want yet," said Raymond

"That's the point. You could be deciding now. You're not a very good multi-tasker." Other pedestrians walked around them. Most wore specs. Many of them working, sub-vocalizing communiques, their eyes flitting back and forth as they read data.

Raymond looked from building to building. Sanji knew Raymond was interested in restored architecture. Why he didn't access the info off the net was beyond him. Raymond actually liked to *see* the structures.

Raymond said, "So, did you ask her?"

Sanji wrinkled his brow. It was such a direct question. "Yes, last night."
"And?"

They crossed the street and entered Reefers. "Good afternoon, sirs,"
said the door as it opened for them. "Your table is ready."

A line shimmered on the floor leading them into the restaurant. On the
walls, outdoor footage of a rock concert surrounded them. The soundtrack
was just loud enough to make other patron's conversations unintelligible.

Sanji said, "She wants to think it over. She'll tell me tonight. I'm
thirty-two. You'd think I wouldn't be so nervous."

"Thirty-two and never been married. As far as dating goes, you're
practically a teenager. Thinking it over's better than a no." They sat. "Can
I get a menu?" Raymond said to the table.

A minute later a waiter, looking miffed, delivered a paper version of
the day's offerings. "Are you new to Reefers, sir? We have a much more
attractive electronic display tailor made for our Concierge customers."

"You'll just have to come back, son. I left mine at work," said
Raymond. The waiter's jaw dropped, and Raymond added, "You must be
the new one. I've eaten here twice a week for four years."

The waiter did the peculiar mid-focus, twitchy stare someone got when
checking a readout in his specs. "Who *are* you, sir?"

Raymond smirked. "I pay cash."

"Ah, one of those," said the waiter with a sniff, as if everything was
clear now. He stalked away.

"Where do you *get* cash?" said Sanji.

"If you go to your bank in person, and present identification, it's still
available. Mostly they keep it around for international travelers."

Sanji shook his head. This was another of Raymond's oddities. He
was so consistently dependable, however, that management had decided
he was eccentric rather than weird.

"But why go to the trouble?"

The waiter appeared again, an order tablet in hand.

"I haven't decided yet," said Raymond, and the waiter turned on his
heel. "That boy isn't going to get a tip."

Sanji toyed with his napkin. Around them, others were eating their
meals, their conversations lost in the projected concert's ambient noise.
On the wall, a new band mounted the stage. A sea of heads stretched from
the foreground to the stage's base.

Raymond said, "That's Woodstock. The 2014 one. I love the classic
footage. The other night they showed the old Who concert that ended in a
riot. Pretty strange to be eating shrimp in the shell while watching cops
beating kids over the head with batons."

"It's the atmosphere," said Sanji. He called up the Marlyss profiler again. Her pulse was down, but he had no fresh information on her other than she only had fifteen minutes left on her parking. The day after being asked to marry, she goes off on a strange errand. The question was, what was on her mind?

"Is it work or Marlyss now?"

Sanji snapped the display off guiltily. "How'd you know?"

"Your eyes get all spastic."

Sanji sighed. "How can you stand it, not being connected? Do you know where your wife is this instant? Have you checked on your children this morning?"

Raymond put the menu down. "Now that I'm ready, where's that waiter? No, I haven't checked them. I don't know how you do it. You can't eternally keep your fingers on everyone's pulse. It'll drive you crazy."

Marlyss's heart rate blinked onto the display again. The Concierge reported it had remained unchanged for the last ten minutes. Analysis indicated she was sitting or standing, probably eating lunch. Was she alone? Something fluttered in Sanji's chest. "I have a right to all the information that's available. That's the law. What would be crazy would be not taking advantage of it."

Sanji's ear plug beeped a pay-attention as new displays scrolled across the bottom of his specs. The Far Eastern division reported a markdown in raw material pricing. If he ordered now, he could cut seven percent on manufacturing, invest the savings in interest-bearing bonds for an extra percent and a half. He thought for a couple seconds about whether the numbers could drop more, decided that they might, but not much, placed the order and shifted funds into the right accounts. In the meantime, a tiny vid window opened up in the upper left corner of his vision. The spider had found Marlyss. In the grainy picture from a bank's security camera she walked up the street, gripping her coat closed at her neck. The breeze whipped her long, red hair in front of her face.

A quick query placed the bank a half block from her car. The Concierge listed three restaurants that were her most likely lunch spot. All touristy sea food places. But she hadn't *paid* for anything. If she wasn't eating lunch, what was she doing there? She walked out of the first camera's view, and the Concierge switched to another camera that caught her back as she walked up the block, then out of sight around the corner.

"You're not going to make it until this afternoon, are you? Man, you are practically comatose when you pay attention to that thing. You're an infozombie. They have twelve-step programs for your problem."

Sanji squirmed. "You can never get enough good data. That's why all information is public. Nothing is private."

"Maybe that's okay for business activities or government policy. You're trying to read her mind. Ah, there he is."

The waiter reappeared, looking bored.

"What's the catch of the day? The menu didn't list it."

Rolling his eyes, the waiter said, "Orange Roughy."

"I'll have that then."

Sanji leaned forward. "You don't get it. If you love someone, you want to know everything you can. How else will she know I care?"

"They used to call that 'stalking.'"

"That's ridiculous. Stalking is following her around. Threatening her. All I'm doing is accessing available data, which is my right. She knows I can do it—everybody does it—in fact, she probably expects me to. This is the information society."

"All I know is in matters of the heart, the more you know the more you don't know."

Sanji sat back. The waiter arrived, pushing a cart, their meals steaming. He put the plates in front of them. When he left, Sanji said, "What the hell does that mean?"

Raymond smiled, cut into the Orange Roughy. "It means that sometimes you don't want to know what's on the menu until you get there."

For the rest of the meal, they ate quietly while rock crowds cheered on the walls. Numbers rippled across Sanji's vision: delivery times, work schedules, stock prices. His ear plug whispered status reports. When he finished, he couldn't remember what he'd eaten.

At work Sanji set a countdown clock in his specs' upper right corner. Four hours until he met Marlyss. She went home. No vids in her house, but her security alarm reported when she disarmed it, electricity consumption went up as she turned on lights, water usage indicated she'd showered. Then, nothing. Her pulse perked along steadily. Her Concierge was in sleep mode.

He drummed his fingers on the desk, baffled. Why wasn't she checking on him? In the year they'd dated she had *never* checked on him as far as he could tell. From her point of view, their entire relationship was based on conversations and the time they'd spent together. No wonder she can't answer the question: she doesn't know me, he thought. A stomach twinge hit, and he flinched. His own med readouts indicated indigestion and suggested an antacid. He wondered what he had eaten that would cause that;

he couldn't recall anything spicy. Last night had been the same though, and it wasn't food related. He told her goodnight, the echo of his proposal fairly hanging in the apartment's air. Her hand rested briefly on his, her fingers warm and long and fine. "I need to think about it," she said.

After she left, he laid in his bed staring at the ceiling, thinking about her beside him. He rubbed his palm over the sheets on what would be her side. They were cold and smooth and empty. He tried to recapture the moment before he asked her, when the words were formed but he hadn't spoken them yet. Even now, only minutes later, he could hardly believe he'd had the nerve to do it. Then the twinge. Stomach acid reflux. She wasn't there, and maybe she never would be. His guts tied up inside him, but he didn't get medicine. He put on his specs, activated the Concierge, started the data streaming. Green text flowing across his eyes. Quick-speak chirps in his ear. After a while, he connected the spider for Marlyss. It picked through the megamillion information strands, and soon he swam in her numbers. All of them. Medical records, shopping purchases, paychecks, tax returns, utility bills, loans, bank statements, school, everything. And the vids he'd saved. Marlyss at the mall. Marlyss in the park. Marlyss coming and going from a thousand places, all captured digitally, stored somewhere, and retrieved, by him.

But nowhere—not a clue—on how she would answer his question. Sanji clenched the sheets. How could the answer not be there? What was left to know?

His eyes grew dry watching the clock count down. He blinked and shook his head. Scrolled through jewelry catalogues, screen after screen of wedding rings. Checked travel brochures. South American beach resorts. European tour packages. What would she like? Briefly he connected with a flower shop, then broke it off. She said she wanted time. Flowers would seem pushy. Or would they be romantic? What was in her head?

He imagined a sensor planted in everyone's brain. Readouts cunningly tailored to track emotion and thought. *That* would be information worth having. There would be no need for guesswork.

Irresistibly, with glacier-like gravity, the clock unwound the minutes.

Marlyss waited for him in front of the Maritime museum. In the dusk behind her a restored schooner attached to the dock with three permanent gangplanks, thrust its bare masts into the cloudy sky. Sanji walked quickly. The wind cut through his jacket, and he realized he hadn't been near the sea in months. She'd suggested Fisherman's Wharf for their rendevous. "I like the seagulls," she'd said.

He'd correlated seagulls to her database and found she'd papered the first apartment she'd rented, years before they met, in Seascape Serenity, a pattern of lighthouses, chambered nautiluses and seagulls.

"I missed you," he said as they hugged, and he regretted the words immediately. It'd only been a day. He sounded needy.

"Me too." She held his hand and they strolled toward the shops and tourist attractions. In the bay to their left a cargo hovercraft surrounded by its self generated mist, thundered past Alcatraz. He sensed the unanswered question between them like a malignant djin.

Glumly he noted the temperature and weather report to give himself something to watch. Even though she walked beside him, he couldn't resist replaying "I'd love to have dinner with you." To give himself courage, he triggered the loop: "I'd love to...I'd love to...I'd love to..."

Beside him, she was a silent cipher, red hair spilled over her jacket, most of her face obscured. Just the edge of her cheek and a bit of her nose visible from the side. Something didn't look right about her. As they walked, he glanced from the corner of his eye several times. Finally it occurred to him. She wasn't wearing her specs! He ran a quick check. Her Concierge was still in her apartment.

Casually he reached up and pulled his own off. He blinked against the breeze hitting him square in the face for the first time. They went into his pocket. He shut down his Concierge, and his earplug went dead.

Sidewalk stands they passed sold cheap tee-shirts and San Francisco trinkets. Crab and beer smells escaped the restaurants. Tourists waited in lines for tables. She led them into a maze of souvenir displays and then onto a boardwalk overlooking a small marina. Private fishing boats bobbed under the dock lights. It was nearly night. The buildings cut the wind, and Sanji didn't feel as cold.

Marlyss said, "I come here sometimes when I want to think." She sat on a wooden bench and when he sat beside her, she looked straight at him for the first time since they'd started walking. Her hand went to his cheek. "Sanji." She traced a line from his temple to the corner of his mouth. "I've never seen you without your specs."

And they were kissing, her lips soft against his, her breath quick against his skin. After a minute, he realized she was crying. His face was damp with it. He touched a tear from below her eye with wonder.

She said, "They told me you were an infodict. My friends told me you were...emotionally isolated." She giggled, a surprising sound in her throaty voice. "Oh, Sanji, I would love to marry you."

And they kissed again, long and silent. Sanji felt the waves beneath them lapping against the pilings, rocking their bench the tiniest bit. Seagulls cried in the bay. He held her close. She trembled, and he trembled too. It was all so huge, the emotion within. In the night, in the artificial light, the boats moved in elegant witness to the moment. Sanji knew he would remember this instant forever.

He didn't know how long they'd sat before Marlyss straightened and pulled away from him. She wiped her face. "I need to tidy up a bit. Do you mind? There's a restroom just around the corner. I won't be a minute."

"Of course not," he said, and even these little words felt different, because now he was speaking them to the woman who'd said yes. Everything was different now: the quality of air, the quality of sound, all of it. "I'll be right here," he said.

She kissed him on the cheek, smiled, and walked to the corner of the building, her footsteps loud against the boards.

Sanji leaned back, the bench a firm support behind him, and he stretched his legs. He sighed. It was good.

Then he noticed a small box half-way up the light pole on the dock across the water, a police unit, an infrared camera turned on only at night for security. Of course, the police would watch closely at night, when most crimes occurred. He looked around. The area was thick with surveillance. Accessible surveillance. His hand snuck into his pocket, caressed his specs. He twitched the Concierge back to life.

Yes, there he was, in reds and blacks as the camera saw him. He expanded the search, jumping from camera to camera. There was the front of the building he sat behind now. There was the side. There was the door to the public restroom. Sanji backed up the infrared vid a couple of minutes. There was Marlyss, entering the restroom. Sanji turned the spider up a notch. Water ran in the restroom. A hand dryer pulled energy.

He thought, what's she thinking now? Is she sorry she said yes? Will she always love me? It would take a lot of data to know. The information would have to flow fast and furious. Yes it would.

When she came out, he put the specs back in his pocket, but the Concierge was ready. The spider was running, and it would never rest.

# The Diorama

lack! Black! He's painting the house black!" Owen glared through his picture window at Gary's house across the street. Emma, reading a *Roads West* magazine grunted as she pushed herself out of the recliner.

"You're smudging," she said. Owen pulled his hands off the glass, then she buffed his marks away with a handkerchief she produced from her jean's pocket. He thought about saying a woman her age shouldn't wear jeans, but decided he didn't want to start that argument again.

She said, "And that looks more like navy to me. No one would paint a house black." She tucked the hankie back in her pants as she looked out the window. "Of course, navy would be just as bad."

"Navy? You're out of your mind, Emma. He's painting it black, and he's doing it to spite me because of the houseboat."

"With all those trees in the way, I can't tell."

"I'm not talking about the trees. Who cares about the trees? I can live with trees. Can't you see what color he's using?"

"I'm old, not blind. Might be navy, might be black. Why don't you talk to him?" Emma walked back to her magazine, removed her brass page marker, sat down in the chair and then adjusted her reading glasses. "Not that he'll listen to you anyway."

"I will. I'm on my way right now." Owen slammed the heavy, burglar resistant door behind him.

He winced at the brightness of the unseasonably warm early October afternoon, and almost instantly a prickle of sweat formed on his forehead and the back of his neck. He tugged at the bottom of his tie while holding the knot firmly against his throat, buttoned his gray suit-coat's middle button, then checked the shine on his patent leather shoes for scuffs. When he reached the sidewalk he looked back at his own house, a sand-tan with sienna trim, plain Colonial two-story, much like every other house on the block. He could see Emma reading inside. She didn't look up.

Owen marched across the street and onto the twigs and leaves beneath Gary's trees where the temperature seemed ten degrees cooler, and the paint-filled air smelled like silver polish. Gary perched awkwardly, high on an aluminum extension ladder. He sprayed paint onto the gutter and then pulled a foot wide swath of black down the side of the house almost to his feet. Then he sprayed the next section of gutter and added another broad ribbon of black to the side of the house. The asphalt shingles on the roof were already painted. From the spray gun in Gary's hand hung a rubber hose that led to a chrome and blue power sprayer hunched like a metal mosquito over a five-gallon bucket, its proboscis buried deep in the paint.

Gary painted the five feet of siding from the corner of the house toward the first bedroom window while Owen, with his arms crossed on his chest, watched, waiting to be noticed. The window wasn't covered, and Owen wondered how Gary was going to avoid spraying the glass when he reached it, but Gary didn't break his rhythm: he continued the same pattern, painting the window and brown frame a solid, flat black.

"You can't do this," Owen announced. Gary looked down, his face covered with a dust mask and oversized goggles.

"Ah, Owen." He clambered down the ladder, dropped the gun in a bucket that smelled of lacquer thinner, pushed the goggles onto his forehead then pulled the face mask onto his neck. Where they hadn't protected his skin, his wrinkled face was gray with over-spray and so were the few normally white hairs that fell out of his baseball cap. He was a tall, skinny man whose most notable features were his hands, long fingered and huge knuckled, arthritic looking; they constantly moved, picking things up, setting them down, rubbing his chin, scratching his chest. The two times Owen had talked to Gary, once at a homeowners' meeting and the other during a short but heated discussion on the street, he had found it hard not to watch them.

"Would you give me some help with the ladder?" Gary asked. Owen pushed his hands deep into his armpits and scowled. Gary shrugged, pulled the ladder upright and clanged it a few feet further down the house. He said, "Still steamed over the houseboat aren't you?"

"What are you doing?"

"Here? I'm painting, of course."

"No, I mean what do you think you're doing."

"You don't like the color?"

"Yes, I don't like the color. I hate the color. What are you doing?"

Gary bent over a box with four one-gallon cans in it, pulled one out and pried the lid off with a screwdriver. He poured it into the five-gallon bucket. "Color's a matter of taste, don't you think? But if it's any of your business, which it isn't, this is just an undercoat."

"You painted the window."

"No law against that. Now, at least, I won't have to clean it." Gary opened and emptied a second one-gallon can.

"Don't think you're so smart. The Neighborhood Association will have something to say about this."

Gary "hmphed." He pushed the screwdriver into his back pant's pocket and slid the goggles over his eyes. "Coming from their impeached past president? Why don't you wait and see what it looks like when I'm done?"

"I won't like it, and they won't either, this breach of the covenants. We have a nice neighborhood."

"Depends on what you like, I guess." Gary covered his mouth with the dust mask. "You need a hobby, Owen. Retirement is making you an old man."

"Old man!"

"Well, I know it's an insult to the elderly, but it's the worst I can think of right now." He picked the spray gun out of the bucket, shook the lacquer thinner off and put a foot on the first rung of the ladder. "By the way, Owen, when I retired I gave all my suits and ties to the Goodwill, but even when I was working I wouldn't wear them on a Saturday." He climbed back to the gutter.

*O*wen's ear hurt from pressing the phone against it for ten minutes. Emma said, "Why don't you hang up and try later?" He turned his back to her. The city building's tape of music for people on hold started over, a medley of old Rolling Stone's tunes done with violins and French horns. He grimaced again at the coincidence of the first song, a syrupy, upbeat rendition of "Paint it Black."

The line clicked. "City Manager Lisa Younger here, what can I do for you this time Mr. Burrows."

"I pay taxes. I vote. I don't expect to be on hold until you get around to answering your calls. That's what you can do for me."

Momentarily, the line between them whispered with tiny sounds, ghost voices. "I'm sorry. They had a hard time tracking me down."

"Gary Guy's painting his house black. Stop him."

"The fellow with the houseboat and the hot air balloon? Really? Black?"

"Yes. Flat black." Owen stretched the cord from the wall phone so he could look out the picture window. "Trim, windows and front door. He started three hours ago and the front's all black now. Our covenants specifically forbid 'decorations that are not consistent with the general tenor of the neighborhood.'" Owen heard a shuffling of papers on her end.

Lisa said, "Decorations, according to city code, are 'Lawn ornaments and seasonal displays associated with holidays,' like Christmas lights or Halloween jack-o-lanterns. Paint is not considered a decoration. What do your covenants say about general upkeep?"

Owen thumbed through the fifty-page pamphlet he had almost single-handedly drafted four years ago when he bought the first house in the sub-division. "Um. 'Homeowners will maintain paint, siding, brickwork or other accruements to the main structure in new or near-new condition.' There isn't anything specifically referring to color, but the *intent* of the covenants is to maintain the appearance of the neighborhood. He can't just willy-nilly paint his house a different color. Earth tones! Natural earth tones are our choices. I give everyone who moves in a list of suggested color combinations if they decide to repaint. Good quality Sherwin-William colors."

"He's not done yet, you said?"

"No."

"Even if we could do something, which I'm not sure we can, as long as he's still in the act of painting we can't very well judge the final job. Maybe he's just putting on a first coat."

"He *said* it was an undercoat, but the windows and door...and the roof! He painted the roof, and it was already black. They don't get painted no matter what he's planning for the rest of the house. He's loony, and he's ruining the neighborhood. You've got to do something now."

"I'm sorry, Mr. Burrows. Maybe your homeowner association should meet with him. The city can't look at the house as long as he's still working on it. If there are no violations of the code, and your homeowners group doesn't appeal to us, there's nothing we can do. He's not doing any construction, is he? If he's building, then we could inspect the work."

"No, just paint."

"We're stuck, then. Sorry. If it's as bad as you say it is, someone else will complain too. With your history with Gary Guy, you might be better to stay away from him."

"I don't need advice, I need the city to do its job."

Owen pushed the cut-off button, ending the City Manager's chance to apologize again and made a mental note to send a letter to the city council about Lisa Younger's job performance. Emma stood at the window beside him. The setting sun seemed to rest on the peak of Gary's house and shined directly through the grove of oak, casting shadows into their living room. The house itself looked like a hole where a house had been, like the house had retreated backward and left a space that hadn't missed it yet.

Emma said, "A completely black house. You don't see that often. What a wonder."

A week later, the neighborhood association's meeting was a disaster, Owen thought. First, President Phuong Kim Nguyen hosted, and his wife served punch in plastic champagne glasses with detachable bottoms that were left over from their daughter's wedding two weeks earlier. Owen felt some obvious resentment from her, which he recognized stemmed from his opposition at the last meeting to the reception in their backyard on the grounds that the street would be cluttered with too many cars.

He was sure that she spilled the punch on him, and gave him a glass whose bottom kept dropping off, intentionally.

Secondly, Roger Bing, who he could always depend upon to second his motions, stayed home with a stomach virus, and thirdly, no one else seemed as alarmed about the painting of the house. Elston Newkirk, the elementary school principal, pointed out that Gary was still painting, and the house was obviously not going to be black when he finished. Elston said, "Why, just today, when I drove by, he was using brown paint."

The real mess, though, came from the next item on the agenda, the treasurer's report. Vonda Heaton read the total from the monthly income of association dues and the expenses, which, besides the normal landscaping service fees, included a large payment to Fenton and Associates, a law firm. Carol Craft asked to be recognized, stood, locked her eyes to a position four or five feet above everyone's head, her normal speaking stance, inhaled deeply and delivered a well-rehearsed speech. Owen saw her husband mouthing the words with her as she spoke.

"I believe that since the debt to Fenton and Associates was entered into by our past president illegally, such illegality being demonstrated by our homeowners group's decision to oust said president, that the aforementioned president should not only be personally responsible for the debt but also repay the treasury the money he used to obtain the initial consultation, such action being neither presented to or approved by said homeowners. Our bylaws giving the president such broad powers as to act without us should be amended retroactively."

Everyone applauded. All eyes were on Vonda. They scrupulously avoided looking at him.

Owen stood, picked up his coat, began moving toward the door and said, "Gary Guy's houseboat didn't belong on the street!"

"You didn't have to try and sue him with our money to prove it!" said somebody, maybe Elston. "Yeah!" yelled someone else, and then the room erupted in angry shouting. President Nguyen grabbed a brass chip-and-dip serving plate and clanged it repeatedly on the top of the coffee table, sending a spray of chip dust and guacamole onto the carpet. "Neighbors, neighbors," he said. The room silenced. His wife looked horrified at the coffee table finish.

"I hope your property values fall," said Owen, as he opened the door.

*I*'m not wrong about this, am I, Emma?" Owen looked out the window. "They hate me, and I did it for their good." He was sitting on the love seat that he had pulled in front of the picture window a week ago. A huge pair of binoculars rested on the windowsill within easy reach. The sun had set two hours earlier, but Owen could see Gary was still painting. A Coleman lantern on a stool to his side cast a harsh light filled with sharp-edged shadows.

Emma had been reading when Owen came in, her feet curled up beneath her on the recliner, and she hadn't glanced up when he sat down heavily. He heard her close her magazine. She moved onto the love seat with him, put her hand on his shoulder and said softly, "Of course not. You're not wrong. You're clumsy, though. You didn't use to be so clumsy. You used to take time to consider."

He shrugged her hand off. "They hate me." He picked up the binoculars and peered through them. Gary bent over a palette, dabbed a wadded rag into a color and applied it to the wall. "What the hell is he doing? Is that a tree he's doing? Here!" He thrust the instrument into Emma's hands. "You tell me what he's doing."

"Don't bark at me, Owen, and I won't peep at Gary Guy because you're mad at the homeowners." She handed him back the binoculars. "As a matter of fact, it *is* a tree. A California White Oak. Some people call it Valley Oak. I asked him about it."

"You *talked* to him? What are you doing talking to him? What was he doing in my house? The maniac might have strangled you, or...or...painted you or anything."

She laughed. "You are ridiculous sometimes. He'd been working all afternoon and I took over a beer. We talked for twenty minutes. He's doing a whole forest."

"A mural. The maniac is painting a mural on the *front* of a house in Cherry Hills. Across the street from me he is painting a mural like the side of a cheap restaurant? And you didn't say anything?"

"What would be the point? You haven't listened to me in years. And if you won't be civil, I won't tell you the rest."

Owen leaned toward her, opened his mouth to speak, sort of coughed instead, and fell back into the loveseat.

She said, "It's not a mural: it's a diorama, and he plans on finishing it by early November. He said he got the idea from the Museum of Natural History." Emma took the binoculars back and focused them. "See, he's doing a limb now. I imagine he'll be on a ladder later to get the high parts. The idea, he said, is to make the trees in his yard blend into the forest on the house. That way you won't be able to tell where one stops and the other starts, just like at the museum with the stuffed animals."

"Why would he do such a crazy thing? He can't sell a house like that. The city will have to act now. That used to be a beautiful house in a beautiful neighborhood."

"Oh, I'm sure he is going to change it back after November. He said that he won't need it after then."

"What does that mean?"

"Just that the project will be done, I guess, and he'll be able to go on to something else. You know he only flew the hot-air balloon once. When he finishes one thing, he dismantles it and starts another."

"A balloon in his backyard was bad. The houseboat was bad. But they were only there for a little bit. He's ruining his house." Owen looked from Emma to the window suddenly. "Ha! The trees! The trees!"

"What? What?"

"He planted the trees a year ago. Are you going to tell me that he's been planning this project for a year? And that he will just clean it up when he is done? He must have some other idea in mind. No one works for a year on a whim. Everybody is the same. They all want to get something. Look at me. Years and years in the bank, and all that time I dressed nice, talked nice, and kept up appearances while you and I lived in rentals, one horrible rental after another, but I worked with a plan. We got this house because of that plan, and now we live in a neighborhood as good as anybody's. So I'll bet he's got some plan in mind. Nobody buys a beautiful house just to paint it black. Either he's after me, or he's crazy, or he's got some plan. Why he can't retire gracefully and enjoy the fruits of his labor is beyond me."

"He said he didn't want to die in that house."

"He's sick?"

"He said that the neighborhood looked like a mausoleum." She laughed again. Owen hated it when she laughed at him. "He said you looked like an undertaker."

"Well I say he looks like an idiot."

Emma walked away toward their bedroom. "Maybe so, but he's a nice man. Very polite. I liked his tree."

*F*our days later, Roger Bing and Owen draped their arms over the top of the fence separating their backyards from their frontyards. They watched Gary across the street on his hands and knees painting in some detail they couldn't discern. Roger wore a shapeless, floppy, wide-brimmed lady's hat that completely shaded his upper body. He had said, when the doctor scraped a small carcinoma off the side of his nose the year before, that he figured the sun was out to get him.

Roger said, "Have you been over there lately? He's got it so the ground just keeps going into the painting. Damndest thing. We're standing about five feet from the house looking at what he's done, and he says to me, 'See those five leaves?' and I says, 'Sure, they're yellow.' And he says, "How many of them are real and how many of them are painted?' Well, this is quite a shock to me because I thought they were all real. So I studied them extra careful, like it's a driver test. Do you know we got to take that damn vision test every time we renew now? You'd think they're saying because we're over sixty-five we're incompetent or something..."

"What about the leaves?"

"Right. Anyways, I'm looking at the leaves, which are in a row, almost lined up, and I can't tell where the base of the house is! He's matched the colors. I mean, there are leaves lying on the ground from those damned trees of his, and he's painted leaves lying on the ground so they look the same. So I check them out from where I'm standing, and I say three of them are real. It's a guess. But he laughs at me and says, 'Only one is real.' I get down to look, and he's right. When I get close, it's obvious, but from more than five feet, you can't tell."

"That doesn't sound so great to me. Sounds like you shouldn't be driving anymore. What does it matter anyways? In another couple of weeks he's going to have to clean it all off. The city will get him, or the neighborhood association. The man's obviously mad." Owen pulled his own hat lower on his forehead. The grass seemed visibly wilted in the heat.

"What's going on between Emma and him?" said Roger.

"There's nothing going on. She gave him a beer and he gave her a ear-full about trees." Owen spoke languidly. The autumn heat made him feel lazy and slow.

"Oh."

A yellow jacket took off from its nest in Roger's gutter and flew almost in Owen's face before veering away. He waved a hand at it.

"When are you going to clean those things out? They start breeding and then you never get rid of them."

"Maybe next week." Roger didn't move. "I've seen her over there several times."

Owen suddenly became alert. "Really?"

"Sure. Ever since he started painting. Most the time in the morning. Don't you go to the Veteran's Hall in the morning? They sit on the ground and yak it up like a couple of gossips. 'Course I can't hear a word they're saying."

"Why should she do that?"

"Who knows. Maybe what's good for the goose is good for the gander." Roger turned his head on its ear and looked at Owen slyly. He was half smiling.

"That was a hundred years ago. And she's an old woman anyways." Owen paused. "And where do you get off with that kind of talk? I have half a mind to paste you one."

Roger sighed and put his chin back on his forearm. "It's just words, Owen. Just a joke." He straightened up. "I guess I ought to finish this lawn. If winter'll ever get here I can quit mowing."

Owen pushed away from the fence too. "Enjoy the Indian summer. Can't last." He headed for the back door.

Roger's voice drifted over the fence. "Even an old dog'll wander off sometimes, Owen."


The next morning, Owen settled into the loveseat next to the binoculars. From the kitchen came glassy clinks and dishwater swishing.

"Isn't it about time for you to go?" called Emma. He imagined her blouse sleeves were rolled up above her elbows and her hands were hidden deep in the murky water.

"Those old fogies. A few rounds of canasta and they're ready for naps. I'll stay home today." The noises stopped for a moment, then resumed.

"Are you feeling all right?" she asked.

He picked up the binoculars and focused them through the window. Gary appeared to be standing at what used to be the front step of his house, except now the gray sidewalk didn't stop at the door but continued on, curving slightly through a flowered meadow until it vanished a hundred yards farther in a dense thicket. All the trees, and there were hundreds of them now, glowed as if in direct sunlight. Their yellow and red leaves seemed almost a flame across the house. The shadows of the closest trees cast purple streaks across the meadow.

Gary pulled a note pad from his overall's pocket, flicked it open and consulted one of the pages. Then he bent down, tugged on what looked like a tent peg with a string running from it to the base of one of the trees and moved it over a couple of inches. He walked down the front of the house, first looking at his notebook, and then shifting each of the pegs with strings on them that stretched from the real trees to the wall.

The binoculars limited Owen's vision so that he could see nothing other than Gary's painting. The illusion of gazing into a mountain oak forest was almost perfect. The real trees blended into the painted ones. Owen rested the eye-pieces on his cheekbones and peered over the lenses. The effect vanished. The neighboring houses, prim, plain and proper gave Gary's property a weird, surreal frame. But Owen had been looking through the binoculars for so long that it took him a moment to shake the impression that the forest was correct and that the neighborhood around it was out of place.

Owen's front door opened, and he sat up. His back popped and he lowered the binoculars gingerly to his lap. His elbows had stiffened. Emma stood, one foot in and one out. A picnic basket hung from her hand.

"What are you doing?" Owen asked.

She held up the basket and nodded her head across the street.

"How do you think it looks, you being seen over there while he's making a fool of me?"

"He's not even thinking of you, Owen. If you thought about yourself half as much as you think about him, maybe you'd see more."

"What do you mean by that?"

"Just that you should pay attention to your own house. That's all."

"So, you're siding with him. Is that it?"

Emma put the basket outside and sat on the doorsill. Owen could see the curve of her back and a fall of wispy white hair that covered her collar. She didn't say anything for some time. She said, "Do you remember right after we married when you wanted to take that job in Ontario, and I said it was a bad idea?"

Owen answered cautiously, "Yes."

"I made lots of excuses: I wanted my kids to be American; I didn't want to be away from my folks; I didn't like cold weather; I didn't know French. But the real reason I didn't want to go was because I was afraid of changing my picture of the future." She hunched over. Owen guessed that she had her arms wrapped around her knees, but he couldn't see for sure. "I had this vision of the way my life was going to go, and Ontario wasn't part of it."

"You were right. Ontario was a bad idea."

"Maybe, except we never had kids, my folks died, and I'm cold all the time now."

"You still don't know French."

"No, I don't."

"What's your point?"

"When we argued about going, you said that you didn't want to live, work and die in the same place. You said that if we didn't keep our options open to 'the magic of possibility,' we'd just fade away. 'The magic of possibility.' I remembered that. You always could turn a phrase." She started rocking. Her ear appeared, then vanished. He glimpsed the side of her face. "It seems to me that somewhere in the last fifty years, we've switched positions."

"I kept you in new clothes. You always looked good."

"I don't want that on my tombstone: 'She wore new clothes.'"

"Jesus! Everybody is talking about dying lately. What's this got to do with Gary?"

She turned, faced him and braced herself with one hand on the floor inside the house. Owen thought it a very girlish maneuver. It reminded him of when they had met. She had been sitting on the end of a dock at Smallee Lake, tossing stale donuts to the ducks. She had turned and looked at him like that when she felt his footsteps behind her.

"He's leaving, I think. Pretty soon. Maybe in the next couple of days. I don't want him to believe that no one cared. You know, he's been our neighbor for four years, and all he's gotten is anger. His wife dies and nobody brings him a casserole. Two months later you're threatening to sue him because he parked a houseboat where you could see it. It doesn't feel just."

"The damn thing blocked the whole street. You practically had to drive on my sidewalk to get around it."

"Well, you didn't have to bring in the lawyers. His children stopped him. He had this idea about selling the house and getting away, and it turns out that his children convinced a judge that he wasn't competent. Can you imagine that? He's on an allowance now. He sold everything to buy the trees."

"Where's he going?"

"I don't know. He says he's getting away from it all though, somewhere the children won't find him." She took a deep breath, held it, then let it out in a rush. "He's not crazy, but I think he believes he can walk into that painting. He hasn't actually said that's what he's going to do, but he talks like that's what he wants to happen. He tells it like a story. He said, 'What if the sun was just right?' I don't know what he means by that. But he said, 'What if the sun was just right? and my attitude was right, and I only had a few seconds where I could slip in?'"

Emma looked at him, as if waiting for him to contradict her, then continued, "When that doesn't work, he'll go someplace else. He's talked about a ranch in Washington where he used to go, an artist's colony. He said you don't have to be an artist to go there, that you don't have to be any more an artist than me, but that the people listen to each other, and they don't push each other around. Either way, his kids will be stuck with a house that needs a new paint job. That seems fair."

"You don't think that's crazy?"

"When he talks, he makes sense. He says you got to believe in what you're doing, and not care what other people say. He says he's on the edge of knowing enough to do what he wants to do and being too old to do it. He says that most people don't even know when they cross the border, but that's what it is. I like listening to him."

"I don't want you going over there."

"I know."

She got up, picked the basket off the front stoop, closed the door behind her and walked down their sidewalk, and across the street. Gary came out from beneath the trees and met her. She said something to him and he shaded his eyes, looking in Owen's direction. Gary waved, clearly a "come on over" wave. Emma stood motionless beside him, then she waved too. Owen clenched his jaw, straightened his back very stiff and didn't move.

*I*n bed that night, Owen opened his eyes and read the time on the digital alarm on the dresser. 1:40 a.m. A distant hum from the refrigerator, and the measured ticking of the "antique" grandfather clock they had bought new at Penny's were all he heard at first. The less prominent background noises soon sorted themselves out: a train passing through a half-mile away, a siren, a breeze wiping the house, his own pulse in his ears, and, finally, Emma's even breathing.

He had watched them eat their little picnic. Gary had spread a drop-cloth under the trees; she had taken from the basket a thermos, a small cheese board, a quarter wheel of Longhorn cheddar (all that was left from a present from the Bings), a knife, two coffee cups and a box of crackers. They smiled often as they ate. Occasionally Emma looked over her shoulder toward him. He knew that she knew he was watching, so, eventually, he put the binoculars down and went to the basement. There, among lumpy, misshapen cardboard boxes filled with clothes they no longer wore and newspapers they intended to give to the Boy Scouts on the next paper drive, he found what he was looking for, a photo album.

Most of the pictures were from a trip they had taken during the summer of '63, twenty-six years ago, to south-west Colorado. Here was a picture of Emma at Four Corners with one foot in Colorado, one in Utah, a hand in New Mexico and another in Arizona. Here was a picture of Owen standing in front of a kiva entrance at Mesa Verde. He had one hand jauntily on his hip and the other pointed down the ladder. Here was a picture of the two of them at the base of Bridal Veil Falls near Telluride. The mist from the falling water nearly obscured them, and they were hunched over, their hands pulling their collars tight against their necks. They were laughing. He couldn't remember now who had snapped the picture.

He hadn't heard Emma come in, and he, in fact, did not come upstairs until the middle of the afternoon. She had been reading and did not acknowledge him when he passed through the room. Dinner was polite.

The album was beneath the bed. He thought about showing it to her in the morning. He thought about what it would be like to lay in the bed without the quiet, continuous presence of her breathing. Yes, he thought, he needed to pay closer attention to his own house.

Things would be better when Gary left.

A sound woke Owen up. Gray morning light faintly illuminated the dresser, the posts on the bed, a bentwood rocker with lace arm sleeves by the window, and on the wall a seascape Emma had painted years ago. He strained to hear the sound again. There was silence. He knew she was gone without looking; he swung his feet out from under the covers and grabbed his robe from behind the bedroom door.

"Emma!"

He walked briskly from room to room. He wanted to run, but what if Emma stepped out of a door and saw him, running? What would she think? What would she say to him?

She would say, "Owen, why are you running? What will the neighbors think when they hear you were tearing around your own house at the break of dawn?"

He threw open a bathroom door and the spring door-stop buzzed on the rebound.

He paused at the top the stairs. The living room was empty. Her magazines were neatly stacked beside the recliner. His binoculars were in the case by the loveseat.

"Emma?"

He tip-toed down, suddenly afraid to make a noise. The carpet scratched at the bottom of his feet. The balustrade slid smoothly beneath his hand.

He looked into the kitchen. The rising sun flushed the curtain over the back door window. The light streaked the polished linoleum.

Then he ran.

The front door was ajar.

Slanting sunlight turned Gary's trees a mellow, softer color than Owen had seen before. He sprinted down the sidewalk, his robe untied, flapping behind him. The street stung his feet.

"Emma!"

He thought he saw a movement at the end of Gary's painted trail, the trail into the mountain forest, a flash of color like a ray of sun on the backs of two people a hundred yards away *in the painting.*

The leaves skittered beneath him. A breeze creaked branches in the trees above, and for an instant it seemed like the trees in the painting swayed too. The sun cast long shadows from the real trees that exactly matched the shadows painted on the meadow.

He skidded to a halt. "Oh god. Oh god. Oh god." He stood on the sidewalk, peering into the painting. In the distance the rising sun caught the face of a snowcapped range of mountains, reflecting orange and blue. A deep purple and black gash marked a pass, a place for the path he was on to go through. "Oh god!" He closed his eyes and ran forward.

The front door slammed him down on his rear, and his left cheekbone and eyebrow swelled his eye shut instantly.

He sat with his legs spread and straight before him, his hands braced on the sidewalk behind. His left hand hurt. He brought it up to where his right eye could see it. A chunk of gravel was imbedded in the middle of a broad, red scrape on the heel. He shook the stone out and then felt his cheekbone and eyebrow.

He rolled onto his knees then forced himself upright. The doorknob was a bright, meadow green, but was easily visible this close. He turned it. Light spilled through into the empty living room. There was no furniture. In the kitchen he found a card table with one folding chair pulled up to it. A single plate and cup rested in the drying rack next to the sink. His lungs felt like they were filling up with water. Each breath bubbled.

His footsteps, soft as they were, echoed. He turned on lights as he went, and for a moment couldn't figure out why the house was so dark, until he remembered that the windows were covered with paint. Upstairs, in the master bedroom, was a bedsprings and mattress lying directly on the floor. The bed was made. All of Gary's belongings could have fit in the back of a small truck.

Owen sat on the edge of Gary's bed. He realized that the house was exactly like his. The design was the same. Without furniture, there was no difference. He lay down on his side, and then on his stomach. His knees were on the floor. His face pressed into the bedspread that smelled of lacquer thinner.

After a while, he got up, shuffled through the house turning off lights and shutting doors, locked the front door, crossed the street, went inside and sat in the loveseat. He stared out the window, unfocused for an hour. Eventually, he picked up the binoculars and pointed them at the forest. The left eyepiece he canted away from the swollen side of his face.

The next morning, just before dawn, Owen waited under the trees. He wore new hiking boots, new jeans, a bright blue backpack over a new flannel shirt, and his old yard-work cap. He shivered. Frost edged the leaves and a wind swirled some of them into the air. He could smell the inevitability of snow although there were no clouds. Indian Summer had broken.

A sliver of sun popped over the peak of his house. He adjusted the shoulder straps. Shafts of light fell through the limbs and remaining leaves of the oaks. He faced the painting, half embarrassed to be standing there but fully resolute to do something insane.

The light grew and he watched. The trees in the painting stood still, exquisite, convincing, but still. They never rustled like they had for an instant yesterday. The wind didn't touch them. He watched the shadows from the real trees. They didn't quite line up to the shadows of them painted on the meadow now. Where they first touched the house the difference was minute, a fraction of an inch, but perceptible. Yesterday, the shadows matched perfectly, but the earth had moved on. They shadowed the painting; they never lay down as if there were no wall there. When the sun cleared his house completely, he took off the backback and dropped it on the ground. He laced his hands on top of his head like a prisoner of war and walked home.

Later that morning, the phone rang. He listened to it for a long time, ten rings, before lifting himself out of the loveseat.

"Mr. Burrows? This is City Manager, Lisa Younger. I have some good news for you."

"Yes," he said dully.

"About the matter of Gary Guy's house, I had a man go by and take some photographs, and I think we can make a case that he's violated the city's sign code. We ought to be able to get the sheriff to serve him papers forcing him to change it, or we can condemn the property and do the job ourselves. Also, your homeowner's association president, Mr. Nguyen, came by with a formal request for the city to enforce your covenants. Either way we go, the place should be back to normal in a couple of weeks."

He said nothing for a moment, then he rubbed his forehead. "You can repaint it without his permission?"

"Yes."

"What if you can't find him?"

"It won't matter. We can condemn the house anyway."

"No."

"Excuse me?"

"You can't change the house." He gripped the receiver tightly. "The house has to stay the same. It has to stay like that for a year."

"But, Mr. Burrows, we wouldn't be involved if you hadn't given me a call. We've gone to a lot of trouble at your request."

He thought. "Do you know the law firm of Fenton and Associates?"

"Yes."

He extended the phone cord from the wall to the window so he could see Gary's house. "Well, if you try and change that house...that...work of art, I'll have a court order from them blocking you every which way to Sunday."

"Mr. Burrows, it doesn't fit into your neighborhood. It doesn't match the appearance of the other houses."

He started to speak, paused, and then said, "Who cares what the neighborhood looks like?"

Her voice was amazed. "You did. Have you lost...I mean...changed your mind?"

Owen saw his new backpack still sitting beside Gary's house. A pile of leaves partially covered it now. He made a mental note to go pick it up.

"We'll have to consider that possibility," he said.

# Nine Fingers on the Flute

What decided it for me was the expression on the painted woman's face.

That afternoon as I walked with Kursh through the marketplace I had thought, this is a narrow city, a narrow, cold city carved out of stone and sitting in stone—a place where the only magic to be had costs too much—a city where no knows me or can touch me. Named after a woman, this ancient city is a deep, unknowable place, built in a canyon, filling it half up to the high edges; reaching dozens, maybe hundred of levels down. Who knows? Even in the crowded marketplace though, on the city's roof, open to the sun and wind, I was alone and hurt and sad. I thought, they all have something to sell, and the one that matters won't take what I have to give. Twenty summers have passed, and manhood is upon me, for what use?

"Now there's one who's worth a finger." Kursh clapped me on the shoulder. "Hell, she's worth a hand at least," he joked.

The girl he talked about balanced a basket of fruit on her hip, which rolled pleasantly as she walked ahead of us on the crowded market street.

"Yes sir, a man could do well by that one I expect." His humor—his stone-cursed, never dying humor—clashed with my dark mood.

"She is too skinny," I snapped.

"Bah! Skinny ones are best. They don't cost a lot to feed, and they're all muscle."

I could smell fresh ox cooking from a tent to our left. Ahead, a deeply wrinkled old clothier hawked his samples to the passerby. Kursh said, "There's another. Look at the legs on that one!"

"Short and fat. You are going blind."

He strode beside me nonplused, scanning the crowd. A bit of unidentifiable food clung to his dark scraggly beard. His leather jerkin was sweat stained, and his pants torn.

"Picky, picky, picky. They're all the same. Just step up and take one."

I glimpsed a bright flash of a smile and heard a lilting laugh under the canopy beside us, and I started in, but it wasn't her so I mumbled an apology and backed out.

Although the sun was brilliant in the clear sky, I found no joy in it. A pot merchant offered me a cracked vase, and beside him, his son or servant stared blank eyed into the throng. A dog with a broken hind leg, poorly splinted, whimpered under a meat table, his eyes filled with fear and hunger.

"You are not making yourself well. Pick another and be done with it." Kursh palmed an apple out of a bin and bit into it. "Your business is slipping away. Customers do not want to deal with a surly blacksmith."

I stared at my hands. Carbon blackened the creases and calluses shaped the palms. I clenched them into fists.

"These look good and strong don't they? You'd think I could make my life work."

He spit a seed and it stuck to the back of a soldier in front of us. The soldier didn't notice. "You are so dramatic. A little trouble and you collapse like an empty sack. Look around you. Do you think there is only one woman in the world? Do you think no one else has felt like you?"

In the gap between two tents, a juggler tossed a series of rounded stones in the air. His female assistant, maybe his wife, lobbed object after object into the whirling group. I tried to see if there was happiness in his eyes, but I only saw his concentration. Sweat smeared his makeup into long streaks. Catch and throw; catch and throw. The stones blurred into a solid ring of rock. Even moving as fast as it was, the misshapened left hand marked him: it only had four fingers. The woman reached into the spinning ring and plucked out a stone. One by one she removed them until the juggler tossed a lone object up and down. Kursh flipped a coin into her bowl.

We turned left up the long set of cobblestone stairs that served as a sidewalk on this steep side street.

"Don't walk this way."

"I want to see her house."

"Why bother?"

I had no answer for that.

The upper canyon edge glinted in the sun as we ascended. I looked to our right at the marketplace spread beneath us where hundreds of tents and temporary pavilions lumped and swooped from one side of the trade grounds to the other. Masses of people flowed between the rows of displays, but from this height they seemed less like men and women and more like toys moving in miniature parody of real life. From this distance, their voices, laughing, yelling, bargaining, were tinny and false.

The shadow line from the west wall cut the middle, leaving half of the tents in darkness. The contrast of rainbow colors in the sun and the tents turned gray in the shade seemed particularly intense.

I thought, I must see her today. That is all that matters.

"Maybe your problem is books. I never held to a working man reading books."

"They relax me."

He "humphed" in the back of his throat. "Drink. I think in the end it would give you more happiness than poetry."

The staircase ended on Edgeway Straight, the longest continuous road in Shuleleigh, which the plain's peasants call "King's Town," or just "The Town," but I have always thought of it as Shuleleigh, after the old queen who founded her. The city is a woman, and her spirit deserves the respect of her old name.

The straight was as wide as six carts, and on her east side were the most prestigious homes. The wall soared two-hundred feet above us, and the apartment windows set into the raw stone reflected the late afternoon light onto the road. To the west, of course, was the drop to the market-place. The wall on the other side was also filled with apartments although the tenants there were of the middle class. The homes above us were often referred to as Edgeway Heights, and the people below, where I lived, jok-ingly called their homes Edgeway Depths.

Because of their outside, western exposure, the apartments of Edgeway Heights were much envied, and practically impossible to buy, being handed down from father to favorite child rather than sold.

She lived here.

I stared up at her balcony, but no one stood there. Although I had come to this spot many times, I hand only seen her here once, yesterday, at sun set, leaning out, perhaps to catch the evening breeze, black hair tumbled in the air, face ablaze in the dying light, gazing into the distance. At what I do not know. There must have been music playing, because she moved slightly at the rail, swayed rhythmically, her head tilting slightly this way then that, her shoulders rolling subtly with the motion. I saw her shape mov-ing beneath her blouse, tightening the fabric here and loosening it there. A long moment I watched; she looked out on the city beyond me, and finally she glanced down. For an instant I saw...a flicker of recognition...a moment of contact, and I thought she smiled—no, not a smile, but a tightening of her cheeks on the verge of a smile, and she lifted her hand from the rail as if to wave; then, she turned away and glided through the door.

Kursh said, "Does she even know your name?"

I backed to the knee-high barrier that marked the side of the road, but sun mirrored the glass in her windows, hiding everything within.

"You think I'm a fool, don't you?"

He sat beside me, careful to test the stone seat first. More than one careless citizen had fallen from roadside after trusting solid appearing walls. "No," he sighed. "No more a fool than anyone else, I suppose. I've heard everyone meets their heart-trap some time." Our shadows stretched nearly across the road; sun warmed my shoulders. "But," he continued, "they've the wit to shake it out of their heads and go on with their lives."

"You don't know," I said. "You weren't there when she came in. I..."

"Don't tell me again," he said, not unkindly. "Her eyes. Her laugh. The smell of her. The touch of her hand when she paid for the latch. The 'lingering look.' I've heard it before. You're a one-note trumpet."

"I haven't slept for a month.

"Pity the waste," he said. "Night after night in bed, awake and alone."

Market sounds drifted up to us: a clatter of pans, a shouted exchange, a steady drum beat from a dancer's tent.

Kursh said, "Lovely daughters of the Heights buy from blacksmiths all the time—that's where the money is—but they don't fall in love with them."

"I've saved," I said. "I can pay the price."

"Bah! You're sick, man. That's fool's talk." He grabbed my arm and dragged me from the straight, away from her unreachable balcony, to the market level, and then down one of the many stairwell entrances into the city. Here, on the western side, the hallway stones glowed light green, a magical effect the city collected taxes for; on the east the light was more orange. Up canyon or down, high in the city or deep, the tone and color changed so that one could tell where one was.

I knew the course. "Not tonight. I've work to do," I said, but Kursh pulled me on, down one sloping street to another, until the ceiling stone pressed nearly to his head and we'd come to the artisan's quarter, a hopelessly confusing maze of alleys, tunnels, stairways, apartments and shops where no one ventured except the residents and a few brave outsiders who were lucky to walk out with their purses, assuming they found their way out at all.

"You've no work more important than a beer with me," he said, as he ducked through a wide doorway into The Nine-Fingered Flute, and into the raucous sound of Shuleleigh's most infamous tavern.

Which is where I made up my mind.

On the wall of The Flute, above the long bar, lays the mural that gave the bar its name. On her side in long grass, twice as big as life, head cocked, a naked woman looks yearningly into the forest. He skin glows with muted lights and darks, and the artist incorporated the natural swells and crevices in the rock to form her, to paint her. I've seen men and women at the bar for many long minutes staring at her, lost in whatever thoughts she provoked, but I've always found myself drawn to her face, the way her eyes look into the forest, the way the corners of her mouth turn down on the verge of some emotion I can't name. Back in the woods, almost lost in shadows, a small figure of a half man, half goat plays a flute. She looks toward him, this mythological figure dancing in the wood, playing a song stopped forever in the moment of the painting. He's captured her with his song, and his hands, clearly, are one finger short. The goat man plays his melody for her, and her undefinable expression shows she is lost to the flute player who's lost a finger, who's paid the love price for her attention.

Kursh tried. He bought beer. He made me sing with him, and he roused the others in the bar to verse. Stories he told. He danced on tables, but it did no good. The woman on the wall still longed for the nine-fingered lover, the cloven-footed man in the shadows. If only I could name the emotion on her face, I thought, I would solve the puzzle the artist painted on the wall. I'd solve myself.

Near the end, after a couple of hours and sensing his defeat, he said, "No one who visits there comes back the same." His beer sloshed out of the mug.

"You know," I said, "that I'm going." The musicians started putting away their instruments. A fresh band warmed up behind them. In Shuleleigh, no one cares what time it is. In the depths, sun light never reaches. The Nine-Fingered Flute doesn't close its doors.

Kursh placed his hand on my wrist, trapping it to the table. "I once thought I'd do it myself, son." His glance dropped to the darkness of the beer. He swirled the liquid around. "I almost went down there myself, and I can tell you this, if you come back up those stairs, gold-free and bleeding, ask yourself what I did; ask yourself what you have gained."

On stage the new band ceased twittering their instruments. Conversation fell. For a moment, silence reigned; only Kursh's question hung on the air. His fingers squeezed my wrist. Again I sought the woman on the wall, her face tilting toward the goat man. The answer seemed obvious; anyone who looked at the painting could tell.

"Why, I will have gained everything." I pulled my arm away.

I placed money for the drink on the table. Kursh didn't raise his eyes from his beer when I stood. "I'll tell you about it when I return."

So I left the Nine-Fingered Flute and headed deeper into Shuleleigh, down the stone corridors, deeper and deeper, closer to the root rock that is the canyon floor.

Led by the queen several thousand years ago, the first men fled to the canyon, seeking protection from the dangers on the plains. She directed the building of the first wall that protected all within. Gradually the canyon bottom filled, and there was no place to go but up. They quarried stone from the wall, making rooms and building rooms. Magic held the structures in place, and the city grew high between the cliffs. Shuleleigh became an underground city.

Down here, in the primitive bowels of the city, the oldest, smallest houses stand, and here people begin to change. Generation after generation were born, grew old and died without ever seeing the sun. Wall light cast most weakly here as I walked steadily down. I passed beyond my farthest exploration. My knees throbbed with the constant downward pounding, and I began to worry about climbing back up. The nature of the stone changed to something darker and denser. Here, the air felt different on my skin, heavier and still, and it smelled strangely more animal, like an old kennel or stable.

A child crossed my path; pale skinned, bulbous eyed, she skittered away. With her huge eyes she looked back at me from a doorway, and I hurried from her. I didn't feel comfortable until I'd rounded a few corners and was far away from her inhuman gaze. Soon, though, I approached two men sitting against a wall like shadows, their white and wispy hair falling across their wide eyes. I slowed as I approached and crossed to the other side of the tunnel from them. One stood as I passed, and a few streets deeper down, I saw that he was following me.

Directions to the finger-wizard's shops are well known in the city. "Go to the bottom," they all say, either as a joke or a curse. But no one talks about what they find there. It is an ill choice to speak of the works of wizards.

Stairs led me deeper. The walls showed no evidence of brick work, and the ruts marked the stone floor showing the passage of millions of feet. I knew I'd passed below the city into the catacombs, the excavations below canyon floor level. A slimy seep coated the wall that were within reach on either side. Round, glassless windows opened into black rooms where an occasional whisper of cloth on cloth or a hiss of breath showed that people lived within them, silenced by my passing. Still the tunnel dropped. I twirled. The man behind me stopped but didn't turn away.

I ran, my feet slapping against the wet stone. Blindly I took turns, always down, and when my lungs could take no more, I ducked into a niche in a wall and waited. Water soaked through the back of my shirt, and my hands slipped on the slimy coating, but I breathed quietly through my open mouth and waited.

Like a crescendoing heart, his steps came close. He'd slowed; no doubt confused about where I'd gone. His breathing was liquid, as if he sucked his air through damp cloth, and I imagined his huge eyes casting left and right, seeking me out. My teeth chattered, and I bit the inside of my mouth to still them. At this depth, I could barely see. When he finally walked in front of me, it was more as if the wall were eclipsed than I saw him, but I jumped and had him by the throat.

We fell to the floor. In my hands, his throat felt as damp and cold as the stone around me. He didn't struggle, but only looked up at me, his eyes wide, like huge eggs, glowing with pale green light reflected from the walls, and the skin over his lips so thin that the shape of his teeth showed through them.

"Why are you following me?" I demanded. A blacksmith's hands are strong; I could have broken his neck with a twitch, but he didn't move, only swallowed weakly.

A sucking sound came from behind me, and I shifted around so I could see. A door had opened from the back of my niche. A figure stood there.

"He is my servant," the figure said. Under my hands, the man swallowed again. His pulse throbbed against my palm. "Let him go. You have come, no doubt, to see me."

And so, I found the wizard's shop.

When I went inside, he said, "You have the color of the sun on your skin. You're a long way from home."

The walls glowed brighter here. The wizard's room surprised me with its size. Oddments dangled from wooden frames, strange looking tools with shining barbs and brass bells, bits of feathers woven together into parchments, leather and wood plates twirling from strings. Animal skulls covered the walls; everywhere else, piles of books teetered precariously. The air smelled of poorly tanned hides and incense.

He wore a badly soiled robe that might have been white once, and his teeth were worn nearly to the nubs. He continued, "A young man like yourself only comes for revenge or love." He studied me for a long time, and I realized he didn't share his servant's large-eyed look. "My guess is that it's love." Reaching into a heavy chest, he rummaged about for a few seconds, then emerged with a small book, an evil-looking candle and a hooked knife. "You know the price, do you not?"

Looking at the knife, I clenched my fists to hide my fingers. It was a natural reaction. I knew the price.

"Yes," I said.

He saw my gesture. "Not just that, boy. There's money too."

I put my purse on the table between us. The gold within clinked heavily together.

He lifted it. "Ahh," he said, and let it drop.

"You have something of hers?"

I took the handkerchief I'd taken when she had turned her back for a moment from my belt pouch and draped it over the purse.

After clearing away the gold with business-like efficiency, he placed the candle in the middle of the table on top the handkerchief. Lighting it with one hand and holding the curved knife in the other, he said, "The spell is simple, a straightforward sacrifice for the boon. Are you left handed or right?"

This was the moment I had come for, the one I wanted with all my being. When I walked out of this shop, my love would love me, and all my pain would be gone. I would never again toss sleepless in bed, aching for the sound of her voice, the touch of her lips on mine. I would be complete. Leaning forward, I placed my left hand on the table and painfully forced it open.

The wizard's servant reached around me and held my arm steady, pressing my hand firmly against the table.

Wide-eyed, gasping, a thousand tingles racing up my arm, I tried to picture her as I'd first seen her, when I'd first fallen in love. If I could keep her picture in my mind, then this little thing, the taking of a finger wouldn't even hurt. I'd make the sacrifice gladly and laugh at the inconvenience.

But nothing came.

I broke free of the servant's grip and tucked my hands under my arms. Now that I'd made it this far, I was having a hard time seeing my love's face as she leaned out over her balcony, the afternoon sun resting there so warmly.

"Is this true love?" I said. "Will she truly love me, or will it only appear to be love?"

The wizard sighed and put the knife down.

"What is the difference? She will want you and only you. She will give up all she has to be with you. Her passion will rival the storied gods. Who will care if it is real or not?" He itched under his chin. "And like any love, you will have given up something for her, but in this case it will be visible."

At the back of his shop, hanging from a wire stretched from one side to the other, was what I had first thought to be decorative fringe, but now I suspected it to be desiccated fingers. It was too dark to tell for sure.

"If you take my finger then, the spell will be complete, and she will love me forever? Is that right?"

"Within certain limits."

I swallowed dryly. "Limits?"

"Other magic, of course. Someone else might fall in love with her and make the same spell. The fresher spell wins, naturally, and you will be out of luck and a finger short." He laughed to himself. "Rivalries are good for business. It happened once that two men came back nine times each for the same woman."

Sickened, I said, "What became of them?"

"The first fellow gave up his arm, and the second one quit. He said, and I always thought this was funny considering he had no fingers left at all, that love wasn't worth it."

The wizard tested the blade against his thumb, then rubbed the edge against a stone he took from a pouch. "What really tickles me, though, is that none of you young men think of the woman."

"Excuse me?" I said.

"The woman might already love the man. This has happened too: I've had a man pay for the love of a woman, and later the same day, the woman visited me or another wizard for the man. Neither would have had to pay anything if they'd only thought to ask first. But there are other variations too. I've had old married men pay for their wives of thirty years because they were afraid that the wive's head would be turned by a younger man, or the old wife will do the same thing fearing her husband has developed a wandering eye. Oh, business can be good if you deal with the human heart."

I heard all he had to say, but while he spoke, all I could think of was his first statement, that 'none of you young men think of the woman.' And, as he droned on about who had paid for what, I thought again of the mural in The Nine-Fingered Flute, of the naked woman with the indecipherable expression looking at the goat man. I'd stared at her face for hour on hour, and the artist's rendition of her emotion floated up before me in dreams. What was she feeling, now that her flute player had cast his spell on her? What happened in her head when she heard his playing now that the finger magic robbed her of any choice?

That word echoed in my brain: robbed. Not until the wizard mentioned what the men think of the women had I even considered the woman's place in this.

That is what it is, I thought. The expression on her face is hidden mourning; on top is the love, and that is all the flute man sees, but underneath the passion and the longing, the artist painted her knowledge of loss.

"What of her free will?" I said.

The wizard paused in his honing of the blade.

"You don't know very much about love."

I backed away from the table. "I want my gold back."

Sighing, he picked up my purse. "There is a consulting fee."

"Take it."

He removed two coins and handed the rest back to me, but didn't let go when I pulled on it.

"Think of this, boy. Think of this." Flickering, the candle light danced off his face. "You worry about her free will, that by casting a spell you are cheating her in some way. It that it?"

I nodded numbly.

"As you climb back to the upper city, toward the markets and the sun folk, think of this: when you fell in love with her, where was your free will?"

He let go of the purse, and I almost fell.

The candle sputtered, nearly went out, but then flared up bright and strong. In the back of the shop, I could see clearly now; they were fingers hanging from the wire, hundreds of them; and behind them hung another wire full, and another and another.

As I trudged up the tunnel, my hands whole but my heart heavy, he called from behind, "I'll always be here, boy. You won't be the first to come back a second time."

He was wrong, I thought. He was wrong. He didn't see her standing on the balcony. He didn't catch that extra instant when our eyes met that afternoon. Magic of all sort floats around us.

The climb was long, and I didn't realize I'd broken out of the city until I was a hundred yards across the deserted marketplace, realized the walls no longer glowed beside me and saw a handful of stars twinkling through a rip in the clouds.

# The Yard God

A week after her twenty-second birthday, Demi sat exactly in the middle of the yard between the oak-tree carpenter ants and the elm-tree blacks, trying to make peace. The war had raged since May's first warm days thawed the soil, and just like last summer centered on the area beneath the sycamore, where the tent caterpillars dropped to the ground and made easy prey. The afternoon sun cast long shadows so her silhouette reached nearly to the chain link fence between her and the street. She pulled at her skirt again to cover her knees. If Mom looked out the kitchen window and saw her sitting cross-legged on the lawn, she'd be sure to yell at her. Not that it was likely Mom would look out. Since January she'd spent more and more time on the couch, surrounded with hot water bottles and warming blankets and medicines.

Even with the ants warring, Demi was happy. One time, when Mom was in a good mood, she'd held Demi on her lap and said, "Life is full of happy-sads. You're my happy-sad." But Demi didn't understand what she meant. You're either one or the other, Demi had thought.

Demi closed her eyes to feel the ants' minuscule lives better. It took a lot of relaxed concentration. She sensed them like tiny red spots in the hundred-yard radius of her awareness, the nest to her left, a loosely tangled ball of thread burrowing into the oak's dead roots, filled with scurrying ants, and the other nests under the elm, reaching nearly a yard deep, with passages more complicated than any human building, even more confusing than the community college's hallways where Demi attended remedial night classes for adults. She was taking Introduction to Reading for the third time.

In the lawn between the two colonies, ant trails wended their ways between the blades. She watched the ants moving to and fro, some foraging, some carrying food, and some battling over a tent caterpillar that wasn't quite dead yet. Demi bit her lip. There was plenty of food for both populations. No need for them to kill each other. But another one died, and then another, their tiny lights winking out in her mind. The only place they didn't fight was at the gift rock on the garden's edge where trails from both tribes intersected. Here they piled seeds, wisps of grass, and once, by Herculean effort, a shiny dime. Demi collected the tiny offerings every day and broadcast her thanks.

She sent soothing signals to them, directed them toward dead beetles, spilled garbage in the alley. "There's feasts awaiting!" she broadcasted, and some turned aside from the combat, but others ignored her. Demi sighed. She put her hands behind her and arched back to let the setting sun bake her face. When she sat very still and quieted her mind, she sensed the entire yard, all the vibrant lives scurrying, burrowing, flying, lying in wait around her, from the sluggish pink haze of earthworms like fat yarn in the dirt, to her favorite, the bright yellow nimbus that was the barn owl in the oak.

Behind closed eyes, she saw Ethan's bilious green aura long before he spoke. As he entered her field of vision, she ordered the wasps off who'd been resting on her shoulders. He moved slowly along the fence and stopped. Maybe he was looking the other way, she hoped, but she straightened anyway, wrapped her arms around her chest and tried to stay small. If I don't make a noise, maybe he won't know I'm here, she thought, but she could feel him staring at her. Had her skirt moved above her knee again?

The miniature life lights winked out, leaving the red-tinted blackness of light through her closed eyelids.

"Hey, little darling. What 'cha doing, sitting in the sunshine like a flower?" His voice reminded her of the squishy sound in the kitchen drain.

She opened her eyes. His arms draped over the fence. He was all smiles and oily hair. Wide-set swampy-brown eyes. Untrimmed, ragged fingernails with burger grease under them. They'd been in school together until the third grade when they started holding her back. Now he lived by himself in what had been his parent's house, two doors down. Twice in the last month she'd caught him peeping in her window. Stiffly, she stood, turned away and marched toward the house.

"Don't go, Demi," he whined. She centered her gaze on the back door's peeled paint, tried not to hear him, but it was like he'd put his mouth to her ear. "Just 'cuz you're retarded don't mean we can't have a special time. I'd be better company than your dead-end mom."

The door slammed behind her. Faintly she heard his last shot, "You won't be twenty-two forever!"

She checked the stove while trying to figure out what Ethan meant. Nothing there. She took a package of dried noodles from the cabinet, poured water into a pot and set it on the stove.

Her mom coughed in the next room. "Demi! Where've you been? I've needed to pee for a half hour."

"Coming," Demi said. The dark living room smelled of old blankets and too much breathing. Mom sucked on a lozenge, her thin lips pursed, the skin on her face stretched so thin that she almost seemed like a skull already. Demi pulled the covering from Mom's thin legs, then put an arm behind her to lift her up.

"Be gentle," Mom gasped.

"Sorry." Demi lifted her, a feathery weight with no substance. Demi remembered a moment from years ago when Mom towered over her, her hand open and coming down. The hard slap. "You're stupid!" Mom had shouted. Demi couldn't recall what Mom had been so mad about. Maybe Demi had spilled the sugar or not picked up her toys. In those days, Mom had been a bulky, ominous presence in Demi's world. "I'll try to be better," Demi had said. Mom hit her again. Later that time, or maybe some other—they got mixed up in Demi's mind—she had sat in the middle of her bed trying to figure out how to make Mom happy. "I'm a bad baby," Demi had thought, and she wept, thinking about how much she loved her mom.

Even then she sensed the other lives: the carpet mites, a family of mice behind the walls, spiders, termites, centipedes, rolly-pollies, cockroaches, bees, all in or around the house, and they were a great comfort. To entertain herself, she made two flies weave an intricate flight before her, cavorting in loops and dives and pretty patterns until they were too tired to stay aloft and they settled on the floor.

Demi helped Mom untie her pajama bottoms and supported her until she sat on the toilet. "Oh, baby, it hurts," moaned Mom.

After Demi carried her back to the couch, Mom said, her voice querulous again, "When's dinner? I think I might be able to eat something today."

"Good, Mommy. Doctor Davis said you needed food to get better."

Mom smiled wanly. "Some beef noodles, maybe."

When Demi got back to the kitchen, she stopped in front of the stove and stood numbly for a few minutes, not thinking, just staring into a middle distance somewhere beyond the kitchen but short of eternity.

A synapse snapped to life in her brain, and she looked around her as if she'd never seen the room before. "What are you doing, you dumb cluck?" she asked herself.

"Dinner, Demi," came Mom's voice from the living room.

"Ah." Demi looked at the water in the pot for a while, then dipped her finger in. Cold. Shaking her head, she turned the stove on, then carefully set the timer for ten minutes.

Outside, Ethan had gone. Demi settled back into her favorite spot. The sun dipped behind the tenement across the street, but light bathed rooftops. The ant war had ended. In the corner under the eaves, a garden spider glowed in her mind like a tiny sun. It must have just fed. With her eyes closed, Demi in her backyard was no different than an astronaut floating in space, the piercing light of a thousand lives beating from every direction. Lines of ants walked the long paths in the grass, heading toward the gift rock. Wasps orbited her. She could even feel the somnolent owl gazing down on her sleepily. In the yard, she felt loved.

Her awareness deepened, penetrated the grass, felt the dandelions' vegetable glow. Even soil fungus wafted a faint light. Something wasn't right. She probed around her. Some part out of place or misfocused. After a while, she found it. The owl was hurt, its wing nearly broken. How did it get back to its high perch? Demi could feel the damaged muscles and the owl's hunger. Had it been like this for a long time without her noticing? She concentrated mightily, gathered a little light from all the lights, sending it toward the owl. Gradually, the hurt mended, while every insect and animal and plant within her globe of awareness was slightly reduced.

She smiled. The owl thanked her in its mute manner. The other lives thanked her for their sacrifice. Demi gave and she took away. She showered them with her affection, and they received it with insect joy.

The stove timer buzzed too soon, and Demi went in to finish making dinner.

"I can't eat this." Mom dipped a spoon into the bowl, stirred it around until a coughing fit took her. When it ended, she said, "My stomach hurts."

Demi sat with her hands in her lap. "Maybe if I blow on it for you? That always makes it better."

Mom closed her eyes and grimaced. "It's not hot, dammit. The smell's making me pukey again. I need my medicine. Come here, girl." Mom waved her hand toward her.

Demi thought, Mom's clothes are getting so big! The blouse's cuff gaped like a cave, while Mom's wrist looked like a pale branch sticking out.

Mom said, "I'm going to pin the prescription to your shirt. Here's the money. You'll have to wait for the pharmacist. It's just two blocks. You can do that, can't you?" Mom exhaled minty lozenge breath, but underneath some other smell lurked, slate-hard and relentless, like the vegetable drawer long after old cabbage had gone blue and liquid.

"A cup of ice first," said Mom. "My throat gets so dry."

After filling a glass with ice cubes, and leaving it on the table by Mom's couch, Demi put her jacket on. A streetlight flickered as she went out the front door, illuminating a pickup truck on cinder blocks and a trash pile that hadn't been collected. A mongrel dog worried something from the pile and hurried down the street with it between its teeth. Demi pulled the jacket close around her neck. She didn't like the neighborhood at night. Boys hung out on the corners or porch steps and called her names, but Mom needed her medicine. How else would she get better? Demi steeled herself. Her mother depended on her. I'm a good daughter, thought Demi.

At the pharmacy, the clerk gave her change for a ten, although Demi was sure she'd paid with a twenty. Outside the store, Demi counted the money twice. A car rolled by, blank faces ignoring her on the other side of the windshield. If she came back with the wrong money, Mom would be mad, and that would only make her worse.

She went back in.

"I made the right change, dunderhead," said the clerk. He leaned against the register, his thumb hooked into an apron string. Overhead, the bare flourescents buzzed

Tears swam behind Demi's eyes. "Mommy gave me twenty dollars, mister. We need that money. Mommy's sick."

"Shit. Everyone has a story." The clerk shooed her away with one hand. "That was a ten spot. Take a hike."

A large black woman came from behind an aisle, a clipboard in her hand. The clerk didn't see her. He sneered, an ugly expression that pressed his eyebrows together and made her think of Ethan. "You got a problem, take it up with management."

The black woman stepped forward, reached past the clerk, startling him, and opened the register. She looked into it for a second. "You don't have a ten in there, Gerald. Give the lady the rest of her money."

The clerk stuttered momentarily. "You going to take this rum-dumb's word over mine?"

The woman snorted impatiently, then counted out two five-dollar bills. "I don't have to, Gerald. You don't have a ten in the drawer. But if I did, I probably would. Why don't you clean out your locker? I'll cut you a check tomorrow."

Demi felt a flood of relief as she stuffed the bills into her pocket.

The woman smiled at her, pulling her face into a friendly map of creases and dimples. She said, "I just bought this store, darlin'. Got one of those investment zone loans. Too bad they couldn't loan us some good help. I'm Marjorie." She put out her hand.

Demi shook it gratefully. "Demi's my name. I've always lived here.

My mommy's sick. I've got to take her the medicine."

She rushed from the store without waiting for an answer. What a nice lady, she thought, and for the first time in weeks the neighborhood looked good to her, the moths circling streetlights, the parked cars like indolent hippos taking naps beside the sidewalk. She whistled part of "Pop Goes the Weasel" as she walked, not paying attention.

Ethan caught her as she passed an alley. No warning. One second she was whistling, and the next, he had his arm over her shoulder, squeezing her to him.

"What's a firefly like you doing out on a dark night like this, Demi?" he said. She could smell beer on his breath, and he reeked of cigarette smoke.

Her skin went scaly cold, and she tried to shrug him off. "Stop, Ethan. I don't like it."

He dug his fingers into her upper arm and kept her close. They were a long way between street lights. No cars. No pedestrians. Every porch was empty. He steered them into the alley. "Don't you get lonely, Demi, day after day hanging out with your mother? I've seen you, you know, sitting at your dresser just starin' into space. Don't you get lonely?"

"Let me go, Ethan. Mommy's waiting." But he held tight and moved her into the deep shadows between the houses. Her legs moved mechanically; her arms seemed incapable of motion. Then, he was pushing her down onto an old mattress that smelled of mildew and dog fur.

"Give a kiss, won't you, sunshine." He pressed his lips to her neck.

Demi turned herself inward. It was like she was at the doctor's office for her yearly visit. "Feet in the stirrups," Doctor Davis would say, and she went away in her mind, far away from the cold instruments, the uncomfortable pinches. She'd listen to the office music, look at the ceiling tiles, imagining she was a cloud floating over plowed fields in winter, everything covered in white, lined into squares. Where are the farmers in winter? Isn't it peaceful, drifting along, disconnected?

Vaguely she felt buttons being undone. Ethan said something incoherent. He pinned her hands above her head, digging her knuckles into a brick wall. She heard crickets. Watched a high haze rush across the band of stars visible between the roofs. It was like the doctor's office, but she was frightened, so frightened that the balloon that was herself shrank up, became a peanut deep, deep inside her, and it was crying.

Ethan's voice from far away said, "We'll have to do this again, buttercup."

It took a long time for the tiny, tiny Demi, who'd fled inside herself, to come back outside to look. At first she was only aware of the smelly mattress. A button dug into her back. She rolled, reached to feel the spot, and was puzzled to find her skin was bare. Her shirt was hiked up around her armpits. Slowly, she pushed it down, then tried to sit. She moaned. Her muscles ached; her crotch burned, and when she felt down there, her fingers came away wet. "And me without a plug, you dumb cluck. What would Mommy think?" she said.

Mommy's alone! she thought, but even with that thought to rush her, it took several minutes to adjust her clothes. A muscle strain in her neck sent searing sparks whenever she tried to look to her left. She limped from the alley and headed home.

When the door clicked shut, Mom sat under the reading light on the couch, blanket-covered and shapeless, her eyes hollow and dark. She opened her mouth to speak, but nothing came out. After a painful swallow, she croaked. "I could have died twice in the time you've been gone. Where's my medicine?"

Demi's hand flew to her mouth. "I had it."

Mom turned her face to the wall, sighed in disappointment, then breathed shallowly without speaking.

She should yell at me, thought Demi. I've been bad. I lost the medicine, but it's not my fault! Not my fault!

Demi shuffled down the street, head down, her eyes scanning the sidewalk and gutter. The prescription came in a white sack with the pharmacy slip stapled to it. She hoped the streetlights would be bright enough to find it. How could I drop it? It must be in the alley. But the closer she got, the slower she went. What if Ethan was there again? Behind the houses and dumpsters and busted-down garages of the alley, impenetrable shadows could hide a dozen Ethans. She stood on the sidewalk, facing the tunnel of graveled darkness and broken glass, closed her eyes, and forced herself to relax. Gradually a sphere of lights brightened around her. It was as if she was coming from an arc-lit room to a dim cave. Her eyes adjusted, and the world that emerged was beautiful, all soft, fuzzy, living lamps that as soon as she saw them, they saw her. A slinky, purple cat wove around a trashcan. Two aqua-colored rats peered at her from beneath a stack of broken pallets. Sleeping flies, creeping millipedes, huge water roaches waving silver antennae in her direction, but no Ethan.

She found the package by the mattress, the paper torn, the plastic bottle smashed, and all the pills crushed to powder.

There was nothing she could do. The pharmacy would be closed by now. She was a bad daughter, and it wasn't her fault. That's all she could think. Not my fault...not my fault. She thought about Ethan holding her, stopping her from going home with her delivery. The cat fled. Insects froze as she strode by.

Demi walked toward home, fists clenched, eyes closed, navigating by mental vision until she passed Ethan's house. She stopped by his mailbox. Her globe of awareness encompassed the house. Cockroaches swarmed in his unclean kitchen; termites gnawed at the floor joists, and in his bedroom, she sensed the long, sickeningly green light of Ethan himself, lying in bed. She hated him. "We'll have to do this again," he'd said. He'd destroyed Mommy's medicine. She rubbed her hand against her neck where he'd kissed her. Won't someone protect me from him? she thought. He's a bad man. He needs punishment, and those thoughts ran over and over until a kind of calm came to her. She relaxed. Her vision had never seemed this clear. All the house's lives stood out as brilliant beacons. She sorted through them until she found what she wanted: in the attic, five black widows; in Ethan's box springs, a brown recluse. He's bad. He made me unhappy. Ethan has hurt me, she broadcast.

*D*emi had no plan. She didn't think that far ahead, but she knew what she felt at the moment she felt it. When the sun was high in her yard, and the lives surrounded her with love, and seeds covered the gift rock, she felt love. When Mommy scolded her or turned away or sighed her deep sigh, Demi felt despair. When she looked at Ethan, she felt simple hate. That's all. No plan. But she knew what was going on as the spiders began to move, climbing from their attic webs, crawling out from the bed springs. The deadliest bite, the brown recluse, he didn't react to, most people don't. It continued to bite Ethan while Demi watched until he rolled in his sleep, crushing it. Forty minutes later, though, when the black widows reached him, he did scream, and his screaming followed her down the street as she walked to her own house. It wasn't until she shut the front door that she heard him no more, but by that time she wasn't thinking about Ethan. He'd slipped from the plate of her awareness. It wasn't until she was inside that she remembered she still didn't have Mommy's medicine.

"Mommy?" she said to the dark room. In the kitchen, the clock ticked. The refrigerator kicked on with a noisy rumble. "Mommy?"

Demi rubbed her hand along the wall until she found the light switch. Mom lay on the couch, propped by her pillows, head to one side, mouth open.

"Mommy?"

Demi's mother didn't move. Her hand dangled below the blanket's edge. Two small pieces of melted ice floated in the cup behind her head.

Her fingers to her cheek, Demi crossed the room slowly to kneel by Mom. She took Mommy's wrist and held it like she'd seen doctors on television, but she didn't know what to feel for.

Demi sat on the floor, her back to the couch, holding Mommy's hand. She'd never looked at the room from Mom's point of view before. This low, Demi couldn't see what was on the kitchen table top. She couldn't see the clock on the table by the door, but she could see her baby pictures. Mom had put them on the wall below the front window's curtain. Demi cocked her head to the side. Three pictures hanging from the wall at knee level: Mommy cradling Demi in a yellow-checked comforter. Demi sitting in a sandbox, holding a blue bucket. Demi on a swing, clinging to a chain with one hand while trying to get a sucker into her mouth with the other.

She closed her eyes. Mommy loved her after all. Gradually, Demi opened her mind to her other world, the household zoo, the backyard jungle, teeming with life, flowing in multicolor dots, and she realized her mother still glowed, dimly, a pulsing watery blue not much brighter than a fungus or a cloud of gnats, but she still lived.

The owl had been hurt, and Demi made her better. It had never occurred to her to try to help Mom this way. The yard world and Mommy's world were separate. The animals and insects loved her; they brought offerings to gift rock. Mommy...well, Mommy was strong. Mommy loomed in Demi's memory like a moving mountain, all loud voice and raised hand.

Demi concentrated on Mommy's color, willing it to grow. She gathered all the light she could, reaching beneath the soil to worms, taking from crickets, stealing from the ants. Frantic, the mice in the wall fled to the far corners of the house, but kneeling by her mother, Demi found them and emptied them. Their lights winked out. The ant colonies died, destroyed more thoroughly than the greatest ant war could have ever destroyed them. Wasps settled in their nests, never to fly again. Spiders dropped from their own webs. A bat, flitting through Demi's inescapable grasp fluttered once, then dropped to the yard, its light extinguished.

Inside Demi's head, the wire of her talent heated white hot, twisted under the strain. She'd never done anything like this before. Directing flies to dance, healing the owl, hating Ethan were like baby steps.

Still, Demi reached for more. Mommy's light wasn't turned up enough. Demi opened every living faucet she could reach, grass, flowers, trees, moss, algae, and the life flowed toward her mother until in Demi's mind, all was black except for Mom, who blazed like a blue ocean.

At the end, the wire snapped in Demi's head. She gasped, for Mom's light disappeared. Demi opened her eyes to be sure Mom was still there.

Mom twitched. She closed her mouth. Demi squeezed her hand, and

Mom squeezed back.

"Mommy?" said Demi, feeling the pressure of Mom's thin fingers against her palm, watching her eyelids flutter.

"Is it breakfast?" said Mom. "I'm ready to eat something. Maybe an egg."

Demi bit her lower lip. She rested her forehead against Mom's arm. "Oh, yes, Mommy. I can make some eggs."

Mom pulled a lungful of air in and let it out, as if she'd never breathed before. "Good." Mom let go of Demi's hand, opened her eyes and looked at her daughter. "For Christ's sake, Demi, your clothes are a mess. If you've been outside like that, I'll die from embarrassment. Can't you at least take care of yourself?"

Demi's cheeks flushed. "Yes, Mommy. I'm sorry."

"And don't burn down the kitchen either."

Demi fled to the stove, made the eggs and fed her mother, who ate with enthusiasm.

When Mom leaned back to rest, Demi slipped into the backyard. The morning sun had just crested over the neighbors' rooftops. She went to her favorite spot, where grass crackled under her hands as she sat.

Demi sighed with exhaustion. Her back hurt, and raising her hand to rub her sore neck sent a medley of sharp pains along her side. Gradually the sun revealed more and more of the yard, and Demi realized the grass was brown-tinged and there wasn't a near-by sound. No crickets or grass-hoppers or buzzing wasps. The air throughout the yard was cool and quiet. A handful of leaves dropped out of the elm, skittering onto a layer of fallen leaves that were already there. Leaves coated the ground beneath the sycamore and oak too. On the gift rock, a few ants lay curled between the seeds.

Mom's voice came from the kitchen. "Dammit, Demi. You left the stove on!"

Demi looked beyond the ants. Dead grass, dead flowers, dead bushes and dead trees. She closed her eyes and relaxed into her private seeing place. Nothing appeared. It was like probing the gap left by a pulled tooth. She knew something had been there once, but it was gone now, as dead as her yard.

A shadow flicked across her face. She looked up. The owl circled the dead oak, crossing the sun again, its huge wingspan blocking the light for an eye-blink. When it settled on a branch, a dozen leaves rained down. The owl folded its wings to its side and looked at her, locking gazes. Demi felt she could walk up to the owl and touch it. It would let her. There was no hate in the scrutiny, no condemnation. It bobbed its head, dropped off the branch in a long swoop directly toward her. A wing-tip brushed her forehead as it passed, and then it was gone. The caress was a gentle one, not a hello or goodbye, but an acknowledgment. Even if she could never see them the way she had before, the ants would return. The grass would renew, and in her backyard, saplings would grow.

Mommy's alive, Demi thought, and she couldn't understand why she was crying.

# Death

# The Death Dwarves

In the midst of life, we are in death.
—*The Book of Common Prayer*

John Minor realized he saw and heard things other people did not six months after a one pound tin of Winchester's Best Black Powder blew up in his face, sending a ball peen hammer off his forehead and across the room. The accident left him with a small disability pension, a large insurance settlement, and a dark dent like a thumb print in bread dough one inch above his nose.

But he wasn't thinking about the accident as he shuffled up to the mailbox by the bus stop. Mostly he was concentrating on his balance, which he knew wasn't worth hell anymore. Yesterday he had fallen on the stoop at his apartment and since no one was around it had taken several ludicrous moments for him to coordinate his arms and legs and the cane into the right motions to stand up again. At the time it seemed vaguely ironic that a year ago he finished the Denver Marathon in two hours and fifty-four minutes, good enough for twelfth in the 40 to 45 age group. The certificate hung in his living room next to the picture of Ann and Christina. They both smiled out at the photographer (him). His wife wore his checkered flannel jacket that she had borrowed when the mountain air had gotten too cool, while Christina was in a blue sweatsuit, her arm around her mother's waist. In the background James Peak rose up, a huge purple presence.

Ann died within a year of the photo—from a tumor that started in her ovary—and Christina moved to Seattle with her new husband.

Forty-five steps separated the entrance of the apartment from the mailbox. Another fifteen to the flaky green bus stop bench. He measured everything in steps now-a-days, which was all right with him. Just two months ago Doctor Ferguson said he might be able to use a walker (Like an old man? said John at the time.) if he was lucky and worked hard with the physical therapist. Of course, this was the same doctor who had told Christina that he would never come out of the coma. "They were checking with heart transplant units all over the country to see if you were a match for anyone," she had told him later and cried so loudly that two nurses rushed in to see if he was alright.

He paid close attention to the sidewalk in front of him and ignored the traffic noises to his left. The problem wasn't that he couldn't walk, really, it was that things distracted him so easily now. His mind was like an open mike, recording everything equally. And sometimes he would daydream, sometimes about his past but other times about things he didn't recognize: a field of wheat, something coming out of the ground, something forming in the clouds. But more than anything else, what the shrapnel of bone fragments had done was remove his power of discrimination.

He lifted his left foot over a crack and shifted his weight so that he moved forward in a kind of lurching motion. The right foot started dragging so he bent his knee and picked it up, making sure that it too cleared the crack, which wasn't any thicker than a dime. His cane never touched the cement. The extra motion of placing and leaning on it caused him more problems than not using it, but the therapist insisted he carry it, and rather than risk her ire, he did.

So went each step: lift, lurch, drag and lift. His hands waved little circles away from his hips so that he maintained balance. Someone watching him would assume that he was drunk, or senile, or one of those unfortunates that the homes didn't have room for anymore in this age of "mainstreaming."

He checked to see if the letter was still in his hand, which it was, though he had crumpled it a bit, and began tipping over sideways as his feet failed to keep up with the shift in his center of gravity. He scrambled back to equilibrium by taking three quick shuffles to the left, and then two to the right because he overcorrected.

When he reached the mailbox, sweat shined on his forehead and stained the back of his shirt, but he smiled. Doctors can't be right all the time.

He first saw the dwarves that no one else could see on the downtown express bus from Mercy Hospital, where he went for his weekly physical therapy. Three teenage boys in letter jackets climbed in at the Alameda stop and behind them the dwarves, two of them, skinny, dressed in blue uniforms, sawed-off pump shotguns hanging from their shoulders, twin bandoliers loaded with fat red and brass shells crossing their chests. They took the front seat across the aisle from him. The door wheezed shut; the bus swung into the traffic, and John, who was sitting sideways in his seat, his legs stretched in front of him, studied the pair surreptitiously over his newspaper.

The closest one twitched his head back and forth like a bird, checking the back of the bus and then the front several times. Half of his shirt was untucked, and John saw now that it needed laundering, but other than that it looked much like a policeman's uniform, all the way down to a black plastic name tag on his chest, but instead of saying "Officer so-and-so" it said "Naggle."

"I hate busses. Why do we have to ride the bus? Can't we just get him outside his house?"

The other one, John couldn't see his name tag, slouched down in the seat, his feet swinging freely above the floor. "Did you see our list! We're all over town today. We walk and we'll never finish, ninny." He took a sheet of paper out of his pants pocket. "Two in Westminister and one in Littleton. Whoever makes up these assignments doesn't look at the map."

"But the bus!" Naggle snapped his head around again and looked behind him.

"Stay alert and we'll be okay. Besides, it's not like we're helpless." He pulled a shell out of his bandolier with a dramatic flourish and chambered it into his shotgun. "Full load: instant, massive coronary thrombosis. This would drop a football player in nothing flat."

John folded his paper onto his lap and glanced back to see if anyone else had noticed that there were two heavily armed dwarves traveling with them, but the bus was almost empty and nobody seemed to be paying attention. He knew he should be nervous, or even scared, but his emotions were flat, and had been since the accident. That was something else the doctors couldn't tell him about. They said that the brain doesn't heal, it makes new pathways, and that maybe it was a blessing right now since it meant he wouldn't become deeply depressed, a common reaction to a debilitating injury.

The description of what the "load" was didn't make sense, but John knew his gun laws and a loaded shotgun in the city was definitely not right. He leaned forward to tell him, but Naggle beat him to it.

"That's illegal! That's illegal! We'll get popped for sure if the Supervisor finds out." Naggle's hands twisted around and around in his lap as if they had a life of their own.

"You haven't been on the street long, have you?" Naggle shook his head no. "First time out?" Naggle nodded yes. "I've been out for sixteen months. Four hitches. And I've learned two things: the supervisors don't care what you do as long as you get the list done, and nobody looks after you but yourself. So if you get a sport-shot off once in a while—just to relieve the tension, you understand—or you pull one to protect yourself, then it's fine. It's part of the job." Naggle took a deep breath and stopped his hands.

"Yeah. It's part of the job, I guess." He appeared unconvinced. "So when should we do him?"

"Anytime. You make the hit, and I'll cover." Naggle took a shell from his bandolier, compared the writing on the side of it to the sheet of paper the other held out to him, and loaded the shell into his gun.

All this amazed John, because the dwarves carried this whole conversation out loudly. He heard them as clearly as if they were talking to him, but no one else seemed to care. The bus driver, who they sat directly behind, never turned his head. A mother with her child in the next seat didn't flinch. The *child*, an ice cream streaked six year old, never looked. Surely a child would stare at such a sight. The teenagers in the back of the bus murmured among themselves.

Naggle pumped his gun with a distinctive "chink-chink," stood on the seat, leveled the end of the barrel at the back of the bus driver's head—John opened his mouth—and pulled the trigger.

The twelve gauge blast filled the bus with a sound so vast and palpable that "sound" would be a completely wrong word for it. John's ears ached. His heart slammed at the surface of his chest, but he could do nothing. The event ended before he even really understood that it had started. Then a number of negative items hit him at once. The windshield of the bus was *not* covered with blood and bone. The bus driver was *not* slumped over the steering wheel, his head a sloppy, hairy sponge. People were *not* screaming at the sudden, incredible violence. No one did anything that they weren't doing before the shot.

"They didn't hear it. They didn't hear it, and only I did. Everyone on this bus is deaf," is what he thought.

Naggle sat down. "What did I get him with?" The other looked at the list.

"A brain aneurysm next Thursday at 2:05 p.m." He looked at his watch. "If we're near here, remind me to take another bus. This one is going to have an accident." He laughed a high pitched "hee-hee-hee" like a manic cricket.

Then he said, "You're no virgin now kid, so what say we celebrate a little? Load up with this one and I'll let you pick the target." He handed Naggle another shell.

"Really? I mean, you think it's okay?"

"Sure. We all do it. Slam it in there and take out someone else. Hell, I remember my first shot. Gave an old fart a brain cancer. Checked up on him every week. Last time I saw him he didn't weigh eighty pounds and he was swearing and crying and wetting himself at the same time. No death with dignity shit for him."

John started at the mention of cancer. He leaned sideways in his seat and groped the floor for his cane, which had fallen when the bus turned a corner earlier. His fingers scratched over the metal floor.

Naggle held the shell up, reading its side numbers. "What's this?" he said.

"AIDS. Standard stuff now. Very nasty. We're doing a lot of them lately. No cure." He grinned showing a mouthful of pointy teeth, like a cat. "You're lucky Naggle. Ten years ago you wouldn't have had this chance. Half of everything was treatable. Now we got this. Those boys in Research and Development scored a real coup here."

John finally found the cane—it had skittered under the seat—and with some effort pulled it into his lap. He thought he should do something, but he didn't know what. He half didn't believe what he heard them talking about, but they sounded sincere. Worse than sincere, they sounded *real* and serious.

Naggle put the new shell into the gun. "Maybe I could get the kid?" He indicated the little girl in the seat behind them.

"Sure. What the hell. Most the time we use it on niggers and druggies. Confuses them. Makes them think there's a pattern to it."

Naggle stood on the cushion, rested the gun on the seat back and pointed the barrel down at the child. The girl's mother was trying to wipe her squirming daughter's face.

John realized he must do something, so he yelled "Don't shoot!" The woman stopped wiping, looked at John and pulled her daughter close. John raised his cane over his head. Naggle, startled, turned to John and shrieked as the cane came down.

To John the striking with the cane seemed less the result of a conscious decision, and more something that he stood away from and observed. It wasn't even that he was afraid for the girl, but that he didn't want to experience another gun shot so close again. He heard himself shout "Don't shoot!" He saw himself lunging forward, one foot on the floor of the bus, the other awkwardly curled beneath him. Naggle screamed and started swinging his gun towards him; the other dwarf fumbled for his weapon that was now trapped between him and Naggle; and then the cane struck Naggle with exactly the same result as a sharp rock hitting a water balloon.

He popped, messily, spraying milky water-like substance everywhere. And the cane passed through him without pausing until it bounced off the bus seat and out of John's hand as he fell into the aisle.

The driver yelled something at John (it sounded like a curse); the child started laughing; the mother looked concerned, and the boys at the back of the bus jumped up to see what the fuss was about.

From his vantage point on the floor John saw his cane lying in a puddle of the remains of Naggle. "I wonder how many gallons in a dwarf?" he thought hysterically.

Chink-chink.

The other dwarf, soaked, jumped to the end of bench seat and pointed his gun at John. "You can't see us! You can't see us!" A single black hole, seemingly wide enough to accept John's fist, was all John could see of the shotgun. The dwarf's eyes, comically huge and rolling in fear, peered down at him. In a moment of insane clarity John noticed a series of inappropriate detail. The dwarf's name tag read "Wisnet"; there were no chest pockets on the shirt; his hair was parted in the middle; the blue trousers had no fly (as if they were on backwards), and "Wisnet" was left handed.

He saw all those things, and at the same time felt grains of sand beneath his back from the dirty floor, and he smelled onions from a discarded sandwich wrapper, and he heard the transmission of the bus shifting gears.

Which saved him.

Standard Regional Transportation District procedure, when a passenger experiences a medical emergency, John found out later, is to pull over and radio for help. The driver down-shifted and swerved the bus into the curb. Wisnet's foot slipped off the edge of the wet seat and he tumbled backwards. The shotgun exploded harmlessly into the ceiling. John reached for his cane but missed. On the second try, he grabbed it and pushed himself into a sitting position. Wisnet, swearing, fumbled a shell out of the bandolier and dropped it.

He said, "Please," just before John caned him into a splash of watery nothingness.

Fifteen minutes later the para-medics arrived and John spent a half hour convincing them that he was fine, and that "No, I've never had a seizure before." After they discussed his head injury, and he tolerated their pitying looks at the dent in his forehead, the bus restarted its route and took him to the stop near his apartment. By the time he arrived, the dwarves' "blood" and everything they carried, paper, shells and guns, vanished. Either they evaporated or were absorbed. It didn't matter. No one else saw anything.

*L*ate that night, John lay on his back in bed staring at the cracks in the ceiling, seeing shapes there as he had in clouds in the summer once during a fishing trip with Ann and Christina. Then, eight year old Christina busied herself in the mud on the creek bank. Ann rolled next to him and brushed her fingertips against his ear. Her breath smelled of pickle and bacon they'd eaten for lunch. "Go away," he'd sighed. "I'm counting clouds." She traced a line behind his ear. "Maybe I can distract you," she said. "I doubt it." But later, when Christina was asleep in the camper, the sky was a high quivering blue and the clouds drifted without a hand to guide them, she did.

He jerked back to his apartment and the cracked ceiling. In the distance, through the open window, beyond the sounds of traffic and the muffled voices in the darkness, he had heard it again, a shotgun, the third one tonight. He wondered how often he had ignored the sound before.

The cracks in the ceiling still looked like clouds, but they were dark clouds, rolling painfully, and something was in them moving down toward him.

The Thompson Insurance Building's elevator swallowed John and whisked him to the fifteenth floor, where he picked up a portion of his settlement money. His former employer, L & R Ordnance, with a minimum of fuss, had agreed that John's accident was the result of their negligence (they violated Federal regulations concerning humidity in a shop where gunpowder is regularly handled), and for his part John did not insist on receiving his money in a lump sum. So he made a monthly pilgrimage to sign for the check, a trip he enjoyed particularly this time because he walked in on his own rather than riding in a wheel chair as he had four weeks earlier.

"Mr. Minor! How good to see you," said the secretary with genuine affection and surprise when she looked up from her desk. She hurried around it to open the inner office door for him. Her hand on his elbow provided welcome support. He feared the humiliation of falling in public. "Oh, this is wonderful how well you're doing."

They joked as he left, and in the elevator he was thinking wistfully how attractive she was when the car stopped on the fourteenth floor to let in a maintenance man wearing a tool belt and pulling a rolling work bench behind him. He glanced dully at John, did an obvious double take at the purple splotch on John's forehead, then put his back to the wall and watched the progression of numbers as they headed down.

Three floors later the elevator doors opened—John was fingering the check in his coat pocket, deciding whether he was well enough to fly to Seattle—and a pair of dwarves scuttled on and jammed themselves into the front two corners of the car. John pushed himself against the wall and froze. The maintenance man punched the first floor button. "Damn kids," he said.

"Kids?" John's voice squeaked. The dwarves were outfitted the same way as the two from yesterday. They watched John and the maintenance man warily. John tried not to meet their eyes.

"Yeah. It happens all the time. You know most people think when an elevator stops and nobody gets on that it is a malfunction, but it's those damn kids. They push buttons and then run."

He could smell them, unwashed, sweating, a gross unsanitary smell. They slid out at the second floor. The maintenance man cursed and slammed his fist on the button. "Damn kids."

*B*ut he didn't start getting mad, until he read a small article on the second page of the city news section of *The Denver Post* a week later, about a city bus driver who died of a stroke while waiting for the light to change on Colfax Ave. and University Blvd. No one was hurt. "Richard is survived by his wife and two children," said the article and then went on to quote a city official who assured the public that this was a freak occurrence and they needn't worry about the health of the drivers.

John sat in the back of the tiny church during the memorial service, and, when he offered his condolences, the dry eyed wife, whose weightless hand trembled when he shook it, said, "Lots of people on his route liked him."

Snow fell at the cemetery. Beautiful wet, white flakes that vanished when they touched the earth or spun into the depths of the grave.

*D*enver International Airport turned out to be the best place to study the "death dwarves," John discovered. Thousands of people daily wandered around the overpriced shops at the end of the concourses, browsing in the news stands, fingering "Ski Vail" T-shirts, or sitting in the lounges watching daytime T.V. And, attracted to this concentration of humanity, pairs of dwarves sidled along the walls, consulting their little lists, marking names when they made connections, like demented and sadistic civil servants, and, occasionally, blasting away at the unaware.

They stayed away from any place people walked or sat and seemed practiced at finding observation points where they could be undisturbed, although John did see one dashing across B Concourse get "splashed" by a United Airlines courtesy cart.

He evesdropped, and the things they talked about sickened him: disease in all its forms, strokes, carcinomas, lingering illnesses, heart attacks, epilepsy, sudden infant death syndrome; and of the lost arsenal they fondly remembered: plague, leprosy, tuberculosis, yellow fever.

They mocked the people as they passed: businessmen with briefcases, family groups towing their bags behind them like Naugahyde pets, lost looking youths carrying duffel bags. The dwarves spit at them. They danced and laughed and called names.

John waited at the foot of the escalator. With his back braced against the polished aluminum base, he waited, cane in his right hand, casual, nonchalant, and when a pair jumped on the top and came gliding down, at the last instant he swung his cane through them. Their wet remains drained into the grooves of the moving stairway. He would have stayed all day, picking them off pair by pair, but a security guard started watching him, probably wondering what this strange looking individual with a dent in his head was doing.

John became a death hunter. For a few days he stalked them, as he had the pair in the airport, but it became increasingly evident that the dwarves firmly believed that he would not, could not, did not see them. His main challenge was in maneuvering them into positions where they couldn't skitter out of his way, something they were expert at. His encounter with a pair in the produce section of Albertson's, between the bins of apples and bananas was typical. They crouched below the overhang under the fruit display, their guns slung clumsily in front of them. John spotted them when he turned his cart down that aisle for peanut-butter. The plastic handle felt cool and solid under his hands, and the cart gave him something to lean against so that to someone observing him he would not appeared handicapped at all, only a little stiff. Fortunately, his physical rehabilitation was progressing well and he seldom fell now. Only the purple dent in his forehead marked him, and when he looked in the mirror it was the first thing he saw. Dark, deep, soft. He examined it closely for changes in color or depth that would warn him of swelling or infection, Dr. Ferguson's last doom predictions. "Head injuries are tricky," he said. "Everything seems fine and then a weak wall on a blood vessel blows out like a bad bike tube and we lose you."

The dwarves under the produce shelf were arguing, which is what most of them seemed to do, as he rolled closer and closer. John pulled his cane out of the cart with his left hand, the side they were on, and when he walked by them he swung the front of the cart into the bin, cutting off their one escape route. Before they could react he had reduced them to a pair of puddles with a casual wave of his cane. They were his forty-first and forty-second kill.

It was easy.

ramed certificates covered the walls in Dr. Ferguson's waiting room: undergraduate work at C.U., Doctorate from Harvard, member of the Better Business Bureau, good citizen awards for eight years, etc. The Doctor's achievements were commemorated with gold-lettered parchment. John saw his own reflection in each pane of glass. He was alone in the waiting room.

"You can come in now, John." The doctor leaned out of the half-opened door. His lab jacket glowed an immaculate white under the florescent light fixtures; the black tubes and chrome joints of his stethoscope looped out of one large pocket. His long face and receding hairline gave him the high foreheaded look that John associated with intelligence.

A series of X-rays hung from clips in the examining room. Doctor Ferguson moved from one to the next, his arms across his chest; he hummed softly. The paper on the examining table under John crinkled when he moved. His shirt was unbuttoned. For some reason the doctor always listened to his chest when he came in. The routine was comforting though. "Breathe in," he would say, and John would. The stethoscope would slide to the next spot. "Breathe in." It made John feel like a kid again. The doctor concentrating on John's chest sounds; his breath smelled of mint; in the background the office music system played.

He turned from the X-rays. "You should be dead you know." John nodded. "There are splinters everywhere we couldn't get."

"So why aren't I?" John could see the X-ray over Dr. Ferguson's shoulder. His own gray and white skull floating on the black background grinned back at him. Just a whispy suggestion of skin covered it. The hole looked like the result of dropping a bowling ball on the thin ice of a newly frozen lake.

"Dumb luck, as far as I can tell. Somehow the bone fragments missed all the vital spots; we managed to not kill you when we operated, and none of the normal opportunistic secondary infections set in. I have seen head injuries half as serious as this one that were instantly fatal. In fact, I am working up a paper on your case. It will give me an excuse to go to this year's medical convention."

"Glad I could help."

"It is in New Orleans. I love New Orleans." He laughed, sat in the chair next to John, crossed John's right leg over his left and tapped at his knee with a rubber hammer. The leg twitched reflexively. "And how is your physical therapy coming along?"

"They think I might be able to jog again in a few months, but my fine motor control is still terrible. Threading a needle, writing, buttoning a shirt, tieing a shoelace—those are hard to do. We're working on it. I'm in a night class that helps me on concentrating. Last night they had me do math problems with a television on behind me."

The doctor put the hammer back in a drawer in the table, pulled out a pen light from his coat and directed it into John's eye. The light glared like a giant sun, and John tried to look away, but the doctor's hand, warm and firm on his face, held his head still.

"And how are you feeling? I mean, emotionally?" He switched to the other eye.

"I've found plenty to keep me busy."

"A hobby?"

"Sort of."

"What are you doing?"

John thought of the last three weeks, the dwarves he had snuck up behind, the ones he had ambushed at blind corners, the ones that he caught in narrow hallways. Most of them never knew he was coming. He was their own unpleasant surprise. And then he had a sudden vision of the state of the world. He had seen parts of it before, but never fully, never with this clarity. He saw the death dwarves being born, some of them oozing up from the ground, from tiny fissures in the earth, weaving thread by thread until they stood whole and malevolent; and others coalescing in the clouds, dark particle piling on dark particle until their own foul weight bore them down to walk among men, and only he could see them. There were millions, maybe billions of them, and in his vision he swung his cane like a scythe until his arms ached with the effort, but they kept coming. A blanket of them covered the plain in front of him, their guns poking in the air, waving aimlessly like wheat. The horizon was crowded with ranks of them forever marching. He could never win. But he saw himself, glowing, a figure of light, swinging around, and they shrank back from him forming a little circle where they did not cover the ground, one place for a moment where they did not rule.

"I struggle with death." He realized how peculiar that must sound. "I mean, I think about ways to defeat it."

"Funny kind of hobby, John, but I am glad you are keeping a positive attitude. Many people would give up after an injury like yours."

"It's not in my nature to quit."

"Good, good." Doctor Ferguson moved his light to the dent in John's forehead. "If your brain has stabilized, which every indication says it has, then we may be able to do something about this too. A plate, some cosmetic surgery to remove the color. I'm afraid you will never look like you did before though."

John thought about the dark place in his forehead, like a badge, like the center of his vision, and he said, "That's all right. I'm getting used to it."

# Eight Words

The lock resisted at first, then clicked with a rusty thud. The door hung freely on its hinges and drifted open a black inch. Deep in the orchard the cicadas droned.

"Are you afraid of ghosts?" he said.

"Who believes in ghosts?" She pushed the door back.

He had insisted on the "traditional" tools, so, when they shut the door behind them, they fumbled for candles and matches, and, after a dark moment, unsure light illuminated a bare room.

He held his candle close to the wall, and a faded gilt pattern shone back at him in intricate, complicated whorls, like the heart of a rose. He looked toward her and saw a candle and her hand floating in the middle of the room, and a reminder of her face drifting above them—eyes black and deep.

"The ghost won't be here," he said. "Not in the *living* room."

Her hand and candle swooped to a banister, and her flame showed the first steps of a flight up, warped paneling of the wainscot, an empty place where a wall switch had been, her arm, her shoulder, her hair a sudden corona around the eclipse of her head.

"It's not like you to be ironic," she said.

"I practice in the mirror."

"So where should we be?" She looked at him; the candle shadowed her face. A drip of wax flowed onto his hand; it seared for a second, then solidified.

"If not the *living* room, where?"

She thought for a second. "The dead room?" He touched his ear. She said, "Oh! Sounds like. The bedroom."

"Where it began..." He lowered his voice. "...and ended."

She laughed and some metal cabinet in an unseen kitchen reverberated. "So melodramatic." She climbed the steep, narrow stairs in front of him. He looked at her back, the pockets on her jeans, the seam, then his own hand scraping along the wall.

"A ghost doesn't like to be ignored," he said. "It's personal. Ignoring it doesn't make it go away."

"Ghosts are in your mind. If you dwell on them they hang around, otherwise they're vacuum." She laughed again. "People see ghosts who can't let go of the dead."

They held their candles in front of them and stepped into the bedroom doorway. A water soaked section of sheetrock bowed from the ceiling, and from it some wires, red and black, dangled from a porcelain light fixture. Along the walls, the yellow lights flickered on a stained dresser, a pile of newspaper, ripped cloth hanging from a bent curtain rod, a boarded window, and a china cabinet on its back, its glass fronted doors shattered so jagged remains lined the empty spaces in the middle.

She cleared a spot off the floor with her foot, sat down, leaned against the wall and put her candle on the floor between her knees, which cast huge, twitching shadows. He sat on the edge of the dresser facing her and scrunched back so that his calves rested against the edges of the drawers. He watched the shadows on her face. The candle light gave her skin a wheat-gold glow and he had a sudden memory of her in a similar light looking across a dinner table at Carbone's when he had said "I love you." He shut his eyes and pressed the back of his head to the wallpaper which crackled. He listened to a branch scratching the side of the house.

"Tell me a joke," she said.

"Why a joke?"

"Who needs a reason for a joke? This is a dreary place. You used to joke a lot. Tell me one now."

"A ghost joke?"

"I don't care. You choose."

"How many ghosts does it take to change a light bulb?"

"I hate that kind. That's not a real joke." She shrugged her shoulders together and shivered. "Does it seem cold to you?"

"Cold spots are a sure sign of hauntings." He brought his feet up to the dresser top and rested his chin on his knees.

She sighed. "Cut it out. I don't believe in them."

"You don't have to. No Tinkerbells here. A strong ghost will get a disbeliever too."

"Have you ever seen one?" She rubbed her arms briskly. He said nothing, but cocked his head to listen to wood beams and old nails creaking. Something skittered in the wall behind him, and he jumped.

"They're around me all the time. Not just in this old house, but it's a good place. Some people need this setting. Some people need to see a ghost."

"You mean me? You don't know what I need." She straightened her legs out, which raised a pall of dust when they flopped onto the floor. She coughed into her hand. "Okay, I give up. How many ghosts does it take to change a light bulb?"

He leaned to the side and blew out his candle. Now her candle provided the sole light. He could see her better. "None. Ghosts aren't afraid of the dark."

"That's stupid. That's as stupid as this one. Knock, knock."

"Who's there?"

"Boo who."

"Boo who who?"

"Don't be sad, I'll tell you in a minute."

Below them, in the kitchen or the living room, something moaned softly. He tried to inhale, but his lungs seemed paralyzed. She looked toward the door.

"I love the wind in a old house," she said.

He listened and the moan began again. Maybe a window in back was broken, a whistle gap for moving air. He rolled a pebble beneath his finger, around and around, tiny motions so that one revolution was the circumference of his finger tip. "Are you ready?" he said.

"Yeah." She put the candle on the edge of the china cabinet. "Go ahead and tell me the story."

"You have to be in a believing mood." He picked up the pebble and held it up to the light across the room. It was a mouse dropping. He tossed it. "You've got to forget who's telling the story."

"Tell it good, and I will."

"No. It's important. Shut your eyes." She did. She leaned her head back, like his. The light distorted the proportions of the room. The ceiling seemed twice as broad as the floor, like they were at the bottom of a square funnel. They seemed so small, tiny legs, baby-doll arms, fingers too short to touch each other. "You feel the wall behind you?"

"Yes."

"It's dry wood, no varnish, rough kind of?"

"Yes."

"Rub your hand on the floor."

"Why?"

"Mood."

"Okay."

"The floor's gritty, isn't it?" he said.

"Yes."

"Do you feel your clothes on your skin?"

"Yes."

"Do you feel the air on your face?"

She turned her head side to side, eyes closed. "Yes."

"Take a deep breath with your mouth open."

She opened her mouth, a black hole, and inhaled. Her chest filled, he could see it rise. "Do it again." She did.

He said, "Say, 'I am here.'"

"I am here."

"Say, 'The time is now.'"

"The time is now."

"There is no other," he said.

"There is no other."

The wind noise stopped. The branch that rattled back and forth across the side of the house stopped. Slowly he breathed out all his air, pushed his diaphragm tight against the bottom of his lungs.

*A stair creaked, distinctly.* She twitched her chin to one side, canted her head, kept her eyes closed.

He said, "It could be something on the stairs. It could be nothing."

She nodded.

He said, "Say, 'All times are now, all times are here, we are in the here and now.'"

She did.

"This is the place it started. This is the place it happened. It is happening now, again, as I speak. It is always happening. All parts of it."

*Another stair creaked.*

He said, "Are you ready?"

"Yes."

The air between us, he thought, all that separates us is the air. Almost nothing.

"If you truly are, then maybe the ghost will come." He spoke the lines the way he'd rehearsed. "This is the story I've been told about the ghost that haunts this house. Others have seen it. I'm not the only one. This is what they say: in the time of the story, when this house was lived in, there was a beautiful man, a Greek god of a man. His name was Theodore and he threw discus in college. But it wouldn't matter if he were plain and unathletic. He could've been any man. He wasn't, though. He was Theodore the beautiful, and everyone loved him except himself. He strode to class, blind to the eyes that followed. His voice was clear and strong. When he spoke, the air quieted around him. Professors paused, not because of his brilliance, but only to bathe in that voice. People who barely knew him stopped to ask him how he was, just to hear him speak. And the music in his voice only hinted at the wonders of his laugh. But when boys and girls hung on him, he shrugged them away, and they loved him even more for his disdain. Like any man, he only knew himself from the inside. He saw nothing special.

"There was one woman, though. Her name was Katherine and she sat beside him in a mythology seminar. She, too, was moved by his beauty. Everyday others tried to sit in her seat, to sit next to Theodore, but she got there earlier than all of them. When the janitors opened the building, she was on the step, her books tight against her chest, her hair combed a thousand strokes, her face scrubbed and powdered, her clothes agonized over, and she sat in her seat, next to the one he always took and waited."

*Two more stairs groaned under a weight ascending, some soft, slow movement upwards.*

"The class met in a lecture hall, hundreds of seats bolted side by side, with swing-up desks for writing. Katherine rested her arm on the edge of his desk hoping he might accidentally brush her; so she could say, 'Excuse me,' and they would talk. He never did. She could not even look at him. Day after day he came to class, and she sat next to him in miserable ecstasy. Then, one time, she glanced over at his notes and saw that he was doodling. Around his notes of Daedalus and Icarus and the intrigue in the court of King Minos, Theodore had drawn tiny rocketships balancing on long lines of exhaust. He was busy sketching in an armada of missiles behind the word *Perdix*, which Katherine had written in her notes too, but couldn't remember what it had to do with Daedalus. His paper was covered with ships and asteroids and cratered moons."

He listened to her breathing. The house was so silent, he thought he heard her heart. But more important, he heard, or sensed, or just knew, that a thing stood on the stairs, not breathing. He heard it not breathing.

"She thought, then, that she had seen the Theodore that no one else knew: the little boy inside, not a cold, stiff, unfeeling marble man. She relaxed. For the first time in weeks sitting beside him, she slouched in her chair. Katherine reached over with her pencil and drew on his page a flying saucer. He froze for a moment, then drew behind it, as a backdrop, a ringed planet. She placed a sun high on the sheet, and he added a single spacecraft orbiting.

"Because she saw his spaceships and played his game, he thought she was perceptive, intuitive, that they had touched on some higher level. She was not like the others. She knew the real him. They left class together, and he took her to his favorite spot, through a door shut with a broken lock and onto the roof of the tallest building on campus. There they met, day after day, and talked of inconsequential things, as men will to women and women will to men, though they never spoke of the spaceships or the ringed planet or the orbited sun."

*In the hallway at the top of the stairs, he heard the quiet press of a foot onto the floor, the hiss of cloth scraping cloth.*

"And, after a time, they became lovers, in this house, which his parents owned, in this very room. And as they were lying in bed, after their first time, he said, 'I don't trust myself to say I will be here for you forever.' And she said, 'We are modern. Nothing is forever.' They met many times in this room, and when he became frightened that she wanted things from him that weren't his to give, she reminded him that nothing is forever, and he was comforted.

"But as they walked together on campus, he saw that no one followed him anymore. The attention he never noticed when it was there, he missed when it was gone. And it seemed the professors were less interested in what he had to say. He laughed and no one looked his way. So it came to him, in a devious kind of logic, that Katherine had changed him, that she had wanted him to be different all along and was subtly working a woman's magic on him. She wanted him to be hers forever. Katherine had told Theodore that he was special, and he believed her, and he believed that she was preventing others from seeing it."

*He felt a movement to his left, in the hallway beyond the door. A ghastly half-speed dropping of a sheet. A stir of air.*

"So he told her here, after they had made love, 'I am leaving. You have diminished me,' and he left. Katherine didn't beg him, she didn't cry out after him, she didn't weep when she was alone, but she was empty. She thought about his little-boy rocket ships, and their private place on top of the building. She thought about that nothing is forever. After a while, she slid her feet out of the bed, wrapped the sheet around herself, wrote a note, just eight words, and left it on the dresser. She knelt, opened the bottom drawer, took out a safety razor and sliced her wrist. She died on her knees, her forehead pressed against the floor."

*The candle caught a gust of air and almost went out as a shape glided through the door and into the room.*

She said, "I'm freezing."

He said, "It's here."

She opened her eyes. "What?"

"The ghost. Katherine's ghost."

The misty shape drifted in between them. The girl smiled. "There are no ghosts."

He had been afraid she would say that, that she wouldn't see the ghost, but he had to try.

"You are not in the here and now, or you would."

"It's cold. Let's go."

The shape coalesced on the floor beneath him. Its back bowed, the form of its head against the hard wood.

"No, I can't. You go ahead and I'll be along."

She stood, carried her candle over to him, walking through the ghost.

"I'm frozen! There'll be snow tomorrow." She lit his candle. He looked at her impenetrable eyes. He remembered her again in a similar light. She said, "Come with me."

"I can't. I'll meet you in the car. Give me a minute."

He thought for a second that she was going to touch him, but instead she said, "Being just friends isn't going to work out for you, is it?" She left.

He and the ghost stayed motionless. Only the shadows moved. He thought about Katherine alone in this room. He thought about her writing the note, the eight words. Then the ghost raised its head from the floor. It looked up. Hair fell down in front of its face, but there was no face behind, just emptiness. He wasn't frightened. He leaned over the dresser. He thought about the girl who was sitting out in the car now; he thought about the eight words.

Then the ghost spoke.

"It's not my fault I fell in love."

The voice was only an echo. He heard it more in his head than in his ears. But he knew the ghost was real.

He said, "I know."

# Parallel Highways

The semi-trailer truck's rear tires rumbled a yard from Jack's window. A faded sign in red, HORIZON TRANSIT, in giant letters, decorated the trailer. In the rear mirror, another eighteen-wheeler's grill loomed just off the bumper, and in the right lane a line of cars slid by, no more that a half a dozen feet between them.

White-knuckled, Jack gripped the wheel. Backwash from the semi rattled his little car, and he fought the tug that pulled him toward the tires spinning to his left. Blurred at the tip, the speedometer needle hung just beyond eighty-miles per hour.

"He's coming over," said Debbie. Her voice cracked. From the corner of his eye, Jack could see she'd balled a handful of skirt into her fist. She sucked in a breath as if she were about to scream, but instead she murmured, "He's coming."

"I can see," he snapped.

The semi's trailer of ribbed aluminum, rivet studded and coated with dust, crossed the line, narrowing the space. In the truck's mirror, dark glasses hid the driver's eyes, but he seemed to be looking right at them.

Jack whipped a glance over his shoulder. The other semi behind them had moved up, now nearly touching their bumper. No break in the line of traffic to his right, but he signaled anyway, stomped on the accelerator and slid over, hoping for a gap. Traffic behind him stretched in a domino row of glaring windshields, and he realized no one was going to let him in. They *couldn't* let him in.

Inexorably, the truck closed the distance, squeezing the lane.

"Oh, no," Debbie moaned.

"I've got it," Jack said. "I've got it."

He dumped into fourth gear, winding the car's little engine into the top of its RPMs; it jumped forward. They passed the trailer's front wheels. A woman in a beat-up station wagon on their right leaned on her horn, flipping them off, but she moved over a bit, and so did the Volkswagen in front of her.

Jack scooted close to them, crossing the lane stripes, passing the station wagon, the semi's wheels roaring in his ear. He juked the car right, bumping the Volkswagen; metal crunched, and Debbie fell against him, her chest heaving, her arm slippery with sweat.

The face in the Volkswagen contorted in anger and fear.

Better you than me, Jack thought. Although his car was small, he knew the Volkswagen didn't have any weight at all. If he had to, he could force himself into its spot in the traffic.

Now, horns all around them blared. Traffic in front of them rippled. Tail lights flashed. A pickup that had been blocking the Volkswagen cut left in front of the semi, and its air horn erupted, but now there was space to the right.

Sobbing, Jack pulled in front of the Volkswagen, clipping its bumper on the way, and another opening appeared on his right, which he took.

Two lanes separated them from the trailer-truck, now bombing along as if nothing had happened. Jack pried a hand loose from the steering wheel and wiped his mouth. His chin was slick.

He checked the mirrors. As far back as he could see, traffic. The highway faded into the blue distance. Same in front. One more lane over, a cement retainer separated them from the city, a numbing series of dirty, gray warehouses.

He took deep breaths, letting himself calm down.

"Missed us that time," he said, and he tried to laugh, but it came out tight and fake, like it felt.

Debbie say up straight, smoothing her skirt over her legs. She looked out the side window, pressing her hand against it. Long brunette hair with just a hint of a curl at the end brushed her shoulders. Her face reflected a little in the glass. Deep, brown eyes. No makeup. A serious woman carrying despair in the lines of her frown.

Beyond, building after shadowless building rolled by. The sun stood exactly overhead, but smog or mist fuzzed away its outlines, so the sky glared hot, white and without form.

"We should have let that car in," she said.

"Which?" He knew what she was talking about. It was an old argument.

"We shouldn't have been in such a hurry."

Jack checked the mirrors again, then closed the distance between him and the next car to get the guy following him off his tail.

She said, "I don't recognize anything."

"I know."

"It could be L.A." She looked at him without moving her hand, her eyes so tired that they appeared as if they'd been punched.

"Or Pompeii."

"That's not funny."

"It's a superhighway from somewhere. Just as well could be Pompeii. Or maybe Rome, just before Nero burnt the sucker."

"Stop it."

"Do you think there was a freeway between Sodom and Gomorrah?" He laughed a little easier this time but bitter.

"Sodom and Gomorrah," she said, "L.A. What's the difference?"

If it were L.A., we might be able to get off. Merge lane," he said. Whatever the junction was, a spray-painted white hand obscured the name. "Should we take it?"

"I thought that was Anaheim we passed yesterday," she said wistfully. "I always liked Disneyland."

"I'm taking it."

Jack scanned his left, tapped the breaks and eased into a space between a Bronco with tinted windows and a guy on a motorcycle. The cyclist's head wove back and forth as if he were listening to a private symphony. Hair spilled out beneath his faded bandanna and streamed in the wind. Ahead of them, taillights blinked and cars jockeyed for position.

Traffic split, and Jack followed the curve of the road beneath an overpass. A green highway sight said, *Carmilhan—76 miles*. Within a few minutes, the warehouses disappeared, replaced by desert and twisted Joshua trees streaking by behind the concrete retainer.

Jack sighed. Highway reached before him straight to the horizon as unwavering as a knife edge. Here, the cars spaced themselves a bit. Twenty to thirty feet between them, but the asphalt still whined under the wheels at a steady eighty miles per hour. He laid his head back and stared at the ceiling for a second, then blinked hard and rubbed his hand across his eyes.

"I'm exhausted. Can you handle it for awhile?"

Debbie nodded, moving next to him, onto the emergency brake. She put a hand on the wheel and arched up as he slid underneath her, the back of her blouse wet with perspiration. Now, almost sprawled across the seat, the brake's handle digging into his back, he kept a foot on the accelerator. She stepped over his legs, careful to keep from turning the car with her hip as she dropped into his place.

"What should we do at the next junction?" she said.

Jack reached into the tiny backseat for a jacket, folded it over several times, then wedged it into the corner between the top of the seat and the doorjamb. He rested his head on it and closed his eyes. Humming wheels whipping over road whispered against his cheek. "It doesn't matter," he said. "Go where you want."

Speed varied as Debbie adjusted for the traffic. Air rushed past the window, whistling a little in some crack he'd never been able to find. After a while he drifted into a kind of false sleep, not quite dreaming, not quite aware of where he was, and he felt like he was floating. Then he said, or thought he said, or maybe even imagined he said, "How come all roads lead everywhere, but you can't get there from here?"

Debbie didn't answer, so he let the car's motion lull him further. He thought about treetops waving back and forth and a time when he rested beneath them, watching diamonds of sun coming through the leaves. All he wanted was to sleep and to wake up there—to wake up anywhere other than on the highway—not to be pounding out the miles and watching the bumper in front of him. Jack wanted to sleep and to wake up and to sleep again far away from the roads and horns. Far away from the zombie motion of driving the car.

He lurched, bouncing his forehead against the glass. No telling how long he'd been asleep. It didn't feel long. He squinted against the pain, then peeked over at Debbie. He chin was down, eyes closed; her hands loose on the wheel.

Too late, he jolted upright, reaching for her. Concrete whizzed inches from the side window. Metal screeched. Sparks fired from the front of the car. Debbie shot up. Overcorrected.

The world keeled over and slowed as the car went sideways and rolled. Jack floated to the ceiling as it crumpled toward him. Glass shattered into the passenger compartment. His arm broke first, a wet snap above the elbow, then his shoulder. Then he hit the ceiling. And last, as the car rolled, he saw through a red veil the semi bearing down, an avalanche of metal and momentum.

*J  ack's consciousness surfaced in the half-death in a white flash of agony, and through the shock he thought, pain slows time. Agonizing second after second. He thought, terminal cancer victims must hear clocks in their blood slowing down. Any minute and every minute an infinite reach. Unstoppable and dispassionate. Waves lapping against the sand. Everyone like the first; none the last. All bones crushed. All flesh mangled. Pain living forever. All of it over and over again. For infinite time, his bones broke one after another, and like Prometheus, without healing and without cessation, the bones broke again. He had no way to tell, nothing to measure it against, but the crash seemed to replay for a thousand years.*

*I*'m sorry, Jack." Debbie held the wheel in one hand and touched herself with the other. First, her face, then across her chest and onto her leg. "Oh, god, I'm sorry."

They passed under another sign, *Carmilhan—8miles/Alice Mar—104 mile/Titanic—156 miles*. On the dunes beyond the cement retainer, isolated Joshua trees spaced themselves between long patches of bare sand. Each like a mutant sentinel, holding mutant limbs to the brilliance of the white sky.

Jack felt his own arms, stretched his back. Nothing broken. Nothing even sore. "It's inevitable," he said. It's not your fault. We're bound to get tired."

She shook. Her hands trembled on the steering wheel. "I can't do that again. It's not fair that I should have to do that again."

Cars bunched up in front of them, closing the distances. Looking in the mirror, Debbie switched lanes, away from the congestion. In a minute, they passed a four-vehicle pile-up, two cars, a cement mixer and a bread truck. Broken glass crunched under their tires as they went by. Debbie looked away.

"Dying's the best rest I get," said Jack. "It's a silver lining."

"I don't know why we get sleepy. We don't eat. We don't go to the bathroom. The stupid car never needs gas!" Debbie said, her voice on the edge. "You know what else? I don't see enough accidents. If everybody's like us, then there ought to be accidents constantly. There are people all by themselves in half the cars. Who gives them a rest? But most of the time, traffic's moving. Why is that?"

"Well, if we're logical..."

"You're not a scientist anymore! I'm not a student in one of your classes. Nothing's logical about this!" Debbie's lips paled; her face was so tight.

Jack touched her arm. "It's okay. It's just conversation."

She took several shaky breaths, then relaxed. For a second, Jack saw in her face a semblance of his wife the way she was aeons ago, when they climbed in the car and left for the commute. They'd been uptight; they'd argued; they were late; it was her fault; it was his fault. He'd cut into the traffic viciously. Someone beeped at them; then they'd settled into the flow, and she'd relaxed, just for a second, like she did just now.

"Not logic, then," Jack said. "Thinking it through, though. If there are solitary drivers, and they're like us, then they ought to be crashing left and right, but they don't. So they're not like us."

"I guess we know that."

Jack peered into the car beside them, a shiny, blue Lexus. Inside, a man in a business suit stared straight ahead. Lots of commuters looked like him, focused in a kind of catatonic way. Locked on the road, frozen into position as if posing for portraits. Lost in their thoughts, he supposed.

But some of the cars that passed...the occupants weren't possible...were painful to see. He noticed that Debbie had quit looking long ago. But how often do we really see the people in the other cars on a commute? thought Jack. Maybe the highways had always been like that. Maybe I never paid enough attention. He had a theory that this is the way it had always been: traffic consisted of demons, civilians, newbies and the damned. Sometimes it was mostly civilians: drivers who got on the highway, went somewhere and got off, never knowing what drove beside them. Sometimes it was mostly the damned, like them, who died and lived and kept on driving. Sometime there were newbies: the damned before they died the first time. And then, there were demons. Jack shuddered thinking about the sunglassed face looking back at him in the semi's mirror. That driver had known there were there, but he came over anyway.

Jack said, "We have to sleep, or we'd go insane, and if we were insane, this wouldn't be so bad."

"You're assuming we're being punished."

"It's like the fate of Sisyphus. He pushed that old boulder to the top of the mountain in the Greek underworld, but it wouldn't stay there. So his curse was to walk after the thing and roll it back up. If he only had to roll it up, and he could never stop, he'd never have time to think about his sins, but the rock rolled down, and he'd go after it. The punishment was in the walk down, while he was resting. We've to sleep so we can wake up and realize again what our task is. It's our walk back to the boulder."

"So, are we wimps or heroes?" said Debbie. "Are we resisting our fate or giving in?"

"Well, I guess if this were a movie, we'd be wimps. We're not solving our problems. But in real life sometimes the most heroic thing you can do is stay even and not give up. So we're heroes."

"I don't feel like a hero. I haven't done anything."

Debbie let her hands slip to the bottom of the wheel. She was steering with the tips of her fingers barely draped. Back in the Joshua trees, a black shape moved; Jack only caught a glimpse of it. It was like a bear, but its arms were loose-fleshed, hairless and yellow. It looked up from whatever it was feeding on. Eyes glinted.

"We're not in our world," he said.

"I'm sure that was Anaheim the other day. Maybe we're there part of the time. If we could find our way back."

"One freeway to another. Merge lanes and junctions—there's never an exit."

"I remember the signs: Hermosa Beach and then Long Beach. We were going west on the 91. Maybe these are like parallel universes, except they're parallel highways. Part of the time we cross over. Do you think anybody saw us? Do you think we looked different?"

Debbie drove for three hundred miles before they switched. She rested her head and closed her eyes immediately. Ahead, a line of hills rose out of the desert, and soon he was climbing steadily. Joshua trees gave way to pinion as the road wove higher and higher. Occasionally he passed a camper or heavy truck laboring in the right lane, belching exhaust. A sign read, *Slower traffic keep right: No stopping on the shoulder*. He smirked. They'd tried stopping twice, pulling against the cement retainer, only to watch the following traffic pile into them, as if they were incapable of stopping themselves. The second time they'd burned. A thousand years in the fire.

Once he'd seen a man jump from a car; maybe he was a newbie, desperate to escape the road. The man slowed as much as the flow allowed— maybe fifty miles per hour—then opened his door and rolled out. Jack had been three cars back, and passed him as he slid and tumbled on the asphalt. Craning his head over his shoulder, Jack saw the man, amazingly, stagger to his feet just before a bus creamed him.

No stopping on the shoulder, Jack thought. No kidding.

A road sign read, *Mary Celeste—14 miles*. "That's a phantom ship," he said. Debbie turned on her seat; opened her eyes.

"What?"

"Sign said, Mary Celeste. It's a ship whose crew never made port. they found her floating around, perfectly seaworthy, but no one on board."

"I know about the Celeste," said Debbie, her eyes closed again. "We're more like Vanderdecken."

"Who?"

Debbie covered her face with one hand. Jack couldn't tell if she were crying or not. "Vanderdecken captained the *Flying Dutchman*. During a storm he swore an oath that he'd sail around the Cape of Good Hope or be damned forever."

"What does that have to do with us?" Jack said. he could feel the anger welling inside him. She's always bringing it up, he thought. She can't give it a rest.

"We should have let that car in. You shouldn't have said, 'Damned if I'll let someone cut me off this morning!' They died because of you." Her voice wasn't angry, but it was flat and tired, as if announcing news she'd accepted long ago.

His heart pounded in his ears. She won't leave it alone, he thought.

It's always my fault. He remembered the morning this started, holding his own in his lane, the early commute streaming toward its destination, when he saw the mini-van coming toward him from the on-ramp. He'd measured its speed, watched it, and saw that it was going to merge in front of him. He was in a hurry. He was edgy in that special manner that driving in traffic made him. The mini-van approached. Jack would have to give way to let him in. "Damned if I'll let someone cut me off this morning," he'd said, and he smashed the accelerator. For a moment, the mini-van paralleled them, the driver leaning to his left, searching for a break in traffic.

He must not have seen the broken-down car on the shoulder. Jack didn't until the last second, just a glimpse of a jack holding up the driver's side read, or a tire laying on the road, of someone on his knees holding a lug wrench. Then the mini-van plowed into the parked car.

Jack pictured the crash. "I don't want to talk about it. I don't even want to think about it anymore." He heard his voice straining.

Debbie didn't say anything. Curves held Jack's attention for a moment. The road had gone to two lanes, and he had to concentrate on driving. Then the hills opened up, and the ocean spread out before them. The highway fell toward the sea. Soon they were driving a road that held close to cliff edges overlooking stony places where waves lapped dully against kelp-encrusted rock. Even through the window, he could smell the salt and rot.

Then Debbie said, "I would have done the same thing, Jack. I wouldn't have let the van in that morning."

Jack remembered the smoke from the accident. As they had driven on, a pillar of smoke had risen behind them, climbing into the sky like an angry spirit, black and red and writing.

The memory of smoke clear in his mind, he drove on.

They stayed on the costal highway for 3,700 impossible miles before a car coming toward them crossed the lane, catching their side, driving them off the road, over the cliff, tumbling against the rocks for five-hundred feet. The last thing Jack heard was water hissing against hot metal. Then the sea rushed into the car.

*N o one knows about pain but those who are in pain. Only the hurting know what it is. Memory of pain is not pain. Description of pain is not pain. Small hurts are not like great ones reduced. True pain lives in the ever-present moment, expecting nothing, owing to nothing, overwhelming all other thoughts. For a thousand years, Jack tried to scream. Water filled his lungs. Everything was broken, and he was always drowning.*

*Y* ou were saying?" said Jack, trying to sound as if nothing had happened, as if not time passed, but Debbie didn't answer. For the longest time she kept her face to the window, so that all Jack could see was the back of her head. He turned inland and the junction to Palatine, and soon the lanes multiplied, and they were in city traffic again.

"Our driving record sucks," she said finally. "They should pull our driver's licenses." She started laughing, and it built on itself, an insane-sounding layering of laughter until Jack couldn't tell if she were laughing anymore or shrieking. It scared him. After minutes of this, she quieted down, although every once in a while, she'd chuckle, and Jack was afraid she'd start again.

She said, "You know what I'm thankful for?" She paused a half beat. "That we don't have to pay car insurance anymore. It's just a relief." The chuckle came out of the back of her throat, and she wiped tears from the bottom of her eyes.

Jack drove for twenty hours straight, 1,600 miles before switching. Mostly they passed through baking desert, their air conditioner battling vainly against the heat pouring in; the glare off windshields stabbing his eyes, but every once in a while, buildings would loom up on either side, warehouses, factories, strip malls, and he could read the signs: AAMCO, QUIZNOS, BIG O, WINCHELLS, AMERICAN FURNITURE WARE-HOUSE, WAL-MART. Sometimes he couldn't read the signs; they weren't in any language he recognized. But never an exit, just junctions. Highway leading to highway; concrete bridges twining over, under and around each other, filled with cars streaming end to end.

Their drivers studied the road with the peculiar dead look of the long-distance traveler. In some cases the passengers slept. In some, they read books. Jack saw kids and old folks and dogs, all closed in, all isolated in their eighty-mile-per-hour fish bowls. And in some cars, he saw monsters.

Debbie covered almost nine-hundred miles before giving Jack a turn, and he went for 1,300 more. They switched a dozen times, often saying nothing for hundreds of miles; often times both awake, watching the road unreel before them.

A low set of hills shrugged up on the horizon, and soon they wound through dry, grass-covered slopes. For miles, rows of giant windmills lined the hills, their huge, high-tech blades spinning in a wind they couldn't feel in the car. Then they passed the last windmill and other highways joined theirs, adding a lane or two each time. Jack was driving when they rounded a curve and a great city sprawled in the vast valley below. Through the haze, as far as he could see, rooftops and roads, and the traffic drew them in.

Something touched his hand on the emergency brake. He looked down. Debbie's hand rested against his, and he took it, pressing his fingers between hers. They drove into the city, hand in hand.

Debbie scrutinized the buildings as Jack eased from one lane to another, always on the lookout for potential trouble. His back ached; his eyes burned with weariness.

"It's L.A. again," she whispered. "We're on the 10."

"They all look the same," Jack said, but he noticed the palms growing beyond the retaining wall and the manzanita in the median. "I haven't seen a sign."

"I think it's L.A."

"I hope it isn't. I couldn't stand it if we were this close." But he sat up more in his seat, a little less tired.

"She squeezed his hand. Malls flowed by and R.V. lots. Trucks filled the road: tankers, movers and the semis. Cars darted like smelt among the shark, moving around their ponderous bulk, giving way, sliding over, clearing a path. In the distance, a series of high rises peeked out of the haze.

"I remember audio-books," said Debbie. "If you weren't with me, I could start one in the morning and finish it on the way back. I used to think my commute was half a book long."

"I didn't know that. For me, the drive was time to get good thinking done. From Banning to San Bernardino I'd formulate the problem. From there to Pomona, I'd come up with various approaches, and by Pasadena I'd have the day planned out."

The traffic flow varied. Cars slowed and came together for miles, crawling at fifty or sixty miles an hour. Then, without any perceivable reason, they would speed up and spread out. Jack thought of it as "accordion traffic," and it took all his attention. Now he drove with both hands on the wheel, watching for the sudden cut, keeping out of others' blind spots. Drivers looked tense and focused. They snapped glances in their mirrors; kept a thumb hear their horns. Blinkers flashed. Cars vied for placement as junctions came up every mile or so.

Jack changed lanes twice to get into position for the Santa Ana junction. It *was* L.A. he decided. Maybe a parallel one, but L.A. just the same. He could get them to Anaheim at least. Debbie could see something familiar before they followed the road back out to alien landscapes and meaningless junctions that led them nowhere at eighty miles per hour.

He could get them to Anaheim.

Traffic flowed slightly faster in his lane. They crept up on cars, taking minutes to pass them. A semi to their right, ahead of them, blocked the signs. Jack wanted the Compton junction that would take them west on 91, but he didn't know if he needed the left or right side of the highway. A sign blinked by, and he missed what it said.

Slowly they closed the distance. The semi's wheels roared by Debbie's window, and Jack suddenly got scared. Everything felt the same as it had once before. He'd heard these tires before.

"What's that truck?" he asked, voice tight.

Debbie pushed her face to the window and read the side. "Horizon Transit. Why?"

"Jesus," said Jack. He couldn't see the driver's face, but a leather-clad arm rested on the driver's door. Only a few feet separated Jack from the car in front of them, a green lowrider with maroon tassels dangling in the rear window.

Jack tapped the top of the steering wheel. Both lanes to his left were packed solid, hardly a hand's breadth between them. No chance of cutting over and away. All he could hope for was that nothing would happen, because there was nothing he could do to protect himself.

At mid-trailer, the truck's turbulence buffeted the and pulled them over. Jack leaned on the wheel, keeping them in the center of their lane.

Debbie said, "That's the same one, isn't it?"

Howling, the trailer's front wheels passed the window in a blur of rubber and spinning metal. They were beside the cab. Jack could see the foot rest and the bottom of the door. They were by.

Closing his eyes for a second, Jack breathed easier. The lane to their right was open for a hundred yards, as if no one wanted to be in front of the semi. Keeping one eye on the truck in his mirror, Jack scanned the road ahead for junction signs. He couldn't remember how long he needed to stay on 57 before hitting 91. It seemed like years since he'd driven this stretch of road. Years of driving and driving, but never arriving.

After minutes more, they caught up to the car that was immediately ahead of the semi, now a hundred yards behind. Jack kept looking for the signs as they inched past.

"Oh," said Debbie. "That poor man."

In the car beside them, a yellow Volvo sedan with two little boys in the back seat, the driver was wide-eyed and weeping. The man rotated his head left and right, and Jack could see in his face disbelief and growing horror.

A newbie, Jack thought, and he remembered when he and Debbie realized they were trapped, how the sickening dread had welled up inside them. The traffic wouldn't let them stop; there was no place to exit, and they were trapped. They must have looked like this.

The man's face was pure anguish. He didn't even appear to see Jack and Debbie looking in at him, and in the backseat the children played, two little boys with their heads down, studying something between them. Maybe a coloring book.

What could they have done to deserve being here? The image of the children waking up in the half-death after their first inevitable crash boiled up within him. A thousand years (it seemed) of pain and death. What could they have possibly done?

Tears glistened on the man's face. He barely seemed to be paying attention to the road as he wandered from side to side.

Jack felt a fist in his throat. He couldn't take his eyes away from the man. Then the car behind Jack beeped, a short angry beep that said, "Keep up, buddy. You're slowing me down." A gap had opened in front of Jack.

He checked his rear-view mirror. The driver behind beeped again, but what Jack saw was the semi closing fast. The hundred yards was now fifty. Black exhaust streamed from the truck's twin pipes above the cab, and the windshield glared like a rectangular sun. Directly in front of it, the unknowing newbie waited to be squashed. He didn't see the traffic. He didn't see anything, and his boys played on.

Debbie saw it too. She looked at Jack.

Their eyes locked, and hers brimmed with sadness.

Twenty-five yards back, the semi leapt eagerly. It growled in triumph.

Jack checked behind him. He put his hand on the emergency brake. Debbie saw, touched his hand and nodded.

He grazed the brakes. A horn blared behind him, and metal crunched, snapping Jack's head against his seat, but the Volvo scooted ahead. Their bumpers cleared, and Jack jerked the wheel to the right, pulling the emergency at the same time.

The truck was on them before they started to roll.

*Pain's the dark flip-side of excitement. It doesn't bore. It's always freshly minted. Blood in the wound glistens, and pain's world opens wide, all-encompassing. Jack squirmed on pain's hook, but there was no place to go, and he was all alone. Like Vanderdecken tied to the rudder off the weather-whipped coast of Africa, beating his way into the knives of wind, never arriving, never making port, and each wave a reminder of the death that had already claimed him. Like Sisyphus with his shoulder to the rock, unable to see around it, having no idea how long it would grind into his shoulder, how long his legs would quiver beneath him, begging to collapse.*

*Pain, as long as it lasts, is unending.*

*I* never believe we will come back," said Debbie.

Jack stroked the wheel. If felt so good to feel anything, even the steering wheel.

"It makes me want to kiss everything around me," said Jack.

Automatically, he moved into the left lane. The sign said *Compton Only*, and he followed the curve around with all the other cars. Four lanes joined them on the left. The highway was congested, but moving well.

"Do you think he survived?" asked Debbie. "Do you think that it made any difference?"

"Maybe," Jack said. "At least for a moment."

They passed under a sign.

Debbie turned and grabbed his arm. "Did you see it, Jack! Did you see it?"

He was already checking his mirror and signaling. "Yeah."

The sign read, *Harbor Blvd. Disneyland exit/Left Lane, 1/2 mile.*

"It's an exit. Can we make it, Jack? Can you make the exit?"

Four lanes of solidly packed commuters moving at eighty miles per hour stood in between him and a way off the highway, the first exit they'd seen in who could guess how many years. At eighty, a half mile takes only twenty seconds.

Four bumper to bumper lanes. Twenty seconds, and the Harbor Blvd. Exit into Anaheim and Disneyland.

"I think so," he said as he made the first merge. "I'm good in traffic."

# Time

# What Weena Knew

Weena waded away from the others into deeper parts. Current pulled at her tunic, threatened to take her feet from the bottom, but she wasn't ready yet. Maybe one of the others would see her and ask why she was alone, what she was doing so close to the dangerous waters. No one did, even though she stood still for some time, letting her fingers rest in the stream, the cool flow pushing them aside like little fish fins. She squinted against the sun's glitter; each ripple caught a diamond point and tossed it against her vision, so the stream's middle didn't look like water at all but more like a glittery ribbon, gently squirming before her.

She licked her lips—they were dry—and even though the day was not yet hot, her forehead felt flushed.

No one will come. They don't care, she thought. They're more concerned with gathering flowers, eating fruit and making love until the sun sets. She closed her eyes. Would it be frightening to fall into the glittery ribbon or glorious? Would she rise up at the end, a thousand diamond points herself, a sparkling display that none could bear to look at lest they go blind? A step deeper. Water reached mid-way up her chest; it tugged her hands. Come with me, it said. Come deep and stay.

So she did, and the current took her. For an instant, it was peaceful, the floating as her feet rose from the gravel, and she knew she'd chosen well. No more nights hiding away. No more mornings convinced the Fear was a dream, that missing friends weren't missing at all, just hiding. She marveled at how light she felt. The river held her like a cloud; a child could not ask for a cradle so soft.

Then, she inhaled. It burned! Her eyes popped open. Her arms waved and feet kicked. Another rush of gagging water down the throat. It wasn't supposed to hurt! Her face broke the surface. She screeched, glimpsed her friends, then tumbled back under again. Roaring in the ears: current pushing through rocks, waves slapping on waves in the turbid middle. Her hand flailed in the air, tantalizingly above the water, but no movements of her arms or legs seemed to move her up. Her tunic's weight dragged. Then an upswelling pushed her face free for another peek and a half-swallow of air mixed with foam. No one on shore had moved! They weren't going to help her!

But she knew they wouldn't; it wasn't their nature.

A calmness crept through her. She hurt still, but an inner part relaxed. This was the last. The river gripped her and drew her to him, and she understood she would not be coming back up. Light faded.

Then a vise clamped her upper arm. A surge. A tremendous force, and she was clear of the stream. Air! There was air to breathe, but all she could do was cough. She was being carried. Her cheek rested on skin. Huge arms wrapped her close until they were on the bank. Gently, her rescuer put her down. Rock warmed her back; her hands lay flat in the heat; her head dropped onto the warmth. Against the sky stood a figure strangely shaped. Weena's vision swirled—she could barely focus—but before she passed out she saw in wonder, he was a giant.


Weena's life appeared no different from the other Eloi. She was raised by the mothers, played with the other children, learned in time not to eat poisonous berries, grew to adult height, lay with the boys when she wanted, loved the sun and feared the night. If there was a variation, it was in her absentmindedness, her willingness to explore beyond the gray home's grounds, to mourn the loss of friends. She cried, which puzzled the others greatly. In the mornings when some Eloi were missing, and the others went off to bathe or play in the grass, she sat by herself. There weren't even words for what she was feeling, but the friends were gone. In the dark the Morlocks came and took them. They would never return. There were no words to explain the space in her chest. It ached in emptiness. Then, later, there was another emotion she had no name for. She envisioned herself rising above the Morlocks, fear banished, the sun in her hands, striding toward them, and they fled.


After he made sure Weena was not going to die, the giant donned strange clothes fastened together with round pieces of bones. Weena watched him dress, all fear of the night for the moment banished. He was *huge*, almost her own height again taller than she was, and broad and strong. The face was rounded and lined with wrinkles near the eyes and corners of his mouth. Oddly enough, his hair was straight. His speech baffled her. When she couldn't answer him, he shook his head, gave up and wandered away.

Weena followed, staying out of sight. Soon she saw that he appeared to be exploring with purpose. He walked in widening circles, stopping only when he came to the river, then reversing himself. Buildings interested him, even the empty ones no one had lived in for as long as Weena could remember. Even the dark buildings no one entered.

He moved with such purpose! She'd never seen anyone go from place to place as if one were more important than the other.

Who was this alien creature? What did he want here? How was it he could go into the dark without fear?

Weena resolved to find out more. She searched the bushes for flowers to string together until she'd made a necklace big enough. Her nimble fingers wove them together. If the giant saved her from the river, he would not hurt her now, and if he didn't fear the darkness, maybe she would be safe with him. When she finished, she approached, and he let her put the flowers around his neck. They spent the afternoon sitting in a stone arbor, where Weena soon learned some of his speech, but not enough to ask questions. He taught her his words for rock and grass and tree and everything he could point at around him, and then taught her hand and foot and face.

When, in the afternoon, the giant went wandering again, Weena tried to stay with him, but his pace was too fast, and he was going too far from the gray home. The sun moved toward the horizon, and even though Weena cried out after him, he did not return. She fled to the gray home just as the sun touched the horizon. A chill shook her as dusk poured over the land. The giant was alone outside, and night was coming.

No one asked her who he was or what he wanted. The Eloi chatted idly among themselves, and even though Weena had spent the most extraordinary afternoon, not one questioned her. She tried to tell some of them, "The giant went into the dark buildings! The giant has stayed outdoors after the sun set!" but none seemed interested. *She* would have been fascinated. If someone told her such a story, *she* would hang on every word.

Late in the evening, long after the Eloi had gone to sleep, Weena sat up watching the shadow on the wall that was the door into the gray home. Would he return, or would something else come through the door tonight? The moon was over three quarters gone. In a few nights, there would be no moon. It would do no good to run. All she could do would be to lie still and hope they passed over her. It was all any of them could do.

Then, a figure came through the door. Weena gasped; he was so sudden. She'd almost forgotten already how large he was. He found a place and lay down. She rose, walked carefully among the sleeping Eloi, and joined him. At first, he seemed surprised, but he let her rest her head on his arm, and soon he was asleep. Weena stayed still, her eyes open. Even his breathing was big; he rumbled behind her. She could feel the heat broadcasting from his chest. His hand, only a foot from her face, lay palm up, each finger a massive curve of strength. She put her hand on his; hers was tiny.

When Weena was young, before she learned about the night, she built a dam on a stream. The rivulet wound its way down a shallow gully behind the gray home until it joined the larger waters. She didn't want to walk all the way to the river to bathe. It seemed so silly. By the time she returned, she'd be just as hot as she'd been before, so she gathered round stones and put them in the water. Methodically she built a wall, and as the wall grew across the stream, the water rose. After the sun was nearly done for the day, a good sized pool had grown behind her wall.

In the morning she took some friends to see it. "Look," one said, "Weena has found a pool for us to play in."

"I did not find it," she said. "I built it."

"Why would you do that?"

Weena didn't have an answer. How could she explain the feeling she had while watching the water rise? Bit by bit it swallowed the bank upstream. Gradually it deepened. Her heart filled too. There was a joy in seeing the rushing water stilled. If the wall was bigger, everyone from the gray home could bathe here. They could bathe wherever they found a stream!

But she couldn't say that. Her friends splashed in her pool for the day, and the next day they walked to the river the way they always had. Weena knocked a hole in the wall.

In the morning, the giant ate with the Eloi, trying to talk, but they became bored shortly and no one remained but Weena. She told him the word for each fruit, for the drink, for the table and cushions, for door and window. He told her his words. Soon they left together, and she followed him as he continued exploring buildings, fearlessly plunging into darkened structures, some that Weena knew contained Morlock passages, but despite her pleas he didn't seem concerned.

Where did he come from? What secret did he possess that made him so fearless? The longer she followed, the more amazed she became. In the afternoon, he took them to the winged statue. He walked around it. Weena sat on a smooth stone bench and watched. He pushed on the bronze base, and from his expression, she knew he was frustrated. Clearly he wanted in. Why would he want that? This too was a Morlock place. If he could open it, he would only face a passage into the dark where no Eloi returned.

Weena hopped off her bench. The giant had placed his ear against the base, then rapped his knuckles against the metal. He moved a foot farther and did this again. Weena touched his back. "What are you looking for? You will wake the Morlocks."

They didn't have enough language to understand each other yet, but he showed her tracks in the lawn. Something heavy had rested in the grass twenty feet from the pedestal. The giant pantomimed dragging an object and pointed to the marks on the ground. She understood. Something of his had been pulled into the Morlock passage, and they'd shut the door to it. After a long series of gestures and using the few words they both knew, she began to understand that the Morlocks had stolen a "vehicle," something the giant traveled in. Weena tried to imagine what the vehicle would look like. Where would he go in it, and why weren't there marks in the grass that showed how the vehicle got there? The lawn was soft from rains and hail storms over the last few days, even their feet left prints, but there was no sign that showed how the vehicle arrived. Did it fly? Weena asked him if he came out of the sky. It took a few tries before he understood what she was asking. He laughed, a booming sound that startled her at first, and he shook his head.

Weena patted his hand, having no words to say to him. If she could just learn what he knew, maybe she could face the night. For the first time since she'd given herself to the river, she shook off its chill. Her throat didn't feel constricted by the water's rush. She could breathe.

That evening, despite her protests, he slept away from the gray home, in the open. Didn't he know about the new moon? But he was determined to sleep on the grass near the winged statue. Weena struggled within herself. He lay down without fear. Shut his eyes. He didn't care if she came or went. He was a giant, safe within himself. She looked at the complex shadows in the bushes, the darkening horizon, and lay down beside him.


Weena learned about boys while gathering flowers one morning in the spring. She'd followed a group of children, and as they spread out down the hill, they separated until she was alone with a boy she didn't know very well. He slept in a different home and had other friends, but he was nice. He smiled at her as they walked together around a pile of vine-choked rubble. Weena smiled back, then moved into low bushes to pick handfuls of yellow blossomed Cheek-daisy.

Something soft hit her ear. She looked up. The boy tossed a flower at her and smiled again. She threw one back, and soon they were wrestling in the soft grass.

Weena knew what was happening. The more experienced girls talked about it, and the adults made love in the open, but she had never done it herself. Some girls said that it hurt the first time. She was frightened, just a little, as she pulled her tunic up around her waist, but it didn't hurt hardly at all, and it was over before she had time to think much about it. Still, it seemed special, and they stayed together for the rest of the day, holding hands and kissing.

The boy's name was Tomey, and when the evening fell, Weena asked him to sleep in the gray home. As the darkness deepened, they snuggled into sleep among the other Eloi, his knees fitting neatly into the backs of her legs and his arms wrapped warmly around her chest.

Then, later, when all was nearly black, something woke her. She didn't move. None of the Eloi did. They never did. The Fear was upon her, cutting her from her muscles, paralyzing her. In the pitchy dark, ghostly figures moved among them. Slyly they slid through the room, hunched over, pale shadows among the deeps. One approached her. It's dry foot scraped the floor. This close, its breath rasped. Its hand touched her shoulder, and she came loose inside. Couldn't move. Couldn't inhale. It reached behind her, pushed its hand along her back and pried Tomey off. His arm pulled out from beneath her; his other dragged across her chest.

Then the Morlock was off, carrying Tomey like a dead thing across his shoulder. Tomey never made a sound.

In the morning, no one talked about their missing friends. Weena looked around her. They rose, ate their fruit, spoke among themselves, made ready to bathe or to play outside. She couldn't speak to them. Instead a pressure built inside her, it filled her lungs, eddied into her throat and pushed at the back of her eyes. Then she wept. Some looked at her as they left, but no one asked her to explain. When they were all gone, the huge room echoed with her sobs.


*O*ver the next couple of days, Weena learned the giant's language as he learned hers. As he continued his explorations, she watched him carefully. He *knew* things; he had an attitude about things. At a brown structure, nearly covered with trees and prickly bushes, a stuck door stymied him. Weena waited to see what he would do. His approach fascinated her. He didn't come to an obstruction and give up as the Eloi did— he worried the problem until he solved it. How would he act here? The door to the brown structure had always been closed. The building was impenetrable; everyone knew that, but the giant dug at the door's base, pulling rock and dirt out by the handful. He jammed his fingers into a crack and tugged again. The door moved! Not enough to let him in, but it had never occurred to her to change the door's condition. The giant found a stout branch, worked it into the wider gap and pulled back on it. Slowly the door gave way. He dropped the branch, then squeezed into the building. Weena looked at the branch for a long time. It was like looking at the stream behind the gray home when she was young. There was a problem: she didn't want to walk to the river to bathe. There was a solution: dam up the current until a pool formed.

Weena crouched by the branch, ran her fingers along the rough bark, fingered the place where the door had stripped it to the green wood. She rubbed the sap between her fingers. It smelled fresh. The Morlocks—now there was a problem, she thought. Was there a solution?

The giant emerged, his face smudged.

"It's empty," he said. "What happened to your people? They built these wonderful structures." He waved his hand. From where they stood, she saw a half-dozen other buildings. Some were homes where Eloi slept at night. Some were like the brown building beside them now, abandoned, useless, *dark* places where Eloi never went.

"We do not build," she said. "They have always been here since the day the world was born."

He shook his head. "No, dear Weena. They were built by people. Your people I suspect, thousands of years ago. By the descendants of my people." He looked sad and said more to himself than to her, "What happened to us?"


*B*y the afternoon, Weena was too tired to follow the giant any further. She returned to the gray home to eat. Thoughtful, she munched a fruit in the warm light that poured through the windows high on the gray home's walls. A boy she recognized but had never talked to sat beside her. "You speak with the giant. What does he say?"

She looked him over. He was younger than her by a year or two. Bright eyes. Curious eyes, something she didn't see in the Eloi ever. In the days she'd spent with the giant, no one had asked her about him. "He asks a lot questions," she said.

"About what?"

"Why do you want to know?"

Around them, other Eloi ate or played or talked their idle chatter.

He squirmed in his seat, didn't meet her eyes. "I'm sorry if I'm bothering you. It's just...well...sometimes I...wonder about things."

The silence stretched between them. She could tell he was on the verge of bolting.

"So do I," she said.

He looked up gratefully. "Really? I thought I was the only one."

"What is your name?" she said.

"Blythe."

"I am happy to meet you, Blythe."

She spent the afternoon answering his questions until evening came, then she went outside to find the giant, who continued to sleep away from the gray home, fearless to the approach of the new moon and the Morlocks.


*O*n his fifth morning with Weena, the giant marched to one of the Morlock portals, a low, circular wall around a bottomless shaft, protected by a sturdy, stone cupola. There were dozens of them in the area.

"I'll come back, Weena," he said, and kissed her on the forehead.

At first Weena didn't understand what he intended, but when he threw one leg over the wall, she grabbed his shirt sleeve and pulled him back. "You can not go down. The Morlocks live there."

He shrugged her off and vanished into the shaft. Weena peered down after him, her limbs shaking. He was already many feet deep. He smiled at her, then continued the descent. Weena watched after him until she could see him no more. A dull thudding vibration came from below, and she could feel air being drawn into the shaft.

Until this time she thought her interest in the giant was to find out what he knew, to learn from him, but as she peered into the blackness, she realized she worried about him. She didn't want him to be hurt.

She sat on the grass near the cupola, determined to wait. Soon, Blythe came and sat beside her. It seemed obvious that he'd been watching them from some hidden place.

"Will he come back?" he said.

"How can he?" Weena plucked a blade of grass, wrapped it tight around her finger until the grass broke.

"He is a giant," Blythe said with confidence.

Weena thought about this with wonder. "Yes, he is," but she didn't believe that he would return.

"He will teach us how to protect ourselves from the Morlocks."

Astonished, Weena looked at him. Although she'd thought such things, she'd never heard anyone say them.

But Weena didn't believe the giant would return until some time later when his hand appeared at the wall's edge, and he crawled out to collapse on the grass.

Crying with joy, Weena kissed his hands and face until the giant laughed at her and hugged her close. Then he fell back and slept. Weena sat with him, holding his hand until he woke much later.

*T*hat afternoon the giant went exploring again with renewed purpose. He wouldn't tell Weena, but something he'd seen underground clearly bothered him. In each building, he examined the doors, the broken windows. In many he found Morlock passages, and he left in disgust. Unlike his trips before, when Weena tired, he picked her up and let her sit upon his shoulder.

Weena wrapped her arm around his head. He set out away from the gray home in a straight line, and his long strides swallowed ground at a dizzying speed. After a while, she could see they were heading toward a distant building, a huge, green structure in the hills that no Eloi she knew had ever visited. Soon, though, the sun slipped behind the hills, and the air grew cool.

"We need to go back," she said. Overhead the first stars glimmered through the dusk. She clung tightly, but he didn't answer. He appeared tireless. Weena wondered if they would walk all night. Could the Morlocks even catch them at this pace? Would they dare attack him? He'd gone straight into their lair and emerged unscathed. Maybe he couldn't be hurt. Maybe they feared him as much as she feared them.

She thought about this as the night swept over the land. Maybe he had no secrets to discover. If all that protected him was his size, then she might as well return to the river and let herself drown. She remembered the moment of peace, the comforting water's roar as she floated downstream. Then she remembered the first gagging swallow. She shuddered. Was drowning better than the Fear when nothing could move her, when her arms and legs betrayed her, when the Morlocks walked among them?

Still, the giant pushed forward. Weena rested her cheek against his head, closed her eyes against the thousand stars and fell asleep.

*I*n the morning they set off again.

After they had covered some distance, he said, "I come from far away."

Weena walked beside him. He had thrown away his shoes and seemed to have picked up a limp. She chose her words carefully. He didn't talk about himself much. Most of their conversations were about her or the Eloi. "I know. You came in your vehicle the Morlocks stole."

He stopped, sat down and rubbed the heel of one foot. A purple bruise marked it. He massaged it gingerly. "My vehicle doesn't travel *distance*," he said. "It travels in time."

Weena didn't know what to say, so she smiled and nodded.

"My house used to be by the winged statue, where we saw the marks from my vehicle. I didn't move an inch, but I traveled many..." He searched for a word. "Lifetimes. Many, many lives passed while I rode. So many that the world was different. None of these buildings were here. There used to be a city, London, and I lived there with others like me. We ruled great machines in my city that would do our work for us. Make tools for us. Take us from place to place without walking. We could send messages across tremendous distances to learn what was going on in other parts of the world."

He kept talking about where he came from while Weena puzzled over the idea of travel through time. How could one live many lifetimes? And there was only one question that mattered, though. "Were there Morlocks?"

He shook his head. "We had our own demons." The green building stood on a hill beyond a tree-filled valley. They would be there after a short walk. The giant looked across the valley, past the building, as if he didn't see it standing there. "We fought them. We didn't wait for them to consume us." He wiped his mouth. "Mankind was never meant to be cattle."

"I don't understand...cattle?"

"Of course not," he said, shifting his gaze to her. He looked tired. She wondered if he'd slept the night before. "You live on milk and honey. *You're* the fatted calf. What does the herd think about when they're in the holding pens, when they're led up the long ramp to the slaughter house?"

His face flushed. Weena touched his hand. She didn't know all the words he used, but she got the sense of them. "You fought your Morlocks?"

"In a manner of speaking, yes." He squeezed her hand. "I don't know why I should tell you these things, sweet Weena. You are not equipped to understand them. Evolution has robbed you of reason. You live a beautiful life here. A beautiful, thoughtless life with something ugly underneath. Maybe it's best if I don't paint a different picture." He stood, grimaced when he put weight on his foot. "It's better when you are happy."

She thought, but I'm not happy! I'm frightened all the time. What can you teach me? What do you know? But she didn't know how to ask the question. He took her hand, and they started down the hill toward the green building.

Weena walked beside him struggling with a new thought. They *fought* their demons, he said. If he would only show her how.

*T*he green building was tremendous! Weena had never seen a structure so large. The first room's ceiling was vague in shadow, and long spears of hazy light cut through broken windows high above the floor. The giant paused beside a pile of bones so old that many crumbled when he touched them. "This was a dinosaur. We're in a museum," he said. At one side of the room, he cleared dust from sloping shelves. Weena peered around him. The shelves were glass, and within the boxes were stones and animal teeth and other items she did not recognize. The giant moved excitedly from display to display, knocking a perfect storm of dust into the air.

He said, "Here is sulphur. If I could find saltpetre, we could build a little surprise for the Morlocks." But he didn't explain what he meant. He moved from room to room, casting about from one side to the other. Weena trailed him, hushed and expectant. He would find a tool they could use against the Morlocks. They wouldn't need to fear the night of the new moon any longer!

But as the giant continued to search farther into the green building's depths, he found nothing useful, and the rooms grew progressively dark. Weena stayed closer, trying to see into the rooms' unlit corners, wary of the cavernous shadows beneath the tables and machinery they passed. Several times she saw narrow footprints in the dust. The giant didn't notice until a stealthy pattering of footsteps echoed in a room. He grabbed Weena's hand, looked around until he found a metal bar protruding from a rusted, useless machine. He broke it off, hefted its weight. "Now I have something," he said.

Weena bit back her disappointment. All this way for a club? No tools like he'd spoke of? No machines that would jump to his bidding? Just a club? Having clubs would not save the Eloi, even if she could convince the others to use them. Once the sun set, the Fear would petrify them, just as it had immobilized her when Tomey was carried away. The Eloi could not defend themselves in the dark.

The giant said, "We will be out of here soon enough, little Weena." Now he moved from room to room with refreshed urgency. Weena stayed close. Dirt blocked the light through most windows, and the afternoon was wearing away. In a nearly undamaged gallery, the giant found something that pleased him: in an unbroken case, a box of matches. He danced with delight, kicking clouds of choking dust off the floor. In another case, he found a sealed jar that when opened exuded a pungent odor. He was nearly as pleased with this new discovery. "Camphor," he said. "It burns."

Weena didn't know the word, "burns," but she recognized the matches. He'd amazed some Eloi with them in his first days, scratching them against a rock and then showing the yellow, dancing light at its end. Why he was happy to find them, she could not decide. More importantly, the sun through the windows was failing. Tonight was the new moon, and she'd seen too much Morlock sign within this cavernous building. Soon they'd be rising from their subterranean hiding places, and the giant had found nothing helpful other than a club and his glowing toy. Could he protect her? Would he protect her?

At the river, the Eloi had watched her swept down stream. She'd screamed, and none of them moved. Why would the giant help her now? Why had he saved her at the river? She held his hand as they retraced their path through the building until they emerged through the broken doors. The sun rested partly below the horizon. By the time they reached the forest's edge, it was fully night. Oddly the giant had gathered sticks and branches until his arms were full. Weena's eyes ached with trying to see into the woods. There! Was that a white shape moving? There! Another one. Even the giant noticed them slipping from shrub to shrub. The forest air rustled with their passing. Leaves crackled under unseen feet on all sides.

The giant set the branches in a pile on the ground. He scratched one of his matches into its tiny, yellow light. Weena hadn't seen a match at night before. It was surprisingly bright. Then he pushed it into the branches. Twigs grew yellow with a luminous vapor. Branches glowed, and a moving, sinuous presence rose from the wood. Weena leaned forward, fascinated. What is this? she thought. It's beautiful, like the sun captured on the ground, like the diamond ribbon in the stream's center. It threw light into her eyes. She reached for it. The giant stopped her, but she'd already felt its heat. It *is* the sun, she thought. He can make day! For a moment, she forgot the pressing dark around them, the rustling steps just out of sight.

"It's a fire," he said. "Didn't you know?" She heard the surprise in his voice, as if what was happening was a common occurrence.

Soon all the branches crackled in flame. Every once in a while a sharp pop sent sparks flying from the damp wood. An ember landed near her foot, pulsing with heat like a tiny heart.

"Come on." He grabbed her hand and pulled her into the wood. She turned to look back. The burning had crept from the pile of branches into the brush beside it. Fire writhed in the leaves, but it grew smaller the farther they walked. "If we get beyond the forest, we'll be safe enough," he said.

Weena looked up. Through the trees there was no trace of moonlight. Only the occasional star peeked through. She could feel the urge building inside, the Fear, that yelled at her to lie down. Avoid notice! it said. Become still and small and you will live. Something soft touched her neck. She twisted away, slapped against the giant's leg, but she couldn't see. Was it a leaf?

Twigs snapped around them. Indistinct voices, animal voices, murmured in the dark. Weena jerked her attention to each new sound. She was touched again. Her throat froze.

Then the giant let go of her hand.

There was nothing else to do. There was no way to resist the Fear anymore than she could stop from blinking if dirt flew in her eyes or she could stop from inhaling when the river her swept her away. She dropped to the ground. Lay quiet, the Fear said. Be dead. They will pass you by.

But another voice in her mourned. She had lost. The Morlocks would have her. There was nothing to learn from the giant with his long strides and strange clothes and talk of vehicles that traveled through time. He was just a big man with a club, and what good was a club to the Eloi who reacted to threats in the dark by falling down?

A Morlock hand touched her. A horrible soft hand that crept down her arm, around her waist. She couldn't see; it was black as a cave. Weena felt regret through the Fear. If she could cry now, she would cry for herself. None of the Eloi would.

Then, a flash of light. The Morlock hissed, let go and ran away. Cracking her eyes open a tiny bit, she saw the giant light some of the camphor, and the little flame was enough to drive the Morlock back. He pulled branches out of the trees, piled them on the flickering patch. Soon a smoky fire illuminated the trees around them. Still, Weena could not move. She felt the Morlock's hand on her.

The giant picked her up, spoke to her, but she kept her eyes shut. Fear filled her. Closed her throat. Don't let them know you are alive, the Fear said. Soon the giant put her down. He sat beside the fire, and within moments his chin dropped to his chest. He slept.

For a long time Weena stayed on her side, her arm trapped beneath her, her face pressed into the forest floor's dry leaves, watching the fire. Gradually, the Fear left. The cheerful flame leapt through the branches. Green leaves curled, caught fire and vanished in smoky puffs. She crawled next to the giant. On the ground next to him was his box of matches. He must have dropped them. Weena held them close, put her head against the giant's leg. The fire bathed her in warmth. Pungent smoke blanketed them. Watching the flames was mesmerizing. They danced like river waves, always moving in place.

he woke to an uproar. The giant was shouting and all was black. The fire was out! Weena heard him running, yelling incoherently. A creature rushed by her, and then another. The woods reeked with Morlocks, their strange cries rent the air. Her body locked into place. Something stepped on her foot as it ran toward the giant. A metallic crunch silenced one voice. Even gripped by the Fear, Weena smiled. So the giant's club worked for him after all. The Morlocks can be stopped. Her smile slipped away. None of the Eloi would ever know. And what good was the knowledge? They came out at night, when the Fear ruled.

More blows in the dark. Not so loud now. The giant moved away from her, by the sounds of it, fighting Morlocks the whole way. She believed he would survive them. He had gone into their home armed with nothing and emerged. With a club, the giant would be unassailable.

Only now she was alone. Maybe they wouldn't find her, if she stayed absolutely rigid, but Morlocks filled the woods. Their footsteps, their cooing voices were everywhere. When the giant escaped, they would take her.

Weena fought against the Fear. If she could only move. The matches were in her hand. A little movement, hardly any effort at all would light one. She could save herself. The box rested against her fingers. I can grip it, she thought, and she forced her fingers to close around its square shape. A triumph! Had any Eloi ever struggled like this before? Giving in was so much easier. Do nothing. The danger will pass. Her breath came in short gasps now. She pictured the sun beating down the grassy meadows, the diamonds in the stream. Painfully, she rolled onto her back. Real pain, like forcing her limbs into unnatural position. A moan escaped her. Weena scrinched her face in effort so hard that she saw red in the darkness.

A roaring sound began to overwhelm the Morlocks' shouting. She couldn't hear the giant any more. Like a wind through the trees, it came, and Weena suddenly opened her eyes. The red was real. The forest was on fire. Their first fire must have spread, and a bright wall of light flowed toward her through the trees. It released her, the light, and her muscles relaxed. She sat. A Morlock broke into the tiny clearing, its broad eyes streaming tears; it slammed into a tree, twirled in pain, and ran on straight toward the flame.

Weena stood, brushed twigs and leaves off her tunic. The fire didn't leap from tree to tree quickly. She had no trouble staying in front of its progress. Every once in a while, other blinded Morlocks would stagger past, some toward the fire, some wandering in circles. She stayed away from them.

When morning came, parts of the forest still burned. Weena could not find the giant. Exhausted, finally, she walked toward the home, but it was miles and miles away, and she didn't have him to carry her. By the time the sun was overhead, she was too tired to go on, so she stretched out on the grass. Wood smoke filled her nose, and she slept.

**B**lythe met her at the winged statue as evening fell. Footsore and hungry, Weena sat on the bench she'd rested on days ago when the giant had knocked on its metal walls.

"The doors were open earlier, and there was a machine behind them," Blythe said. He sat next to her on the bench. "The giant went in. Then the doors closed. The Morlocks must have got him."

Weena put her hands behind her and stretched her back. She had never walked for a whole day before. Her body was a medley of aches and surprising stiffness.

"I don't think so, not if he got to the machine first," she said. The giant had told her he could travel through time. She imagined him vanishing from the Morlocks' grasp, just as they descended upon him.

"Either way, he's gone," said Blythe. His shoulder slumped. "We've learned nothing. We're just as helpless as before." He looked at the sun as it slid below the horizon. "The night's coming. We should go to the home."

In the distance, the hills glowed pink. A line of skinny clouds in the west flamed brightly in the sunset.

Weena said, "No. We should gather wood and pile it by the home's door." She fingered the box of matches. There were enough to get them through this new moon, or they could keep the fire burning constantly. They had time to solve the problem of making fire for themselves.

"What good will that do? We need the giant to save us," said Blythe.

Weena looked at him. The giant had said that her people had built the structures. They had commanded great tools. Once the night had been theirs. If she could see it; if Blythe could see it, there would be others.

"No, Blythe, we don't."

# *Voices*

ome things happen that you have to figure out how to live with. If you don't, they will kill you," said Pierce.

"You can't keep taking equipment without getting into trouble," said Linda, from her work station. She looked concerned and grandmotherly. "It's not ethical. There are laws."

Pierce glanced up from the briefcase full of electronics. His face dragged against the bones—full of exhaustion and whatever had taken the place of grief—and his brain moved too slowly to lie. It had been weeks since he'd slept more than an hour or two in a row. "You don't always think about consequences. Go ahead and report me," he said, snapping the lid shut. "Besides, her voice is everywhere," he whispered.

He coughed twice. Spring and summer allergies had settled into his lungs and turned into a dry, whistling hack he hadn't been able to shake.

In the hallway outside of the lab, he heard Linda say to his back, "Nothing you find out will make it any better."

She's probably right, he thought as he drove to Denver's City Park. Even with the Aural History Institute's capability of going back in time to record sound, history was still a mystery. Sound records only provided more questions: why did people do anything? Why did they behave the way they did? Why did events turn out one way and not another? Human actions weren't always the result of cause and effect, and motivations were still only guessed at. Sometimes people just acted out. History was a joke.

He shook his head. Surely there must be answers, he thought. We only have to keep searching. History is about making sense of the chaos.

Yesterday's recording of two days at the Chocolate Liqueur's manager's office a week and a half before Sarah's death, had been a wash. Fourteen phone calls, all business related: a long bull session with one of the waitresses about house hunting and tropical fish and several short talks with restaurant employees over hours or what needed to be done for the day. Evidently, Sarah hadn't spent much time in her office.

No mention of his name in two days, though. Nothing about her up-coming wedding.

He turned automatically. Today's recording wouldn't require subter-fuge like yesterday's, where he had to sit in the new manager's office, pretending to fill out a job application while the sensitive instruments in the briefcase below him searched for the time he had preset, recording all the sounds that had taken place in the room then. The mechanism whirred slightly, and he had kept shuffling his feet to cover the sound. Annoyed, the manager took his application wordlessly and waved him away from her desk.

As good as the computer's search engine was, picking Sarah's voice from the hours of silence or other conversations, listening to everything she said had still taken several hours. He'd played back parts, adjusting the mix, enhancing sound quality, identifying who she was speaking to. A printout tucked into the back of the note book listed one hundred and three voices from the hundreds of days of recordings he'd made, but only twenty-seven had names beside them. The rest were unknown.

And in all those hours of voices, of Sarah talking, he hadn't heard her once say why she changed her mind.

If I can reconstruct the past maybe I can understand it, he thought. Maybe I can understand my part in it.

That morning, as the sun washed coldly through the lab's window, Pierce had found himself listening over and over to the same irrelevant sentence: Sarah asking someone in her crystalline clear voice, "Are any of the avocados soft at all?"

He fell asleep on a couch beside the Aural History file cabinets, and Linda found him there when she opened the lab.

City Park slid by on his left, and he almost missed the parking lot. He set the dates before he got out of the car: February 17 and April 28, the day they were engaged, and the day she broke the engagement. The best of times and the worst of times, he thought.

Pierce squeezed the handle of the briefcase as he walked toward the park bench where both events had occurred. Mid-morning on a weekday in August, the park was mostly empty. A handful of toddlers with a single supervisor ran around the marble dolphin sculpture on the street side of the park. On the other side, a row of high rises bordered the bike path and neatly trimmed grass. A scattering of solid wooden benches stretched from Broadway at the east end of the park to Lincoln at the other.

He sat heavily on "their" bench. Dark green paint absorbed the sun's heat, and its warmth baked the backs of his legs. His fingers rested lightly on the briefcase while he sat motionless for a long time.

Somewhere in time it's February, he thought; she's still sitting on this bench. She's wearing the yellow ski parka I bought her for Christmas, has her hands underneath her because we'd cleared the wet snow to give her a place to sit. Two kids play on the bike path, except it's snow covered too, and they're having troubles with their sled. Its runners keep digging in instead of riding on the top.

Tiny heat waves danced off the bike path's asphalt now, but he could see the snow there too; the kids laughed, tugging at their sled, and beside him Sarah's breath came out in little fogs that danced around her face.

Through the smell of summer grass and cars on the street, he could also feel the sharp bite of winter air in his nose. He took another deep breath, then coughed loudly, a pair of seal barks that trailed into whistles.

What did she say, though? he thought. What were we talking about before I asked her? What did her voice sound like before she knew I wanted to marry her? What, exactly, did it sound like when she said yes? Can I hear in her yes a hint of the confusion that would come in two months?

He opened the case and pressed the record button. He imagined a tiny microphone hurtling back to rest at this same spot six months earlier, recording everything that was said then. Nothing physical really traveled, though. The device reached back into the continuum to record what had happened in the past. It didn't go there itself.

The readouts confirmed the device was functioning correctly. A short distance presented no problems in chronological drift, not like his current project at the Aural History Institute, which was finding early Denver political speeches. Going back a hundred years meant he could miss by as much as a day.

His problems were tiny compared to the work some groups were doing, like the one trying for George Washington's inaugural, or the ridiculously ambitious group in Israel who hoped to capture the Sermon on the Mount. Not only were they dealing with incredible chronological slop, but no one was sure when or where the sermon occurred, if it did at all.

Still, a six-month jump presented no challenge. He wouldn't miss by more than a few minutes, and the device could hold two-days' worth of sound.

Pierce shut his eyes. He almost felt Sarah beside him, her cheeks flushed in the cold air, her wide smile lighting the rest of her face. She had rested her hand on his wrist. He remembered how warm it felt. "Yes," she had said. "Yes, I'll marry you." She put her head on his shoulder.

On the same bench, though—on the same bench two months later at the end of April she'd cried, holding her head in her hands, refusing to look at him. Crusts of old snow, blackened with city soot surrounded the bench. On Broadway, the cars splashed grimly through dirty water, and the clouds scudded across the sky like tattered ghosts.

Time held them both.

On July 2 she married Baylor, head of the Aural History Institute, and on July 7, while Baylor was in Dallas working on the Kennedy project, her Victorian house with its crummy wiring she'd planned on replacing in the fall burned down with her in it. Baylor flew back on the red-eye when he heard the news. Now, in August, Pierce was sitting on the same bench, gathering the echoes of her voice solidly anchored in time. Why did it all happen? he thought. Where's the sense in it?

It all existed at once. The bench beneath him now was warm, but once it was wet, and another time it was cold. Sarah held his wrist and leaned against him, breathing winter in and out in fog and whiteness, and she also shook in tears, her face buried in her hands. Everything, all of it, tumbled around and around. But time wasn't like memory. It didn't fade and mix. It didn't change with perception or become disordered. Sounds in time's continuum, at least, were measurable and retrievable. In five years they might be able to capture visuals too, but presently they were limited to sound. Sound would have to be enough, he thought. In sound he would find the reason for the emptiness now.

The mechanism chirped softly, and he knew that it had finished with the February recording, capturing four hours in a few minutes. The recorder moved on to April.

That afternoon, Pierce plowed through several hours of spidery sounding recordings of state senate from the previous century. The new recordings of Sarah at City Park waited on his desk, but he couldn't work on it until after hours.

Baylor's office stood open, revealing a corner of his desk and a droopy fern in a pot on the floor.

Through Pierce's headphones, Henry Teller, one of Colorado's Republican senator's boomed out a speech he gave several times in 1893. "We are neither cast down nor dejected, but this is mindless destruction," he said repeatedly, as a lead in to each point attacking the repeal of the Sherman Silver act, which would close hundreds of mines and put much of the mining industry into bankruptcy. "We do not disguise the fact that we are to go through the valley of the shadow of death," he said with his particular hyperbole.

Baylor stepped into the doorway. His gray suit seemed more businesslike than academic, and the athleticism of his build and stance only accented his nearly white hair and silver-rimmed glasses. He scanned the room, nodding when he caught Pierce's eye, then said something to Linda that Pierce didn't catch through the headphones. They laughed, and through the thundering conclusion of Teller's speech, Pierce watched his boss and Linda chat amiably.

Baylor didn't look like a man whose wife of one week had died in a fire a month ago. He was relaxed and tanned. He seemed well rested, at ease, and, as always, oozing with a breezy confidence that calmed potential clients, nervous about the thousands of dollars a thorough aural search cost.

He'd come to work the day after, Pierce had heard, while Pierce himself spent the day in the waiting room at Denver General, consoling Sarah's parents and being consoled himself.

Pierce categorized the speech, stored it and moved on to the next step. The computer displayed a circular grid with sound sources highlighted. Teller's voice was loudest and brightest on the screen. The other spots were coded and some tentatively identified. Pierce ran the speech back, this time isolating on the weaker sounds. One was a fan, he decided; another was a conversation between what was probably a pair of state dignitaries. He entered his observations mechanically into the computer. Maybe some grad student doing a paper on politics in the west would be interested later.

A third sound puzzled him. It rumbled for a few seconds, then paused, over and over. Pierce tapped a pencil against the monitor, switching from one sound filtering routine to the next. The display next to the circular grid showed the pattern of sound waves in the familiar pattern of jagged lines. Finally he decided it was a man snoring.

Baylor flicked off his office light, and with a start, Pierce realized how late it was. Linda waved as she left, and a moment later Baylor closed his door, strode across the room and sat on the corner of Pierce's desk.

"You don't look good, Pierce. Are you okay?" Baylor's voice was soft, which made it harder to find and record in time.

Every day since Sarah's death, Baylor had made an effort to make small talk with Pierce. Pierce couldn't remember him being nearly as friendly before.

"Fine, yes," said Pierce. A long pause stretched between them. "Thank you," he added finally.

Baylor shifted on the desk, bumping his knee against Pierce. "I know how difficult this has been on you. Get through the Teller speeches and take a week off."

Pierce forced himself to smile. "I appreciate the concern, but really, I'm all right."

"Maybe the weekend will help." Baylor stood, then leaning over Pierce's shoulder, glanced at the computer display. He pointed to the sound source Pierce had just been studying for the last half hour. "Looks like a guy snoring."

After he left, Pierce loaded in the first recording, the proposal.

"Hey, buddy," she'd said. They were her first words.

"God, it's cold." Pierce didn't sound nervous to himself, but listening with his eyes closed, headphones clamped solidly, he remembered now how tense he'd been. Every word was just delaying the question he wanted to ask. He remembered thinking that at any moment she would want to know what was the matter, but she didn't say a thing. She laughed instead.

"Here, sit on your hands like I am. It's warmer, and you won't get your pants wet," she said.

He'd already forgotten how optimistic she had been. Never, it's cold, but here's a way to stay warm.

"Of course, when you're older, like me, you'll know these things," she had continued.

He laughed, and it sounded easy. "By a week!"

When he finally got to the proposal, it was just as he remembered. He listened to her acceptance a dozen times. It was always the same: totally sure, totally in love. What happened in the next month? How could she go from loving him to leaving him? How could she possibly have married Baylor?

He let the recording run on, and she said something he didn't remember. After she'd said, "Yes, yes I'll marry you," there was no conversation for a few minutes. He remembered holding her; his throat tightened thinking about it, listening to the silence of their embrace. Then she said, "You could go back in time and record us, couldn't you?"

"I suppose," he'd said lazily.

"That's nice to know—that it's always there."

"Like a contract," he said with a laugh.

"Would you ever do that?" She sounded lazy too. Her voice carried no edge. Pierce remembered her forehead against his cheek.

Pierce joked, "That would be breaking the law."

"Yeah, but would you?"

"It's possible" A tumble of snow fell from a nearby tree, thumping solidly to the ground. "I might, for you."

He ran the whole conversation through again, this time with a different filtering equation, trying to get the essence of her voice, the pure stuff. The truth. Were the seeds of her decision to leave him present even then?

They'd left the park holding hands inside his coat pocket, and instead of going back to work, had gone to her house and made love. It was only the second time they'd been together, and they were nervous. He'd gotten into her bed first, and when she came out of the bathroom, she had a bath towel wrapped around her. She'd let the towel slip a little and said shyly, "How do you like this?"

The afternoon had passed in languorous glory in her old house. He drowned joyfully in bedsheets and warm breath and moist pleasures.

Pierce shook himself and pulled the headphones down around his neck. His ears ached from pressing the phones so tightly to the sides of his head.

He popped the recording out of the player and turned it over in his hand. The other conversation would be there too. The beginning and end of their love. Bookends, so to speak, of sound.

Florescent lights buzzed softly in the deserted office. It was long past midnight; he'd lost hours playing back the old conversation, listening for any clue to put some sense to the last few weeks. But it hadn't helped. Her words rang in his ears, "Yes. Yes, I'll marry you."

Her twenty-fifth birthday would have been next month. They'd celebrated Baylor's fiftieth at the end of January. Thoughtful, Pierce opened the recorder, set new coordinates, then checked the office one more time to be sure he was alone. Feeling paranoid, he moved softly across the room to Baylor's door, opened it, then slipped through the darkness to his desk. The whir of the device sounded monstrously loud in the quiet room, and Pierce jumped at the click of the air-conditioning when it kicked on.

Pierce listened to the new recording. The morning of Sarah's death, Baylor received Linda's condolences politely, refusing her suggestion that he should go home. After Linda left the office, Baylor made quiet sounds as he worked at his desk. Drawers opened and closed. A pen scratched on paper. He took some calls and made some others. If Pierce hadn't known, he wouldn't have been able to distinguish this day from other days.

Mid-afternoon, on the day after Sarah died, Baylor made a call to his insurance agent. Pierce listened intently.

"I'd like to report a claim," Baylor said, his voice matter of fact and calm.

"Right. My wife died in a fire yesterday." Baylor paused. "No. No, I'd rather do it now. It's better than thinking about it." He answered all the questions, then hung up.

"Linda," Baylor called. Pierce winced at the high volume. "I think I will go home early today."

Linda's voice, very faintly replied, "Oh, I think that's best, dear. You should get away for a while."

Dawn broke gradually, and the sun was well up before Pierce listened to the April recording. She'd started crying after Pierce had said, "I can't wait for the spring melt."

"What's wrong?" he said. Cars mumbled in the background. The bench creaked. She'd continued sobbing. He coughed in the recording. The allergies were bothering him even then, each cough sliding into the airy whistle that just tickled his throat and provoked the next one.

Pierce opened his eyes; scratches marred the desk's surface. The computer display showed the orientation of the sound sources. Lines jumped, and she said, "I'm not happy, Pierce. I've got to call it off."

He hadn't answered. Hands clamped against the earphones, he couldn't even hear his breathing anymore, just the hitches in Sarah's throat as she cried. He held his breath now; it was like being there, her sounds were so clear. A hot iron fist bunched in his chest, and he shut his eyes again. Then she said, "It's not you. It's me. I'm not ready."

"Why?" Pierce said to the emptiness of the office. He coughed and his lungs hurt. Everywhere he'd recorded in the past weeks, he'd searched for that answer, and he hadn't found it yet. She hadn't told anyone why, after six weeks, she decided she didn't love him. She hadn't told anyone why she married Baylor.

Pierce took a recorder and went home. He fell asleep without undressing, and when the phone woke him, it was already dark outside.

It took a few seconds for him to recognize Linda.

"One of the machines is missing," she said.

"I've got it." He rubbed at his eyes. Nothing in his brain functioned right yet, and he was afraid he sounded incoherent.

"Someone at the restaurant recognized you. They called the police, and the police called Baylor. I think they were just checking up on the complaint, but if they find out you took unauthorized recordings, you could be arrested. You could get our license revoked."

Pierce blinked hard and shook his head before he answered.

"I was asleep. Sorry. Why'd they call Baylor?"

"People are afraid of aural historians. It might seem like harmless work to you, but they're worried that everything they've said in the past could come back to haunt them. Haven't you noticed how much harder it is to get the permits? You know how many states have passed laws forbidding sound sampling less than fifty years old? You can't walk into a place that knows what kind of work you do without them worrying that you're going to record them too. A waitress recognized you. She didn't know your name, but she remembered where you worked. They figured you weren't actually trying to get a job, so they contacted the police."

Pierce took a deep breath. "Did you know Baylor called his insurance claim on Sarah the day after she died?"

Silence hissed for a long time on the line. Finally Linda said, "Well, he's a cold fish."

"I don't think he loved her. What kind of guy would be out of town without his wife a week after the wedding?"

"Pierce. There's nothing you can find that will change what happened. It doesn't matter."

He said, "I know, Linda. Listen, I've got to get some more sleep. I haven't been myself lately."

"Good. That sounds like the best plan. Monday we can straighten the restaurant thing out with Baylor, and we can get this behind us." She sounded relieved.

When he hung up, Pierce rechecked the charge on the batteries in the recorder, then headed for his car.

At Sarah's house, yellow, plastic ribbon still surrounded the burned remnants. In the streetlight's garish illumination, the broken timbers stuck up like a pocket lunar landscape. He ducked under the ribbon, then carefully picked his way through the rubble. His feet stirred ash and the smell of burnt wood. A menthyl cough drop coated the back of his throat. The neighborhood was too close together. If he were heard, someone would call the cops.

Her house had been a perfect reflection of her. She'd hung art prints on the wall, mostly impressionists, and black and white photographs she'd taken herself of falling down barns and old country fences. Standing in the remains of the house, Pierce tried to orient himself to what he remembered. The burnt patch of land seemed much smaller than the original house. He figured, approximately, that he now stood where the living room used to be. She'd had a phone on a delicate cherrywood end table. He placed the recorder about where it might have been and activated it.

A car turned the corner onto her street, and Pierce ducked low. Charred wood flaked beneath his fingers as long shadows swept past him. He stayed down until the tail lights vanished.

A chirp from the briefcase told him that the first recording was done. Using a penlight, he reset the instrument and started it again. He didn't bother standing up. Cars came along often enough that he figured it wasn't worth the effort to get out of the ash, and he didn't feel he had the energy to do it anyway.

Finally, lying back, he stared at the stars. The device hummed quietly beside him. Complicated electronics were right now holding a position in time, recording everything that they could. *They* were there, where Sarah still lived and breathed.

Pierce remembered once when he was a student, he'd been taking an exam that he wasn't well prepared for, and as he struggled with the little he knew about the subject, the professor had walked by his desk. The answers are all right there, so close I can almost reach out and touch them, Pierce had thought. But the professor had walked on, and Pierce knew nothing more than he had before. He could feel Sarah's presence like that. She had walked through this burnt out space a thousand times. She was all around him, in time, but he couldn't touch her. The best he could do was send the recorder back and let it do its job.

Moving the briefcase into where the bedroom used to be, he recorded a few hours of the past. Twice a police car drove by, sweeping the ruins with a searchlight, while Pierce hid himself behind a low remnant of wall.


**P**ierce let the computer kick out dead air time. Then an index of sounds scrolled onto the screen, labeling when each section was recorded, how long it was, and, where possible, what it was. Many of the segments were Sarah's voice alone. Some were Sarah and Baylor. A handful were not voices: refrigerator, air conditioner, telephone ringing, etc. And some were labeled "anomalous"—the computer didn't recognize the sound.

Hand trembling and a little sick, Pierce picked July 2, the day Sarah married Baylor. Linda was right, thought Pierce. People *should* be afraid of the aural technology. It is, essentially, limitless eavesdropping. What person could stay sane knowing that anything he or she said could be retrieved later? How could any moment remain intimate if a microphone out of time could drop into your room, into your life, for someone else's consumption? He thought, what right do I have to listen to Sarah's final days?

For that matter, what if the technological advances delivered on their promise, and in five or ten years *visual* records of past events could be made? What if the current prejudice against the admissibility of pre-present retrieval of criminal information changed? For all he knew, his actions right now were being recorded for a trial in the future. As soon as he played back the recording, he was committing an illegal act, albeit at this point a minor one.

He pushed playback anyway.

In the recording, a door opened. Sarah's voice. It was 4:30 on July 2, an hour and a half after the wedding. She was too far away from the pick up, maybe standing outside the door, but clearly she wasn't happy. The tone sounded upset. She was arguing with someone, Baylor.

"It's our honeymoon night," Pierce heard her say clearly. The reply was incomprehensible.

After more words, the door shut. Her dress swished loudly as she passed the recording point. Drawers slammed open. A lot of clatter. Then the shower turned on. As far as Pierce could tell, she was alone. Baylor hadn't come in. Pierce knew he left for Dallas the next morning. Until her parents called him on the night of the fire, he had assumed that Sarah was with him.

Later, she picked up the phone and punched in a number. Then she hung it up immediately. She did that twice more.

By 10:15, she was in bed. Nothing on the disk after that except household creaks and groans. It was an old house, after all, and as the night cooled it shrank against itself with plenty of protest.

The 3rd and 4th were a repetition of the first night without the argument at the door. She took a phone call on the 4th; it sounded like it was from Baylor.

"I'm doing fine," she said, her tone cool and reserved. "And you?"

"That's good...How's the project going?...That's interesting...Uh huh ...Uh huh...Yes...I'll expect to hear from you." She hung up. She didn't move from the couch; the recording point was only a foot or two from her. Pierce heard her suck air between her teeth. Then, distinctly, she said, "The shit."

Pierce drew back a bit and played it again. Sarah never swore. Never. And it embarrassed him to have heard it from her. Or worse, it embarrassed him that he'd intruded into her privacy to hear this. Still, a little part of him exulted. What if she were unapproachably happy in the marriage? How would he feel about that?

On top of the embarrassment, he felt horrifying sadness. He could taste it in his mouth and feel it in his face. Her final days were not good. She married, and her husband left town for a week. Would he have wished that on her?

Why didn't she call him? Everything would have been different if she had only called him.

Pierce listened to her side of four more phone calls in the last days, each one more bitter than the last. Sarah sounded baffled and frustrated. Pierce couldn't hear Baylor's end of the conversations, but he could imagine his calm voice, reassuring her, calming her, refusing to argue.

"I'm not being a little girl!" she yelled once. "This isn't what we talked about before."

They argued about money. He wanted her to sign papers at the bank on the house and car. She had stock.

"Maybe when you grew up, men behaved this way," she said. "It's different now. How about you sign over your mutual fund to me instead?" That ended one of the conversations.

Pierce had lain awake the week after the wedding in agony. It made his cough worse, and he hacked so hard that he thought he would throw up. He didn't know she was still in town. Every time he closed his eyes he could see them together. He couldn't wipe it out. Partly it made him desperate, although there was nothing he could do. But most of all it maddened him. Pointless, hopeless, boiling anger that made him want to punch holes in walls, to tear things down.

He went to work instead, and imagined them in Dallas. Pierce pictured her sitting on the park bench in the yellow jacket. He pictured her in bed, and he could feel her hands on his shoulders, but they weren't his shoulders, and it wasn't him. It was Baylor.

He had to sleep with the lights on.

Pierce looked around the office. The late afternoon sun cast a butter yellow on the walls and equipment. In the cabinets were thousands of files of sound samples, every one marked and sorted. All of history waiting to be observed in its honesty. No interpretation. No prejudices of memory and subjectivity. The actual sounds. The real thing. Unavoidable. Undeniable. Never to fade away.

Like the sounds of Sarah on July 7, her last day, crying on her couch.

She'd placed two calls to Dallas, and left a message both times. "This is Sarah. Please phone."

Pierce's eyes were shut. He cried too. She picked up her phone again, punched in a number, then hung up. Was it his number? He couldn't tell. He tried punching his number on the phone to see if the tones matched, but they all sounded the same to him. The recording didn't give enough tonal difference to be sure.

She cried on the couch for almost an hour, never moving. Pierce didn't fast forward through the section. He laid his head on the scratched surface of the desk, and listened to the rise and fall of her despair. She'd always been so happy that it hurt to hear this coming from her.

Finally, she stopped. The computer showed that a section of her voice was coming, but it didn't show any other sounds. No telephone ringing or knock at the door, just her speaking.

Her breathing was soft and even. Then she sighed. "Pierce," she said. Pierce jerked his head off the desk. "Pierce, if you ever come and listen to this, I want you to know I was wrong about us. I was wrong."

Pierce held the earphones to his head in disbelief. He fumbled at the keyboard and played it back. He clutched double handfuls of his shirt as she said it again.

He whispered into the empty office, "Oh, god, I'm so sorry." It didn't matter why she changed her mind anymore. At the end, she still loved him.

The file played on. She stood from the couch, her clothes swishing, and she walked into the kitchen. Pots clattered. Water ran. Pierce listened to the clink of silverware against a plate.

Outside, the sun set. Pierce listened in real-time. No fast forward. Time crept in the recording at the same pace it occurred. He heard her last hours.

She walked from room to room. Light switches clicked on or off. The shower ran. Then, silence. The computer showed that it was 10:30 in her world. She was sleeping.

Hand shaking, full of dread and resignation, Pierce skipped to just before a sound at 12:15 the computer labeled "anomalous."

Through the headphones, the house was quiet. Not even the creaks that were a part of the early evening. No wind blew. Then, a scratch. The computer barely registered it as a jump in the sound levels. Another sound: the tumblers on her front door turning. A squeak of hinges. A stealthy step.

Pierce sat straight up, eyes closed, seeing the blackness that was the interior of the house in his memory. Another tiny click, a flashlight going on. He could see it in his mind's eye, a handkerchief blocking most of the light.

More whispery hisses like cloth on cloth. A metallic clink. Then, a crackling buzz: the kind of sound a shorted wire would make in an old house where the wiring was ninety years' old and the wood as dry as abandoned dreams.

Then, a cough. A dry, awful cough that ended on a tiny whistle. His cough.

Totally numb, Pierce listened to his own footsteps retreating across the living room—to the subtle rustle, like rainfall on cement, of fire building in the wall.

Still gripping his shirt, he heard the ravenous sound in a few minutes build into a roar. Suddenly she began screaming. It went on and on.

Sarah wasn't supposed to be home. She was supposed to be in Dallas. And why did he go to her house? What did he hope to accomplish? He didn't know. It was just anger and acting out. Even now, having just heard it all, he could barely remember who he was that night.

The last thing she had said was, "I want you to know I was wrong about us."

It was there, always, without explanation, in time.

# The Comeback

*"The art of fiction is dead. Reality has strangled invention. Only the utterly impossible, the inexpressibly fantastic, can ever be plausible again."*
—Red Smith in the *New York Herald Tribune* commenting
on the 1951 Giants snatching the pennant race from the
Dodgers after being 13 1/2 games back on August 12.

This game will teach you things. I can tell you that.
In 1951, the underdog New York Giants beat the Brooklyn Dodgers in a best of three playoff set to go on to the World Series. A hundred years later, in 2051, our manager, Old Deacon O'Doul, who had a keen sense of baseball history, pasted that Red Smith quote on the locker room wall and growled at the boys, "We're only nine games behind and it ain't August 12th yet. If any one of you have an ounce of quit in you, tell me now so I can give up hope and start dusting off my fishing gear."

Baseball's changed some since 1951. Vids everywhere, floating over the field, watching the dugout. Heck, there's vids in the bat and the ball. The home audience can switch views whenever they want. Players are stronger. New ways of cheating. In 1951 you didn't worry about genetically enhanced players, that's for sure. You didn't worry about being traded to Buenos Aries or Cape Town. Nobody knew about guys like Spooky either or humanity evolving. But more about the game is the same than is different, and a coach yelling at his club in the locker room humbles ballplayers the same way in 2051 as any other time.

In the silence that followed, Spooky Earl Waters leaned over to me and whispered, "What 1930s ballplayer said, 'There'll never be another one like me?'"

I said, "Dizzy Dean."

But other than a leaky shower head dripping in the background there was no sound, and the team looked glumly at the floor. The speech worked; we took both ends of a double-header against Cincinnati that afternoon.

Spooky had a career day against Cincinnati. He stood next to Deacon in the dugout and called the defense before the pitch, "Second base, two steps left, one hop," or "Deep right center." Deacon would run through his signals, shifting an infielder to one side or the other, or he'd move an outfielder. Poor Cincinnati failed to get a single base runner in the opener; everything went straight to a forewarned fielder. Spooky didn't miss once. They were quite a pair, Deacon, the gray old man leaning over to get the call from Spooky, who looked like a towheaded kid, his brows all wrinkled up in concentration.

It was a great game: the reason I loved baseball in the first place. At the end, the sun cut across the field; the smell of infield dust and chalk and grass filled my nose, and the home crowd raised a ruckus.

In the nightcap, they only scored one run, and it was unearned. Blue Blackburn walked a pair in the seventh inning, and then scored the first on consecutive wild pitches.

At the end of the inning, Blue stormed into the dugout, knocked over the water cooler, and kicked the bats. He grabbed the front of Spooky's shirt, picking him up before anyone could stop him. "You lost my shut-out for me you miserable excuse of a...prostate-rater!"

"Prognosticator," said Eddie "Crouch" Potato, our catcher, who put his hand on Blue's fist. "Put him down, Blue. You tossed those wild ones all by yourself."

Crouch was a quiet man, very gentle, but he weighed over two-hundred pounds with no fat. He looked like the kind of guy who'd crush your spleen if you crossed him. The year before we had a rookie pitcher who refused to come into the locker room after a game because he thought Crouch was mad at him for shaking off a signal. Blue was nearly two-hundred himself, but he knew it was a bad idea to rile his catcher, so he dropped Spooky and stalked down to the other end of the bench. "What good is he if he doesn't warn me about this kind of stuff?" As he went out to start the eighth, Blue slapped Spooky on the back of head. "Should have seen it coming, freak."

The vids picked up his behavior and replayed it on the big screen several times, which didn't help his mood. The crowd booed him.

Blue had won a lot of games, and he was a darned good pitcher, but he'd never earned a shut-out. Not in Little League, not in high school or the minors. Never. It was just one of those weird things. Weird things are a part of baseball. Take Richie Ashburn of the '57 Phillies. He was playing in a game where a ball he fouled hit a fan. Ashburn, naturally was concerned, and he waited until they started to take the fellow out of the stadium. Then, on the next pitch, he fouled off again and nailed the same guy.

Afraid that he'd jinx himself, Blue never told anybody about the shut out, but we all knew he wanted it more than anything in the world.

Blue plunked the lead off batter in the shoulder. No good reason for it, he was just mad.

The part of the crowd hooked into the batter's point of view winced on the pitch. They passed their V.R. goggles around so others could see it themselves.

Blue wasn't the brightest pitcher I'd seen in my twenty years as equipment manager. Somebody once said, "Open up a ballplayer's head and you know what you'll find? A lot of broads and a jazz band." That was Blue.

He never really did figure out what prognosticators did for the club. In '51 they were still pretty new. I mean, the whole idea of psychic *Homo Telepathis*, which is what the papers called them, as a branch of humanity confused the heck out of a lot of people. Spooky and others like him who got little peeks into the future had only been in the league for a half dozen years or so at that point, and a few teams didn't even use them. Heck, some people argued they would ruin the game, but baseball's survived all kinds of change. I mean, look at the designated hitter and artificial turf! You still have to throw and hit and catch, for crying out loud.

I'd asked Spooky once why he only knew where hit balls were going but no other part of the game, and he kind of hummed and hawed without saying anything. He was a shy guy anyway, and darned small at a bit over five-foot, but he knew baseball like nobody's business—we'd swap trivia and stats all the time—and could tell a great joke. That's how he got hooked up with young Annabelle Martin in the front office. He made her laugh, and even though she was eight or nine inches taller than he was and looked like a model (which she had been her last two years of high school), it was understood they were an item. They'd meet for lunch in the hotel restaurant to split a sandwich when we were on the road. It was cute. I almost expected them to order one malt with two straws afterwards. At any rate, and not to get too far off the subject, Spooky said a hit ball released a distinctive and sharp flash in time he could track. Almost nothing else worked the same way, and he could only predict maybe twenty or thirty seconds into the future on a really good day, so he was no better at the race track than I was.

But he knew his trivia. Once I said to him, "Where'd the term 'Charlie Horse' come from?"

He grinned at me, that real open faced smile where his face looks lit up from behind. "Charlie Esper. Pitched for the Orioles in the 1890's. He ran so badly his teammates thought he looked like a lame horse, and ever since then a player with a leg cramp uses his name."

I thought for sure he wouldn't know that one.

After the second win, Spooky danced a jig on a bench in the locker room. Deacon gave him a game ball; only Blue refused to sign it.

Of course, Spooky had his slumps. Like all ball players, percentages ruled him. Sometimes he'd have streaks too. Baseball's a streaky game; who can forget Joc DiMaggio, for the love of Mike? The day of the double-header against Cincinnati Spooky killed them, but other days he was useless. He carried a little towel, and if he wasn't seeing so good, he kept twisting it, like he was trying to wring out a vision of what was coming next. When his inner eye was working, he'd stick the towel in his belt or leave it on the bench.

After Cincinnati, Spooky went into a dry spell. About that same time, the tabloids ran a picture of Blue at a local dance place planting a big kiss on Anabelle Martin. She didn't look like she was struggling either, her eyes all bright and adoring. Don't know whether the slump had anything to do with the confrontation in the dugout or Anabelle, but I know Spooky started looking real distracted, and his eyes were red-rimmed.

He quit playing trivia with me, even when I tossed him some pretty easy chestnuts.

Over the course of the next few weeks, Spooky worked his way through towel after towel until they were no more than a tatter of threads. He got another from me and started on it. Didn't matter much to the club, though, even if he wasn't helping. We swept the Braves in four, split two games with the Mets, took all three against Tokyo in Tokyo and went twenty-four for twenty-nine to finish the season a half-game back of the division leading Chicago who hadn't played badly in the final stretch themselves.

And wouldn't you know it, our last game of the season was in Chicago to make up for a rain-out in July.

Blue won five of his six starts after Cincinnati, and Deacon scheduled him in for the Chicago game. All that winning didn't make him any sweeter, though. The gossip columnists were making a fuss about Blue and Anabelle, him being a big name ball player and all, and she being so young and glamorous. Blue would bring in the clips, mostly to get Spooky's goat, I think, and then he'd talk dirty about her to the rest of the guys loud enough for Spooky to hear.

Spooky moped around like a whipped dog. Like I said, his average dropped way off, and he started getting a lot of "false positives," where he'd tell Deacon to shift a player wrong; Deacon would flash the signals, and the ball would shoot through right where the fielder had been before. Deacon started to not trust in him so much. Still, Spooky produced in a couple of key situations. He never put down the towel though. Worried it pretty good, he did.

Most of the team caught on pretty quick to what was going on, but there's three or four like Blue on any squad, mostly second stringers, and they'd yuck it up at Spooky's expense. Crouch didn't like it, naturally, and he started tossing the ball back to Blue in the dirt or to the left or right so he'd have to step off the rubber until Deacon told him to cut it out.

"I don't know what's happening here, Crouch, but you're just hurting the ball club. I don't care what you think of the guy off the field, but he's a part of this pennant drive. You toss it up there nice and don't break his rhythm."

So it came down to the final game. Winner makes the playoffs. Loser gets to think about it all winter. After the national anthem, the team settled into the dugout except for Lemon Smith, our shortstop who batted lead off, and Crouch who was on deck. On the bench, Blue started spouting off about Anabelle. "I finally pegged her," he said to his cronies real loud.

Spooky sat up like he'd been shot.

The players around Blue chuckled and slapped him on the back while Blue worked a ball in his hand.

"Wasn't worth the wait, though," Blue said. "All those looks, and I don't think she'd been round the block before."

Somebody said, "How'd you know, Blue?"

He turned away to answer, so I didn't hear, but his buddies burst out laughing like they'd never heard something so funny.

"And get this," said Blue. "She thinks I *love* her. She's probably registering silverware patterns right now. Hell, I haven't spent two nights alone this month."

Made me sick just to hear it.

By this time, Lemon stepped up to the plate, so they turned to watch. A couple of them yelled encouragement. In the other dugout, their coach was signaling like crazy. The pitcher wound up, and as he delivered, their second baseman took off toward first. Lemon slapped a perfect line drive to the gap, but the second baseman snagged it on the run. Spooky's Chicago counterpart had anticipated the hit, and Lemon was out. Our next two guys went down swinging, so we took the field.

Spooky didn't move from his spot on the bench. Deacon looked around after a bit and spotted him. "Get up here, Spooky! We got a game to play, if you don't mind," he barked.

I'm no soothsayer like Spooky, or mind reader or anything else, but he was furious mad. I'd never seen him like that. His face got red and screwed up, and I could see it in the way he held his shoulders, how his hands moved in close to his side and clenched. I thought, it's a good thing Blue's a foot taller than Spooky, or Blue wouldn't have a chance.

Baseball players aren't supposed to let their feelings about each other get into their game, but it happens all the time. It's inevitable. Left fielder gets mad at the shortstop, so he quits hitting him for the cut-off, or third base is pissed at first base, so he short-hops his throws. When personal feelings *don't* enter the game, it's remarkable. Take the Tinker to Evers to Chance double play combo: Johnny Evers and Joe Tinker disliked each other so much, they didn't talk for two years, but there they are, a legendary pair of teammates. Most of the time, it's the other way around. Some days the game is *all* personality.

Blue coaxed a pop up out of their first batter. He walked the second, and the third grounded into a double play Lemon didn't have to budge an inch to pick up. Spooky didn't say a word. I don't think his head was in it. He was holding his towel, but he when he wasn't glaring at Blue he was looking up at the club's sky box where management and their big wig buddies watched. Of course, Anabelle would be up there too. I didn't figure they hired her for her computer skills. But I couldn't see anything behind the mirrored glass.

From the second to the fifth, Blue mowed them down. I don't think I'd ever seen him keener, catching the corners, running the ball inside if they crowded the strike zone. Change ups floated like marshmallows, sliders broke a foot away from the plate, and man, his fast ball was nearly invisible.

He was tight, though. I could see it in his jaw, the way he kept wiping his forehead with the back of his hand. It can't be argued, Blue was a competitor, and when the game was on, nothing existed for him but the ball and the batter. After five innings, I knew he was thinking about not just a shut-out, but a no-hitter.

With two gone in the top of the sixth, their pitcher walked our first baseman, and he got all the way to third on a bad hop single through second base. Nothing a fielder can do about a bad hop. Spooky could call it, Deacon could signal it, and the fielder could be there, but a bad hop can go anywhere and get there fast. Bad hops are a part of the game. Ask Bill Buckner of the '86 Red Sox about bad hops. In the sixth game of the series, with two out in the 9th, Mookie Wilson tops an easy play grounder up the first base line, but the pill slips under Buckner's glove to give the Mets the game.

The ball does funny things.

Runners waited on the corners now; Crouch worked the count full, then fouled off five in a row. Finally, he planted the eleventh pitch into the twentieth row, straight-away center. We poured out of the dugout like the game was over, congratulations all around, and with a three run cushion, Blue looked like a man who'd stepped off death row.

I could feel the change in the dugout too. We started the game *pretending* to be loose. The loud jokes. The relaxed postures. They were a pose. But the way Blue was tossing them in there, three runs looked good. No one would say it, but I knew they were thinking cork popping and champagne baths. The playoffs seemed a blink away, and our remarkable comeback would be complete.

Spooky woke up on the home run too. He started twisting that towel around, watching the field a little sideways. Three pitches into their first batter, he said something to Deacon, and the old guy flashed signals quick as could be. As Blue delivered, left field turned and sprinted for the corner to catch what would have been a sure double at the wall a foot from the foul line. The crowd roared on the hit, then quieted to nothing.

Blue didn't look in, but he had to know he owed that one to Spooky. The second guy fanned at three high ones, and the third popped to shallow right. Our second baseman was camped under there before the hit, so we were out of the sixth.

Chicago called on their bullpen to shut us down through the top of the ninth, but Blue answered back with flawless control, the whole time with Spooky leaning against the rail, watching him.

In the stands, the crowd grew frantic. I could hear it in their cheers as batter after batter sat down. Blue walked one in both the seventh and eighth, but we got them in double plays Spooky set up. No one else reached. Deacon watched Blue too, but he was looking for a change in his delivery. Anything to indicate he was weakening.

"How are you doing, Blue?" asked Deacon at the end of the eighth.

"I can finish it." Blue draped a warmup jacket over his arm. He was so into his pitching, I don't think he knew any of the rest of us were there.

"What do you think, Crouch?" said Deacon.

"He's got more snap on the ball now than he did to start the game. He's on auto-pilot."

Deacon nodded, and I could see the wheels turning behind Blue's eyes. He had a sense of history too. A no hit shutout to win the final game of the regular season would make his name the answer to a lot of bar bets. So Blue led the team out of the dugout at the bottom of the ninth, three outs away from a berth in the playoffs.

Spooky took his place on the rail next to Deacon. Everybody else was up too. I could almost feel them willing the crowd to silence, sending all the bad luck they could to Chicago's batters, praying to the baseball gods.

Blue took his stance, and with three evil breaking balls sat the first batter down. I checked Spooky. He wasn't twisting the towel and he wasn't saying anything either. No hits? I thought. He looked up at the sky boxes again. I'd almost forgotten about Anabelle, but Spooky hadn't.

Somehow the ump saw four perfect strikes on the outside corner differently than we did, and he awarded the next man first base. He promptly stole second.

Deacon signaled for an intentional walk to put the double play possibility back on. Crouch set up wide to take the pitch-out, but instead of tossing the ball out of the strike zone, Blue reared back and beaned the batter with a fast ball.

"What was that?" screamed Deacon. He hates purpose pitches, but I knew what was going on. Chicago's next batter loved to crowd the plate, and since we were going to put this runner on anyway, Blue must have thought, why not send the next guy a message? Maybe he won't dig in quite so deep.

Besides, I think Blue liked to hit batters.

The crowd stood. In the second tier, they stamped their feet so it sounded out like a quick, huge pulse.

I wanted one of Spooky's towels to twist myself, so I looked around for something, and there was his towel. He'd neatly folded it and it was laying on the bench. Deacon asked Spooky something, and Spooky shook his head. Deacon nodded, then signaled Lemon who slid to his left six feet.

I thought, double play ball, and I was right. The ball shot straight to Lemon, and he gobbled it up, but somehow he couldn't get it out of his glove, and when he finally did it slipped out of his hand to drop to his feet. By the time the play was over, the crowd was screaming and stomping too loud for me to hear anything else, and the bases were loaded.

Deacon started to walk over to the bullpen phone. It was only natural to pull Blue now. We needed two more outs, and Chicago had eight innings to learn Blue's timing, but Spooky grabbed his arm. I couldn't hear anything above the crowd. Spooky gestured and yelled, then Deacon yelled back. Finally he shrugged his shoulders. They went back to the rail.

Baseball is filled with incredible performances, like the '77 series when Reggie Jackson hit four home runs in four straight official times at bat. A player's not supposed to be that good. Later, I thought maybe Spooky had a kind of Reggie Jackson game to beat Chicago. Maybe more than twenty or thirty seconds of the future opened up for him just then, but I don't think he cared how the game played out.

No, considering what happened, I don't think he cared at all.

The bottom of the ninth. Bases loaded. One out, and Chicago had the potential winning run at the plate.

Blue's first pitch was a ball. Deacon flinched. The crowd roared. Now the pounding feet almost hurt. Our bench players crowded the rail. It all seemed so intense. My skin ached from the tension.

That's what you play baseball for, or course, for moments like that one.

Spooky, though, he didn't look tense at all. His fingers tapped lightly on the rail. One foot rested on the first step out of the dugout. He smiled, and I realized that was the first time I'd seen him smile since Cincinnati. He smiled, then he yelled something in Deacon's ear.

Deacon went through a complicated series of signals, all to Blue. I couldn't see most of them, but the last one was a hand to his right ear, the signal for "high." The player would have to jump to catch a ball over his head.

Blue nodded, then faced the batter.

Spooky turned to me and yelled, "Herb Score."

The name rang a bell, but I couldn't make the connection. Blue brought the ball up, held the pose for a blink, then unleashed a hellacious fast ball.

Every image that followed is blazed for me like those old time sepia photographs. Blue fell off to the right as he always does. The batter brought back his hands to swing, and as he started the bat forward, Blue recovered, his face a picture of desperation and hope, gathered himself and jumped up, glove above his head. Connection. The crack of a perfectly struck ball. A line drive up the middle just as Spooky had called it. But not high. Dead center.

Blue reached the top of his leap, anticipating the catch above him. His mouth was open. I don't believe he ever saw the ball. It caroomed off his forehead with a horrible, wooden thud. The ball went up. Blue went down.

Behind him, Lemon charged forward. Caught the ball at his shoe laces. Fired to first to double off the runner.

We won.

They carried Blue off the field on a stretcher.

And all the while, Spooky never moved from the rail. He kept the same smile on his face, and I suppose everyone thought he was happy because we'd beat Chicago.

The myth is that in 1932, in the series between the Yankees and the Cubs, Babe Ruth called his home run hit, pointing where he was going to blast the ball in center field. It doesn't matter eye-witnesses don't back up the legendary story. It's the myth of the called shot that survives, and it's the story everyone knows.

After our game ended, and all the interviews were done, I looked up Herb Score. He was familiar to me because he led the majors in strike outs for the Indians in both '55 and '56. But he only had three games in '57. In the third game of the season a Yankee batter, Gil McDougald, blasted a line drive back through the box, shattering Score's cheekbone and ending his career as a ball player.

The story of Babe Ruth and his predicted home run is just a legend, but I know for a fact Spooky Earl Waters called his shot in the last game of the regular season in 2051. We won the game, but that was incidental. There was another contest on the field.

And that should end the story, but I really should mention the next day a grieving Anabelle Martin went to the hospital to pay Blue a visit. She couldn't get in because six other women were there arguing about who he loved most.

Spooky gave her a lift home.

Leo Duroucher said, "Nice guys finish last," but I say, a lot can happen in a season, and if baseball's taught me anything, it's that you should never count someone out until the last pitch.

Doesn't matter if it's 1951 or 2051. Those underdogs have a way of coming back.

# Resurrection

There is no beauty in a starship. Nothing obvious, anyway. A cold efficacy in the numbers, certainly. An aesthetic satisfaction in the way the hull rounds our lives, the curved corridors, the rhythm in waking, working, then sleeping again, the long cryonic near-death. But no beauty. Out the ports, frosted emptiness. Twelve-hundred years of interstellar erosion scars the view. Not a star visible. Not even perfect blackness. All we have is the half-million-ton ship filled with frozen genetic material, farming equipment and us, the Custodians, slumbering through the implacable distance, fleeing despair, pursuing a slim chance or none. My own artistic attempts fail. No comeliness motivates the creative temperament in the metal, sturdy shapes.

Not that there aren't problems to solve. It isn't just engineering taking us to new worlds. Trust the hardware, they said, and the software too, but not the peopleware. Although we are awake for only two weeks every hundred years, when we reach Zeta Riticula after 4,000 years we will have lived over a year and a half. We were picked partially for good genes, long lives and patience, for our willingness to wait, but it would be unreasonable to expect there wouldn't be disagreement, grudges, relationships. So there are protocols for law enforcement, for therapy, for on-board marriages even. Everyone has certification beyond their specialty. We have doctors, counselors, a pastor, and me, a keeper of the peace. You can't go to the stars without people. What would be the point? But I don't like it.

What the engineers didn't plan on were William and MaryJo.

Their romance must have festered long before I noticed. After six months aboard The Resurrection, lived in two week snatches, MaryJo developed cryogenic phobia. Some do. It should be no different from sleeping and waking, but you know you're lying in a chamber filled with cooled gasses, and your body is corpse still. No test can detect a life's thread, while the finest balancing act biotechnology provides keeps you teetering above the abyss. It hurts too. Before you lose consciousness, the cold pierces, and when you wake...well...it's like razored ice everywhere. For a second, you feel it. Then it's gone. Tolerable discomfort. It's efficient. A small price to pay for interstellar distance.

Occasionally, Custodians can't take it. They refuse to enter the pods. Nobody can make them. It's sad. Peopleware. As far as the other sleepers are concerned, it's suicide. For the phobic, they lead a full life—as full as wandering around the Resurrection can be—alone, greeting each crew as they wake for their custodial duties, pursuing whatever studies or hobbies intrigue them, until they meet us again, if they live, a hundred years later. Our bios are good, and we're long-lived anyway—we're a long way from the traditional three score and ten—but a hundred-and-twenty-five years is pretty much the limit. No one makes it through two cycles.

William, a tall, olive-skinned physical-fitness buff rushed by me. He was stripped to the waist—clothing is optional on board—a scowl in his eyes. I'm the peace keeper, so I dropped the ion engine reports and followed him down the corridor. The living area's small. Fifty crew members work on top each other, so disagreement is inevitable. It's a long trip any way you look at it, even when you skip fifty-two-hundred weeks for every two you are awake. As far as we were concerned, we'd spent six months in confinement, and there were twelve to go. Psychological testing can give us the most compatible crew in the world, but human nature is human nature. Someone is going to blow sometime.

I passed other Custodians, some sitting at their stations, checking repair records, fine tuning the Resurrection. Hardly any human artifact lasts 4,000 years. The ship would be built and rebuilt dozens of times before we arrived to colonize the new star system. The hull had to be recoated; the automated routines checked and reestablished; the few moving parts replaced; the computers themselves, eventually, needed a complete overhaul. For us the trip so far had been six months, but the ship had been moving forward for over 1,200 years. One old ship, a quarter-million fertilized ova, and four fifty-member crews, one of whom woke every twenty-five years. Quadruple redundancy. Four sets of workstations. Four sets of living quarters. If we had to, we could all be awake at the same time. Colonial equipment filled the holds, while the amazing computers did most the work, striving toward a distant star.

William lost me at a split in the corridor. I don't think he knew I was following, but he strode forward so angry that people moved out of his way, and they all stopped me. "What's going on with William?" "Do you think you should say something?"

"I don't know. Let me get to him, and I'll tell you." I went a few steps up one path before realizing it would take me to cryogenics. Unlikely he'd be going there. Nothing but chilled crew members and our long-sleep pods. The other passage led to the gym and dining room. If he was searching for someone—and he looked like a man on a mission—that's where he'd go. That's where she'd be, waiting for him, ready to give him the news.

I'd known three cycles ago she was refusing cryonics, just as I knew about their relationship a month out (our time). The fitness profiles go by my station. They exercised in the gym together. I'd passed them holding hands, his dark complexion a pleasant contrast to her china-pale skin. I'd come upon them in a junction in a corridor, William half-bent at the waist, Maryjo on her toes, their lips just touching. I should have seen the emotional explosion ahead.

When I got to the cafeteria, he'd found her. They sat across from each other at a narrow table, their foreheads together, staring at their clasped fists between them. I leaned against a wall, arms crossed, watching. He could do anything, anything at all, but I knew what he wouldn't do—he wouldn't join her. He was a fanatic. Zeta Riticula or bust for him. It was in his profile. He would choose to see the trip to the end, to be a part of the settlement. He had the lowest predicted bailout numbers in the crew. William would row the Resurrection there if he had to.

So I watched them, cool metal against my back. I smelled vegetable soup. Coffee. An outside crew sat at the room's other end, getting ready to go out. Eating big. They'd spend a ten-hour shift checking hull plate, supervising maintenance bots, spreading nanonite paint that burrowed into the ship's skin, remaking it. They ignored the couple.

I keyed my wristcom, arranged to cover their work. William cried. Tears glistened on his cheeks. Maryjo whispered, dropped her head so her hair covered her face. What was she telling him? There was nothing to say. She'd refused the pod. William would go to sleep, and when he awoke, she'd be ancient or dead. I stepped closer.

"It's not my fault," she said. Where's the fault? The ship would move on without her, but she would move on without William.

"You have to go," he said. His hands shook, holding hers. His elbows bore down on the table; his knuckles turned white, gripping her, and she grimaced but didn't pull away. The crew at the other end left. Maybe they knew what was going on too. Maryjo was saying goodbye to us. She was dead in a way already. Tomorrow we slept in the pods. The day after that the Maryjo we knew would be gone. Maybe she'd write us novels as a phobic several cycles ago did. Fifty-four books before he died, while we dreamed slow dreams. I read a couple. Not bad, considering. Maybe she'd paint—we had supplies for it—I dabbled in my rec time, a landscape or two. Of course, she might wander alone through the ship for a year, then climb into a pod to join us, a year older, a little wiser. No phobic had done that so far. No hope for their future motivated them strongly enough to sleep again.

I saw reason for hope, but William didn't. He looked into her eyes as if searching for the answer. What he saw offered no compromise. She was staying.

"I can't," she said, but William already knew. His shoulders collapsed. All emotion drained from him, the anger, the passion. It leaked away. He kissed her hands between his own. I knew I could go back to my station. There was no need for me here, and I had more figures to check. The engines had to stay steady in their work, processing air, keeping us warm throwing us outward faster and faster. Our distance to go was indescribable—it would take 4,000 years—but it could take 40,000 if we didn't slowly accelerate every day until the turnaround point. The engines had to work. The people didn't. We'd get there if the people didn't mess it up.

At my station I finalized the ion thruster numbers. They were good— the engines were good. Techs had gone over them inch by inch. Another twenty-five years of steady thrust until the next crew woke up to check them again. I knew the numbers were fine, just as they'd been fine a week ago, but I had a job to do. What saves us is efficiency. Work keeps our minds off the pods, off the hundreds of years we'd already traveled and the thousands we had left. I studied my cubical. On the walls I'd stuck postcards from Earth: Monterey Bay's south beach; a Dogwood tree in the spring, a waterfall tumbling behind it; a sunset in the Tyrolean Alps. By my desk light they generated no magic. I stared at the Alps for a long time, willing them to come alive for a second, but they didn't. No beauty, as I said, in a starship. Even lovely pictures offer no transcendent moments. I didn't go to bed that night. For the next hundred years, I'd sleep, and that seemed enough.

I didn't see the final goodbyes. Maryjo didn't come to the closing. The technicians helped me into position. When we were secure, they'd help each other into their pods. The last one would climb in by himself. It was doable—going to sleep without help—but it was easier with aid. There were sensors to attach, adjustments to be made. William climbed in five pods down from mine, a fragile neutrality in his face. He didn't talk as they hooked him up. Was he waiting for her to come? How did they spend their last night together? During my melancholy the night before, I hadn't checked. I told myself it didn't matter to me. The crisis had passed in the cafeteria. Besides, numbers had to be refined and verified. My counterpart on the next crew twenty-five years from now had to have clear figures to work from.

I shut my eyes when the lid came down. I'm not cryophobic, but it's hard in those last minutes. The imagination does its wondrous job. A hundred years! Disaster could happen. The ship could fail. Equipment could seize up. A thousand tiny things could kill me in my sleep. And what was the difference between this and death? I remembered what I always remembered just before I went to sleep: when I woke up the last time it was to a lingering memory that I'd been dreaming for the whole hundred years, and the dream had been a nightmare.


*I* followed William again after we awoke. He shook the sensors off his arms. Slapped them to the ground. This would be the other rough time. A minute ago he'd shut his eyes and Maryjo was a young woman, his love. They'd held hands and he'd kissed her. The skin had been smooth, as his was now, and their hearts had beat in heady rhythm. A minute ago for him, but most her life would have passed if she hadn't bested the phobia, if she still lived.

He wouldn't lose me this time. I hustled after. He was blind to my presence. To the cafeteria. It was empty. To the gym. No sign. To her workstation. Nothing. He grew more frantic. Pushed by me without seeing. Past the gardens. Through the infirmary, through the labs, through the rec room. There wasn't much ship to search. I followed into the living quarters. At her apartment, he paused. She could be dead within. Maybe dead for years. I touched his arm, and he jumped. He genuinely didn't know I had been there. He took a shaky breath, then opened her door.

I entered behind him, and we stood silent for a moment.

"Why don't you check the records?"

He sat on the edge of her empty bed, reached across the bare desk, and turned on her station. I was glad to see it come to life—there's always the suspicion it won't.

"She's not dead," he said. The screen flashed results. "She's in my room."

Seconds later, he held her. Maryjo had grown small in the years, and her hair had thinned, losing all color. Her eyes were rheumy, her knuckles huge and arthritic, but she rose from the bed when the door opened. She met him in the middle. William murmured in her ear, and she squeezed him back. Her arms shook as they held him. No wonder; she was one-hundred and twenty-four years old.

"I should have stayed with you," he said.

Her voice had vigor, even if her body had thinned away. "I couldn't go to the pod then. When I changed my mind, I was old, and you were...." She traced a finger along his firm, unwrinkled cheek.

And they both were crying.

Finally, she said, "I missed you."

William gathered her like a child, sat on his bed. "I missed you too."

And I thought about the hundred years of dreams I couldn't remember. What had William dreamed in his time? Could he bring the images up? Was there regret even in sleep?

I left them. Walked the long corridor to my station. I'd forgotten to store the postcards, and the other crews had left them up. The color had faded. All that remained of the Alps was a yellowed shape provoking no memory. I leaned with one hand against a bulkhead staring at it. No reason to be upset, really, the cards had lasted 1,300 years. I sat, called up the figures. Did my job. Efficiency is the key word. Being busy keeps one sane. Progress reports distracted me and repair programs and the notes from the other engineers. At first I worked my work, and I tried not to think about William and Maryjo.

The reports crossed my station anyway. William abandoned his station. He spent every waking hour with Maryjo. I'd glance at the monitors and see them sitting in the cafeteria, heads bent in conversation, his fingers resting on her wrist. Sometimes it was if there was no age difference. She'd speak to him, then pause, waiting for his reaction, just as she had a hundred years earlier. If it weren't for their differences, I'd say they were young lovers. They remade themselves in the first week. In the second week the tenor of their talks changed. He became more vehement. I didn't eavesdrop. I could have. My job allows me. But they were no danger to the ship or anyone else. He must be saying goodbye again, I guessed. She wouldn't live to see the next crew awake. Her days were running out. William must have seen this time as a second life for them. She had changed on the outside, but her spirit remained.

The monitors showed all. I didn't want to see, but I had to. I tried to stay away. Painted instead. My station displayed the Alps, Monterey Bay, Dogwood trees with waterfalls running to mist behind them. But my paintings remained flat. The ship offered no relief. Not one beautiful image. They should have known, on Earth that is, I would not be happy in the ship. Eighteen months without a mountain to climb or a stream to fish in. Maybe that's why they chose me: they knew I would always return to the pod. The idea of growing old in this falling barrel, this sterile cage, sickened me. If I could keep taking the long sleep, I would again walk on land, a sky above me and not a ceiling. Zeta Riticula held the promise.

Two days before the shift ended, I asked the medic what he'd learned about Maryjo's health. He said, "She's remarkably strong. If she takes care of herself, she might go another ten years. There are precedents." He shook his head. "I don't think she will, though. I get the impression that all that kept her going was to see William again. When he goes off shift..." He shrugged.

Taking a late dinner, I sat next to them in the cafeteria. William raised his chin when I came in, but didn't speak to me. Maryjo hunched in the seat next to him. Their dinner plates were untouched. It was if I'd interrupted a long dialogue. For a moment I considered leaving, but there was no point. Whose feelings would I be protecting?

They turned toward each other, eventually, and resumed their talk. Their voices murmured, mostly William's. It rose and fell like a distant soloist, his words indecipherable, but the tone relentlessly intense, pleading. From the corner of my eye, I watched. He gripped her arm, moved his head close, talking, always talking. He reached some crescendo, his words broke into coherence. "I only want to be with you," he said, then stopped. For so long it had rumbled on, I paused in mid bite. The silence in the cafeteria rang. Then, she nodded to him. She agreed. To what, I didn't know, but I was there at the end of their long debate, and whatever it was, he won.

William sat back, stretched. He faced me and smiled. I smiled back, wondering what sad mini-drama I'd missed.

With just a day left, I began a new painting. Fruitless, really. I didn't call an image from the vaults; I composed from memory, but there wasn't time. Like all art, the idea fled before me, eluded my brushes, seeped away from the canvas. Beauty's memory existed, but memory is not enough—we need these wells renewed, and without them the hunger for unutterable moments eats away at us. I yearned for more. My painting wouldn't hold it. It was just colorful dabs, as all art is—dabs of reminiscence. Interesting in some ways on its own, the soul's shadow in a weak, echoey reflection, but not enough. We need renewal. I found nothing in the corridors, nothing in the Custodians' pale, preoccupied faces.

On the last hour, the paints were put away. My station tidied once again. My perishables were stored for their hundred-year wait. I rested on my bed frame, my hands on the solid metal anchored in the ship's walls and imagined the engines, hum through my hands, or Custodians' footfalls shaking the ship, but there was silence. The engines don't hum—no devices move within them but the super-accelerated particles pushing the Resurrection to slowly greater and greater speed, and even when you stand next to the reactors, there's no sound.

When the signal came to repod, I trod toward the sleep pods. I arrived late so I wouldn't have to see William and Maryjo's parting. Hopefully, he would be asleep already. But when I got there, William wasn't there.

Maryjo was. The technician patted her hand as he fastened the last sensor. She smiled up at him, a warm, old face.

I didn't have time to ask. I was late, and the technicians wanted to get me ready so they could sleep themselves. As I was fastened in, finally, I said, "Where is William? Why is Maryjo in a pod?"

The tech shrugged. "I don't know the whole story. William refused. Maryjo requested a spot." He leaned in close, "She's very, very old. She might not be able to take the stress, but she has a right." He lifted my arm, rolled me a little to the side so he could fasten a sensor to my ribs. "It'll be an interesting experiment."

The pod shell came down, cutting off the light. As the rising cold swept over me, I wondered what it meant, and then, for an instant, all was pain.


**W**illiam lived too. When I awoke, he was waiting by Maryjo's pod, a hunched and withered man. No juice left in him. A technician checked her pod's readout, entered commands on the touchpad, then stood back. The pod's gray hood rose. William leaned over the edge. For a long time he stood in the pose. I couldn't see into her pod, and I wasn't unfastened yet. Then a hand appeared from within, fell on William's hand, and he held it.

The two weeks passed quickly. Half the engines were due to be pulled and refurbished. Careful calculations had to be made. All the ship's structural elements needed reassessment. I almost didn't see William and Maryjo until the shift had ended. I was walking from the gym to my station. For once there was too much to do—I'd hardly had a moment to think about my postcards, about the painting. So my figures and schedules filled my head. For once I barely noticed the artless, gray metal in the hallways, the harried Custodians too busy to talk. I had to work.

Then I turned a corner, and there they were, William and Maryjo. They faced each other, he still a head taller, she looking up. William lowered himself—she rose on her toes—and they kissed.

She said, "We have so little time together."

I froze. I couldn't go on.

He looked at me, just for a second, then pulled her close. "No," he said. "We have the rest of our lives, all of it." And they tottered away, their arms around each other.

When I went to the pod the next day, I knew, I knew what I must paint when I awoke, and it would be beautiful.

## About the Author

James Van Pelt was born 1954 in Akron, Ohio. He graduated from Metro State College in Denver, Colorado in 1978 with a bachelors degree in English and history, and a high school teaching degree. He earned an M.A. in creative writing from the University of California in Davis in 1990. His poetry, non-fiction and stories have appeared in numerous magazines and anthologies, including *Asimov's*, *Analog*, *Alfred Hitchcock's Mystery Magazine, Realms of Fantasy, Talebones* and many others. His stories have been recommended for Nebula and Stoker awards, and honorably mentioned in both Gardner Dozois's *The Year's Best Science Fiction* and Ellen Datlow's and Terri Windling's *The Year's Best Fantasy and Horror*. In 1999, he was a finalist for the John W. Campbell Award for Best New Writer.

When he's not writing, he teaches high school and college English in Grand Junction, Colorado. His wife and three sons have grown accustomed to his long, motionless moments hunched over his laptop, punctuated by wild bursts of typing.

More information about current projects and upcoming publications can be found at James Van Pelt's home page at http://www.sff.net/people/james.van.pelt. He welcomes e-mail about writing, teaching and science fiction at Vvanp@aol.com.

Printed in the United States
1042800004B/349-366